Dying For Crystal

Katherine Black

Best Book Editions

Best Book Editions

1 3 5 7 9 10 8 6 4 2

Copyright © Katherine Black, 2024

The right of Katherine Black to be identified as the author of this Work has been asserted by her in accordance with the Copyright, Designs and Patents Act 1988

All rights reserved

First published in 2024 by Best Book Editions.

Paperback ISBN 9798329637878

This publication may not be used, reproduced, stored or transmitted in any way, in whole or in part, without the express written permission of the author. Nor may it be otherwise circulated in any form of binding or cover other than that in which it has been published and without a similar condition imposed on subsequent users or purchasers

All characters in this publication are fictitious, and any similarity to real persons, alive or dead, is coincidental

Cover by Best Book Editions

A CIP catalogue record of this book is available from the British Library

---

The Silas Nash series has some character evolution throughout the books. However, each novel is a contained story that stands alone and the books can be read out of sequence.
I hope you enjoy my books.

To get in touch you can email me at katherine@bestbookeditors.com

If you enjoy my book, I'd appreciate it if you would leave me a review on Amazon/Goodreads

While I don't consider there are any major triggers in this book, I suggest reader discretion.

Contents

1. Chapter 1 — 1
2. Chapter 2 — 4
3. Chapter 3 — 10
4. Chapter 4 — 18
5. Chapter 5 — 26
6. Chapter 6 — 32
7. Chapter 7 — 40
8. Chapter 8 — 46
9. Chapter 9 — 55
10. Chapter 10 — 61
11. Chapter 11 — 68
12. Chapter 12 — 73
13. Chapter 13 — 82
14. Chapter 14 — 87

15. Chapter 15   95
16. Chapter 16   102
17. Chapter 17   109
18. Chapter 18   117
19. Chapter 19   121
20. Chapter 20   128
21. Chapter 21   137
22. Chapter 22   148
23. Chapter 23   155
24. Chapter 24   160
25. Chapter 25   165
26. Chapter 26   170
27. Chapter 27   177
28. Chapter 28   186
29. Chapter 29   192
30. Chapter 30   199
31. Chapter 31   207
32. Chapter 32   214
33. Chapter 33   221
34. Chapter 34   227
35. Chapter 35
36. Chapter 36
37. Chapter 37
38. Chapter 38
39. Chapter 39
40. Chapter 40
41. Chapter 41
42. Chapter 42
43. Chapter 43
44. Chapter 44
45. Chapter 45
46. Chapter 46
47. Chapter 47
48. Chapter 48
49. Chapter 49

Chapter One

Tammy wrote a letter to herself.

Therapy session 3; Tammy Logan; The Priory; December 2024.

Some silly cow who hasn't got a clue about my life is making me write this.

The town was rotting like fallen fruit. The only place I felt safe was at my grandma's table, where the smell of hot scones and sweet jam filled the air.

But Grandma was dead.

I remember when it started. 1995; the long-hot summer. They were happy childhood days back then when everything was right. But that was then. Now the world has changed.

As I grew, I watched the decline of the town's well-kept surroundings. Flats went up and gardens came down. The orchard where I skinned my knees on rocks had been cemented over. A drop-in centre for addicts stood in its place, but nobody dropped in because the innocence of the damned youth was beyond redemption. Hundreds had dropped out of society and more every year. Poverty and puke stained the pavements, growing with every new-build estate of cardboard boxes. The upper-market homeless had pop-up tents, but only the new bastards. They were looked down on by the guys who were weathered from years of living on the streets. They were hard-core and weighed the cost of a night's shelter against their money from begging. Their habit won every time and they bought what they needed to escape the world for another few hours. Hostels were for losers.

Tammy was fifteen—me. I was fifteen. It's hard, you know, writing this stuff. What does it matter? In my search for a new way of being, I envied the boys I saw hanging around the car park. They were tight, a gang. I was seduced by the putrid stench of weed because it stopped the other kids from seeing the rot around them. I wanted to stop seeing it too. I joined them, and while they didn't throw a red carpet on the vomit-stained pavement for me, they let me in. They made me open my legs and serve a purpose. A dark path was unlocked.

Jerod 'Scorch' Mathis, Jed, was the influencer—the fool at the head of the lowest-tier gang, but there were others with equally stupid names if these lads didn't take me in. They governed the town.

Jed, at seventeen, had the swagger. He corrupted me with his smooth words. He replaced my innocence with a twisted sense of family. Grandma was dead—all hail her replacement. I transferred the attachment I had to my grandma to a seventeen-year-old boy. I needed somebody—anybody—to care.

I learned the ropes as I ran with Jed and embraced the web of crime, seduced by the thrill of petty theft and low-level drug dealing. But he was a big fish in a tiny puddle, and his success was soon replaced. He said he was The Man, but he said it with the decayed aftertaste of regret at the back of his throat. There was only one way for the likes of him to go—after he'd covered himself in *tattoos and a criminal record—and that was further up the ladder of serious crime.*

I yearned for the love I felt in Grandma's kitchen and upgraded my addiction from keying Coke to using a syringe to dull the pain. I still smelt her, though. She was beauty among the urine, and rot, and pulp of humanity. Sometimes, I turned my head on the cold ground and Grandma was there, a waft of sunshine and apples on the stinking wind. But each time she was fainter, a fading memory, like bleached denim.

The night I left, I had an encounter with a man—and a knife, I robbed him and ran—it shattered my fragile hold on owning myself, and I took off. Locked in at Scorch's flat, my heartbeat was a train that couldn't take me anywhere. It was lost in the corrupt core of the town, just like me. I stared into the sunken eyes of my reflection—I was a hollow gourd, taken from virginity by Jerod's darkness—I realised the cost of my loss.

I made a choice. I broke free of the suffocating grip of Jerod's world. Then I was going to reclaim the remnants of my happy childhood. I'd cling to redemption before it was too late.

One day I'd have a kitchen.

But Grandma was dead.

Futility came with Scorch and a bag of injected escape—but it was never too late to do something different.

'That's good, Tammy. It's a start. But it's impersonal, cold. Where are you? You're standing outside your life looking at you through the window. You need to find Tammy.'

'Tammy died a long time ago. I don't know who I am.'

Chapter Two

Silas Nash was lying on the living room sofa scrolling down the BBC News website as Kelvin checked out the streaming services—and cruises.

'Let's get on a big ship for a few days and sail the seas,' he said.

Nash spluttered his coffee. 'What? Are you mad? You know I get seasick.'

'They have medication for it these days. You'll be fine. Just imagine it. Lying on the sundeck, being fussed over by bronzed waiters. It works for me.'

'Yeah, you keep playing with those little wet dreams, babe, because you're not getting me anywhere near a boat,' Nash said.

'If you loved me, you'd think about it.' Kelvin pouted and Nash laughed.

'Okay. Look into it. I'll think about it. Medication first.'

'Already have.' He presented Nash with the evidence of little pills and big boats, and Nash had to admit it looked luxurious.

The scent of ground coffee filtered through their contentment, and two mugs—with VW Camper Van decals—sat on coasters on the coffee table. They were a novelty birthday gift from Kelvin in homage to The Good Lady Diana, their van

'A what? Are you mad? Look, Dad, I've made plans, and you're a part of them. He is not. You need to put your children first. We've discussed it between us and it's settled.'

Kelvin laughed to take any sting out of his next words and to turn them into a joke, but it fell short of hitting the mark. 'There's plenty of time to decide what I'm doing. It's so like you to ask me three months ahead of time. You're so organised, sweetheart.'

'And there you go, straight in with a criticism.'

'I was joking, love. I'm proud of you. Your achievements and methodical approach have a lot to do with you being ahead of the game. However, I'm not discussing Christmas with you now. You're all adults with your own lives, and I have mine. Silas is my partner, and any arrangements I make will include him.'

'What would God say?'

'I beg your pardon?'

'You heard. What would God think of your relationship?' Nash squeezed Kelvin's hand. 'What would Mum say?' Imani's voice was loud enough for Nash to hear everything. 'It's disgusting, Dad.'

'I appreciate that you're trying to make plans, but let's keep God out of this, shall we? He may have a thing or two to say about stone-casting. And please keep any opinions about your mother's views to yourself. It's not appropriate. This year will be different. Si and I will be spending this Christmas together, and you're going to have to get used to that.'

'You're choosing him over us?'

'No. I'm choosing happiness. Silas is part of my life, and that includes holidays.'

'You're throwing away our traditions for him. What about your granddaughters? What message does this send them? Zola doesn't want Honey and Serena to be subjected to what you've become.'

'Imani, this is my life. And my granddaughters understand that love takes different forms. We're not throwing away our traditions. We're expanding them. And I hope that my family, on the African and Western sides, can accept it.'

'Mummy would turn in her grave.'

The argument escalated as they clashed over values and expectations. Kelvin stood firm, asserting his right to happiness, while Imani told Kel that she couldn't accept the changes she'd had no say in. Nash had picked up that, since her mother's death, Imani had appointed herself as the mouthpiece of all situations and had to be at the head of every decision. Nash felt it had everything to do with jealousy that her dad was happy and didn't need her as much as he used to. It was hard for her—for them all.

'We'll see everybody at your house on Christmas morning with presents. If Si isn't working, he'll be with me. This is non-negotiable and it's your choice whether you open the door.'

'This is ridiculous.'

'Indeed it is, Princess.'

The unresolved tension mounted. Imani pressed her point regarding family matters, and the atmosphere was charged. Realising her dad wasn't backing down, she changed tack, her tone taking on a calculated edge.

'We've been talking.'

'Is that we the war council?'

'Your children, Dad. The kids you don't seem to care about any more.'

'Imani, you're being silly.'

'It's time you made a will.'

'What? Where the heck has this come from?'

'You need to ensure your children are your beneficiaries and not your new friend.'

Kelvin's face showed how caught off guard he was by the sudden shift. 'Imani, this isn't the time or the place to discuss that. But rest assured that my affairs are in order and you will all be taken care of. My business is just that. Mine. And for the foreseeable future, they are no concern of anybody else.'

Nash's phone rang and he excused himself, patting Kel's shoulder, a silent reassurance that he wasn't angry as he went into the kitchen. They could both use another coffee and he flicked the kettle on.

It was a call from work.

'Nash, they're pulling a teenager out of the lake at Barrow Park. You'd better get here,' Renshaw said.

'I'm on my way.' Nash hung up.

He grabbed his coat and waited for Kelvin to look up. 'I've been called into work. There's been an incident.'

'Go, Si. I'll see you later.'

Nash kissed him on the top of his head and left. Family matters would have to wait, as duty called.

This was the fourth dead kid in as many months.

Chapter Three

Jay Bowes had a reputation for being inseparable from his phone and Nash always gave him a hard time about it. Today had been no different.

But work was finished. It was Friday night, and he was getting ready to go out. The Jay Meister was getting his Gen-Z on. He was going to pull tonight. Jay was in his bathroom getting ready to meet the lads when it died in the middle of his favourite song to get him in the party mood.

He put it in his pocket in the hope of finding a charging point in one of the pubs. He couldn't hang about for it to charge because his taxi was waiting outside, so he shrugged, slicked some extra wax into his hair, blew a kiss at his reflection, and ran out of the house.

It was turned midnight when he got home, which wasn't too bad, and he was remarkably constrained considering the lads were ordering Jäger bombs when he left. The last thing he needed was Nash yelling at him in the morning. He'd struck out on the pulling front and was home alone—but he was philosophical about it. It was probably a good thing considering he had to be up early. It was hell having to work at the weekend. And he can't remember shit. She just knows it was bad, and she's freaking out.'

'I'll come over,' Jay said. The weight of responsibility settled on his shoulders and he only gave a passing thought to being up for work in six hours.

'Cheers. That'd be good. With you being a copper, you might be able to get through to her.'

Jay realised his bed and dreams of Debbie in the traffic department would have to be put on hold. The conflicting pull of duty and personal life collided, and he accepted the inevitable.

The screaming in the background wasn't calming.

'I'll grab a taxi and be there as soon as I can.'

The residue of his night out lingered in his system, but Jay peeled himself out of bed. He splashed his face with cold water to stay awake, dressed and got a taxi to his friend's house.

When he got there, the atmosphere was manic. Liz was a mess and Jay took charge, guiding her to the sofa with a gentle hand on her shoulder while Paul hovered in concern. 'Jay, mate. I've never seen her like this.'

'It's okay. She'll be fine.' Jay put his hand on his friend's shoulder and gently pushed him into a seat.

'Can you find out what's happening with my dad?'

'They won't tell me anything about the investigation, but I'll make a call and should be able to find out when he'll be released.' Paul looked exhausted and Liz started wailing again at the mention of her husband.

'Cheers, man. Do you want a drink?'

Jay declined the offer of alcohol. 'I'll stick with a cup of tea, thanks.' He settled into the role of comforter in the chair next to Liz and noticed that she was nursing a large glass that she'd always moaned when the rota came out and he said that Patel and Woods should do weekend mornings because they were old and didn't have a life.

He smiled as he remembered saying it and Nash going purple and yelling all kinds of rubbish about what was PC in the workplace and what could be defined as bullying. Bowes didn't have an aggressive bone in his body, but he loved a good night out and hated when it was cut short because of work. It was lucky for him that working all weekend only fell once in every six weeks, but he still sulked.

He'd forgotten about his phone while he'd been out, but settling into bed, he plugged it in and checked for messages the second it had enough charge. 'Woah.' There was a list of missed calls from his friend, Paul Gibson. Gibbo didn't go out that night because his girlfriend had put the hard word on him about spending more time together. He'd get some ribbing for it from the lads, but secretly, Jay was jealous that Gibbo even had a girl.

'Hell, Eddie,' he muttered to his pet rat, who blinked at him with interest. 'Look at these missed calls, mate. Paul must have changed his mind and was ringing to find out which pub we were in. I bet he fell out with his missus.'

Jay was laughing at Eddie's reaction to hearing his name as an incoming call came in from Paul. 'Speak of the devil and he'll appear,' he said. He heard screaming in the background. Somebody was wailing.

'Gibbo? What's up, mate?'

'Jay. Talk to my mum, will you? She's bloody hysterical. I can't calm her down. Dad's been arrested, and something bad happened to her in the Crystal Club toilets. She blacked out and picked up from the side table next to her armchair. The tart aroma of alcohol wafted across to him when she brought it to her lips. It was gin, and strong if the smell was anything to go by. He watched her behaviour, wondering how much of the night's events were down to alcohol consumption. Paul had turned the heating up and put the fire on for her. The room was unpleasant and hot. 'Liz,' he said. 'You might want to go easy with that.'

She shot him a fierce glance, her eyes glazed with distress and intoxication. 'I need it, Jay. I can't cope without it.' Her grip on the glass tightened and her knuckles turned white as she shivered. He'd known Liz and Andy Gibson since he first met Paul at primary school. They'd grown up together and often spent days on end at each other's houses. Liz and Andy had thrown some great Christmas parties, but one thing he did know—Liz Gibson wasn't usually a heavy drinker. She was terrified.

'What can you remember, Liz?'

'Nothing. I can't remember anything.'

She wailed and Jay spoke to her firmly. 'Stop that. It's not going to help you. What's the last thing you do remember?'

Liz was defensive. 'I'm not drunk. Honest.'

'Are you sure, love?' Jay wasn't convinced.

'Mum, just tell the truth about everything.' Paul stood up and went over to his mother, he knelt in front of her and took both of her hands in his. 'Tell the truth,' he shouted.

She pushed him away and he went back to his chair. 'I wasn't drunk, not then. I can't remember anything after trying to get a taxi.' Liz took another drink and started sobbing again.

'Let's take it from the beginning and it'll come back to you. Where did you go?' Jay brought the tension down by speaking calmly. If he was going to get to the bottom of this, he had to keep them calm.

'We went to Salvanna's for a meal.'

'And wine?'

'A bottle. But that was between both of us.'

'Okay, and then what happened?'

'I don't know. I just went blank.'

'It's okay. Calm down. Let's go back to Salvanna's. You've put your coat on and you've come outside. Now where do you go?'

Paul's expression implied that he was impressed and it made Jay feel proud. 'Yeah, tell him where you went next, Mum.'

Liz's voice was shaky. 'I swear, Jay, I wasn't drunk when we were out.' Despite the assurance, her dishevelled appearance and the smell of gin lingering in the air told a different story.

'It's okay, having a couple of drinks isn't a crime. Where did you go next?'

'I'm blank about what happened. Everything's so fuzzy. We had our meal and then called into the taxi office. We were coming home. But because it was Saturday night, they were busy and said it would be half an hour before they had a taxi available. So we went to the Crystal Club for a drink.'

Jay nodded, prompting her to keep going. He sensed the frustration and the bewilderment from the gaps in her memory. Or she was spinning a damn good yarn.

'That's the last thing I remember. I had a couple of drinks, but nothing that should make me blackout like this. I was fine.'

Jay dealt with alcohol-related incidents every day, but this was different and Liz's confusion added unusual elements to the situation.

'We need to figure out what happened to you. Did anybody approach you at the club? Was there anything unusual about it?'

'I don't think I talked to anybody,' she said.

Jay remembered his training. Saying "I don't think" was something called statement affirming. Putting a vague response at the beginning of a statement meant that she could retract it later.

'We were just having one drink to kill time and I think I nipped to the loo while Andy was at the bar.'

'Liz, are you saying that somebody drugged you? Do you think you were spiked?'

'No. I don't think so. I just can't remember anything.' She said she couldn't remember but her head was nodding yes as she said it. Jay had been trained to spot this clear tell that she was lying.

He wasn't buying it. He absorbed Liz's account, but it wasn't ringing true. His friend's mum was terrified of something, and he doubted that she didn't know what it was.

He was only a constable, but he was going to work his way up to detective and he'd developed some good instincts from being with the Serious Crime Team. 'Let's go through it one step at a time. You went to the ladies while Andy ordered drinks. Did you see anybody?'

Liz screwed up her face in concentration and then she started to tremble again. A tear rolled down her cheek—and Jay could see that her distress was real.

'There were some girls on the stairs. Outside the bathroom. It's narrow and I had to get past them.'

'Walk through it with me. You went up the narrow staircase and had to squeeze past a group of girls on the stairs. Do you remember if they said anything to you?'

Chapter Four

The cold bite in the air seemed fitting for the grim events at the water's edge. Floodlights cast a laddery glow over the dark water as Nash got out of his car at the crime scene. His breath was visible as he chose his footsteps carefully and squelched over the patch of damp grass leading to the path circling the lake. It was dotted with duck and goose droppings, and he was grateful for putting on strong walking shoes when the call came in. The late afternoon had succumbed to the encroaching darkness, and the urgency in the hurried movements of the SOCO team reminded him of frenetic ants.

They wore white paper suits and moved with methodical precision along the bank as they looked for evidence. They'd photographed the body in situ and had been told to leave it until Nash and the coroner arrived. The grass had been cleared of bird excrement and litter. Nash felt the ripple of tension, a confirmation that this wasn't a routine call. The team was in the process of retrieving the body from the lake with some officers leaning over the path to pull it up, and two more in an inflatable dinghy on the black water. The lake was only chest deep, so there was no need for diving gear.

Looking into the water, Nash couldn't make much out, it was a murky abyss beneath the lights, and it held tight to its secrets. The body had attached itself to the struts of the metal bridge. It looked like once-living art. The reflection of the floodlights danced on the surface, casting distorted shadows, and mimicking the turmoil going on around it. Nash watched as they hauled the boy's body out of the water. He felt the familiar surge of adrenaline at the sight of a corpse. It was something he'd grown a thick skin for but never got used to.

The boy was pulled out of the lake and lay on the embankment, a haunting sight under the pale sheet that covered him. Nash knew him from the neighbourhood. It was Noah Ross. He was dressed in skinny jeans that had been torn and a black hoodie—the standard uniform of the young. He had one tattered trainer on his left foot, the other was missing. Nash shook his head at the sorry sight of the metal prosthetic beneath the kid's knee. His features, frozen in tragic stillness, highlighted his youth. His life was cut short, probably after his first leg-over, but long before a legal drink. He knew this kid was fifteen, a reminder that vulnerability often rode with adolescence.

The coroner, Bill Robinson, separated from the group of men in the shadows. His expression was grave as he greeted Nash. 'We've got a mess on our hands.' As if to emphasise the point, he was wiping his fingers on a handkerchief as he walked.

Nash nodded. His focus was riveted on the lake. The victim, who'd been draped in a surgical sheet, looked ethereal in the artificial glow of the SOCO lights.

Bill was talking about the suspicion of drug use, a well-known spectre in town that added complexity to the investigation. Drugs were a problem in every town in the country, and Barrow was the same. But recently, drug-related crime among the youth was on the increase and Nash's Serious Crime Team had word that day that they'd be working with the countrywide vice squad to try and curtail trafficking.

Bill's breath was making patterns in the air. 'It's not every day we pull someone out of the lake. The ducks look disgruntled. It's most likely foul play, but we'll need an autopsy to confirm. We're getting ready to move him, but you can inspect him first and I'll let you know when I have something more concrete.'

Nash and Bill talked as the SOCO team worked around the body. The corpse—Noah—rested on a tarpaulin to protect it from ground contamination. It lay under the sterile shelter of a white tent erected to shield it from prying eyes and preserve the integrity of the scene.

The air was acrid with the smell of disinfectant and forensic chemicals as Nash put on a PPE suit, gloves, and protective shoe covers. The onlookers, settling in for a show and drawn by curiosity, were told to go home.

Inside the tent, Bill directed a SOCO member to turn the body over for further examination. He manipulated the corpse, revealing the extent of the lividity.

The bloated and discoloured skin, a result of post-mortem changes, made it difficult to discern his features. Nash knew what was coming, there weren't many Nigerian fifteen-year-olds with a false leg in a town this size. However, as the body was repositioned, Nash's reaction was still marked and Bill was quick to respond to the change in his stance.

'The boy is Noah Ross, Aiden and Sebastian's friend,' Nash said.

The kid wouldn't be playing table tennis at the centre anymore. He was wet and lifeless. He'd recognised Noah immediately, and the identification had hit Nash like a physical blow, and sorrow clouded his features.

'You know him?'

'He hangs around with the lads at the refugee community centre. He's a good kid.'

The tragedy had a face and a name that connected him to the lives of the people who loved him. Nash couldn't bear to talk about him in the past tense, not yet. A pall of grief settled over him as he grappled with the fact that Noah was full of potential. Nash ran workshops at the centre, and Noah had talked to him about a career in politics. I mean, politics, for Christ's sake.

Noah's clothing had been checked, and a baggie of white powder was found in his pocket. Nash couldn't understand how a kid with strong opinions on the town's regeneration project could be implicated with drugs. This wasn't right. Nash bloody loved this town. It was on the tip of the Lake District, historical, beautiful, surrounded by wild ocean, and the people were good. 'What the hell is messing up such a great place to live?' he asked.

Bill put his hand on Nash's shoulder. 'We'll do what we can to find out what happened. Let's get him to the morgue, and I'll do the autopsy tonight.'

Nash was torn between professional detachment and personal grief. He nodded in acknowledgement and the SOCO team secured Noah for transportation, while he wrestled with the memories stirred by the loss of a familiar face. There had been too many of them in his town lately. He thought about Kelvin at home where he'd left him in front of the fire. This would hit him, too.

Nash surveyed the lake, the stillness disrupted by the occasional honk of a settling duck. A spout of water gushed from the fountain, and in the background, he was aware of the distant sounds of the town going home for dinner.

What happened to you, Noah?

The murky water guarded the secrets of that afternoon and like Nash's moving reflection, it threw his questions back at him. Answers lurked in the form of evidence beneath the surface and around the flattened blades of grass. Noah Ross, who protested the drug problems in town, had ended up in a lake with a bag of drugs in his pocket.

He watched the SOCO team. He was only fifty metres from them, but far enough for the exclusion he needed. Their voices carried to him as they worked to catalogue the evidence.

The first threads of Noah's narrative were laid bare as the last remnants of daylight vanished. The white tent billowed in the breeze, and Nash's thoughts turned dark. The shadows of Barrow Park bore the weight of personal connections. The boy's death wasn't an isolated case. Chemical marijuana was still the hit of choice in the town, its distinctive stink settling like a green fog over the rooftops. You'd catch it on the breeze first thing in the morning. It came on the tang of sea salt and the stench was known as cheese. But along with cheese, spice and cocaine, there was a new drug in town, again chemically modified from its earlier and purer form. A new strain of heroin-infused crystal meth had infiltrated the town, taking names and decaying teeth. It aged people twenty years in a matter of weeks.

Nash knew Noah's mother. They went to the same school and she was never one of the mean girls. He felt it was his duty and responsibility to be the one to tell her. It was never easy. But when you knew the family, it was much harder. He'd make sure Jean Ross was given information that wasn't too sensitive to the case when he could. He walked away from the crime scene, dreading the task of delivering the terrible news to another loving mother. He rang Brown.

'I need you with me for a house call. We've got another dead kid.'

Chapter Five

Liz took another hit of her gin.

'One girl sounded more forceful, as though she was the leader. I was in the toilet, hiding. Then she punched another woman. The sound was horrible. It was so loud. I've never been so scared in my life and I needed to get out before they turned on me.'

'What happened next?' Jay asked.

Paul slammed his fist on the arm of his chair, making his mother jump. 'Mum, that's awful. Did they hit you? If anybody hurt you, I'll kill them,' he said.

Jay put a hand out to stop him talking. He didn't want Liz to cloud over and clam up again.

Her voice trembled. 'I was going to make a run for it, but the leader heard me coming out of the cubicle. I saw the girl they'd been bullying. She was lying on the floor by the sink. Her face and clothes were covered in blood, and one of the others blocked the door to stop me from leaving. I ducked back into the cubicle.'

'Did you recognise anybody?'

She shook her head.

'Did they say anything that might help us identify them?'

'I don't know them. They were just a group of girls at the club. I didn't expect any of this.' She was crying again, sobbing into her hands, and Paul sat beside her and put his arm around her. Liz drank the last of her gin and held the empty glass out to him. He took it and went to the kitchen to refill it.

Jay had something to go on and steps he could follow, 'I'll get onto Crystal and find out what happened to the girl they attacked.'

'I don't know any more,' Liz said. 'It all happened so fast. I should have helped her, but I had to escape. I just left her there.'

'You had no choice, Mum. They'd have killed you if you didn't put yourself first,' Paul said coming back into the room.

'Think, Liz. How did you get out?'

Liz stammered over her answer. 'The leader threatened me. She demanded to know what I'd heard.'

'What did she say?' Paul asked butting in again and holding out the glass to Liz who took it and gulped a mouthful.

Jay frowned. 'I think you should make her a coffee, mate. She's had enough alcohol.' He tried to keep the judgment out of his voice.

'I don't want coffee, I want this.' Liz clutched the glass and then carried on with her story. 'The leader, the one with blue hair, heard me and banged on the toilet door. When I opened it, she leaned in close. Her eyes were fierce. "What did you hear?" she hissed, and she was close enough for me to smell her breath. I was terrified, Jay. I didn't want any trouble, I just wanted to get away.'

'Did she mention anybody else? Any names or details that will help us find them?' Jay was careful not to give anything away in his expression, but for a woman with a memory blackout, her recollection was tumbling over itself now. It was too convenient.

Liz strained to remember, her forehead creasing. 'No, she didn't mention anybody. It was all about me keeping quiet. She said, "Cry and you'll die." And I believed her, but here you are. I hope ringing you doesn't make it worse.'

'What were they bullying the girl about? Why were they attacking her? Did she say anything other than that she'd killed somebody—a man?'

'I can't remember. But I think it was something illegal. The more I try, the further away it goes. There was a terrible noise. One of the girls had banged somebody's face against the sink. I heard it, and she screamed. I think it was the girl that had been on the floor. She must have stood up at some point,' Liz shuddered and swallowed something that had risen into her mouth.

'It's okay. Take your time.'

She closed her eyes. 'The girl blocking the main door to the bathroom lifted her hand.'

'What do you mean?' Jay asked.

'She raised it in defence. I think the leader was going to hit her. She was protecting herself.'

'Go on.'

'The second she moved, I got away and flew down the stairs. I remember now, I fell down the last three and hurt my back.' She pointed to where it was sore. 'I think the treads have given me a carpet burn.'

'Let's see, Mum.' Paul said getting out of his chair again.

Jay motioned him back in his seat and encouraged Liz to go on. He didn't want to interrupt her.

'And then I told Andy we had to leave. I was terrified. I can't remember anything else.' She was getting tired. The hand holding her glass tilted, sloshing the gin over the rim. Jay lifted it out of her hand and put it on the table beside her.

'Let's retrace your steps from that point. I'll go to the club tomorrow, maybe somebody saw something.' Jay continued questioning her to jog her memory, but it wasn't ringing true. 'After leaving Crystal, what happened next?'

'I don't know. It's fuzzy.'

'Try to remember. Did you leave the club with Andy and take the taxi you booked?'

She stood up, swayed, and sat down again. 'I think we left together, but after that, I don't know. Andy was arrested, so we couldn't have got a taxi home. Why can't I remember?'

Paul said, 'Is it the shock, Jay? You're good at this. She couldn't tell me anything at all. With Mum in this state, and Dad getting arrested, I didn't know what to do.'

Jay kept his face neutral. If this blackout fiasco was true—and he doubted it—Liz's shock wasn't the issue. Paul was blind to anything but his mother's distress and Jay laid the blame in the bottom of the gin glass that was almost empty again. 'It's a good job you were home when Liz got back.'

'I'd just got in when she pulled up in a taxi. She was alone.'

'So she did come home by cab. I'll get on to the company for a statement in the morning. They might have seen something. Liz, let's focus. What happened when you left the club?' He needed to get to the facts about why Andy had been arrested.

'You keep asking the same questions. I can't even remember getting home. Everything is blank.'

'Let's do what we did before, one step at a time. Go back to when you joined Andy at the bar. Picture it. You told him you had to leave. Then what happened? Does anything stand out? Even if it seems minor.'

'It was just a normal night—until it wasn't.'

Jay balanced getting the story with using a delicate approach. He saw the emotional toll it was taking on Liz. She was coming across as an alcoholic seeking attention, but he knew that wasn't her character. They'd never been anything other than ordinary social drinkers. Fear made her clamp her eyes shut as she brought back another pivotal moment.

Jay saw a chill run down her arms as goose pimples appeared on her skin. The blackout may have been false, but she couldn't fake those. 'The leader appeared at the end of the bar. She was glaring at me and banged her fist in her other hand as a warning that if I said anything there'd be consequences.'

Liz's next revelation made her swallow hard and she made a strange sound in her throat. Jay worried that she might be ill and moved back to give her space. He didn't want her throwing up all over him.

'Oh my God.' Her voice was muffled and her fingers trembled. 'It's coming back.' Here we go, Jay thought, as Liz said, 'The girl they'd beaten up was part of their gang. The others forced her to sell drugs, and she'd overdosed somebody. She was threatening to go to the police and hand herself in. But the gang leader stopped her.'

Liz's voice rose in hysteria as she shared the horrifying details. 'They were selling drugs, and she wanted out. But the leader controlled her. They were willing to do a lot of physical damage to keep her quiet.'

Jay and Paul looked at each other. 'Mum's a witness,' Paul said. Jay put his hand on Paul's arm and shook his head to stop him from saying more.

She was on the brink of a meltdown. 'It was drugs, Jay. They were pushing drugs, and they'd forced that poor girl to sell them. And somebody died. She wanted to do the right thing. She was going to the police, but they beat her up to silence her.'

Liz's voice wavered with fear, and Jay calmed her. 'Liz, breathe. You're safe now. We're going to handle this. Did they say anything about where they operated, who was in charge, anything that could help us find them?'

'I don't know. It was chaotic. But they're dangerous, Jay. They won't stop.'

Chapter Six

Nash drove to Jean Ross' house in silence. The weight of the impending house call made him long for the comforts of home. A media ban had been put in place until Jean was told, but he couldn't control the public. It would be all over social media by now.

Damn. He'd indulged his shock and had sat by the lake, composing himself, when he should have got in the car to beat Facebook and get to Jean. The chance that she hadn't been near her phone in the last half hour was slim. He admonished his selfishness and put his foot down.

Memories of Noah played with him. It was a cruel game. He was a vibrant young man with big dreams. They'd talked about the town's drug problems sometimes. Nash remembered the anger on his face. He was furious with the dealers. 'The youth here doesn't have to worry about stepping on landmines or being gunned down in the streets,' he'd said in his thick African accent. He looked like a Prime Minister in Adidas. 'It was good coming to this town. A safe place for us—but these people bring evil. They destroy its beautiful history and the good clean air we breathe. Why, Detective Nash?'

Nash had no answer for him then. And Noah raised too many questions now. The kid was one of a kind. Old before his years from things no child should ever have to see. He wasn't an addict. And that fact alone, made this case stink, but until they had more to go on, nothing made sense. Thoughts played in Nash's mind like a ghostly movie reel. He wasn't aware of the drizzle coming on, but the streetlights blurred into veiled rain halos as he navigated the town. He turned his wipers on without thinking about it and dropped a gear as he approached the hill. Each corner brought him closer to ugly words he didn't want to say.

Arriving at the modest ex-council house, he didn't want to get out of the car. This one was too personal. Nash tried to summon extra strength. He'd seen too many broken mothers in his time, and that night it was an overload of somebody else's pain to absorb. He thought about what Kelvin would say and drew courage from it, but a different voice spoke in his head.

Come on, Nasher. It's your duty, man. Do it for the kid. And if it was his imagination, the glovebox wouldn't have snapped open, scattering a couple of Werther's Originals into the passenger side footwell. *Have a toffee, mate. Steady the old nerves. Shit, you're predictable. Still carrying a bag of sweets in the glovebox, and tissues in case you get a bawler.*

He remembered a similar conversation with Max Jones. Nash was vexed about him raiding his sweet stash and then leaving the wrappers in the door caddy that day. Nash was a clean freak while Jones was a wild hippie slob. 'Have a toffee, mate. Steady the old nerves,' he'd said.

Max was still alive then and had used the same sentence that day in the car, and despite his sorrowful mood and the rain like a mother's tears on the windscreen, Nash smiled at the memory.

He was an arsehole to Max that day. 'For your information, they aren't toffees. They are boiled sweets.'

'For your information, Nasher, you have no idea how much of a dickhead you are. You need to get laid, mate.'

He wanted to shake his head to clear the memory, but people didn't do that in real life. It was over two years since he'd held Max's hand as he died from cancer. But he still missed him. The air was heavy with more rain as he pulled his collar up against the onslaught of the weather. Molly had just driven in behind him and together they knocked on Jean's door.

'Silas. Oh heck. What brings you here?' Jean asked.

And he prepared to break her heart.

The words caught in his throat. The weight of the news he brought was suffocating. 'Can we talk inside?'

'What is it, Nash? Is it Noah? Oh, dear God.' He guided her into the house. He still had to say it. They always knew, but the death sentence had to be spoken. Time froze as the words left Nash's mouth, and wrapped themselves around Jean's neck to strangle her. She choked on them until her eyes were swollen.

In the living room, Nash felt the warmth of familiarity. He'd been here before. Last year, just before Christmas, when Harry was still alive.

Family photos hung on the walls. They'd survived losing him, and the pictures painted the story of a family getting on with things. Jean's husband still smiled down at them from three different images. He had been killed in his car the year before and Jean's life was about to be shattered again.

The town's four dead children were young—and high. You wouldn't expect good homes with overstuffed cushions and antique dressers. Jean's house didn't fit the picture of squalor and addiction. Nash caught Brown's eye. They shouldn't judge—but people did. He did. They were trained to see everything and build an impression of the victim's lifestyle, and Jean, and Noah, didn't slot into this. It was wrong.

Jean's mum had owned an antique shop in town and Jean inherited a collection of Victorian dolls—the kind that gave you nightmares. One was a life-sized little boy who stood three feet tall on the stairs. He was facing the wall with his head on his forearm, and Nash wondered what he'd done wrong.

He came back to a real question. What had Noah done to end up cold and alone in the park boating lake?

A movement drew his eye back to the doll and as he turned away with a grimace, it slumped down the wall becoming less, smaller and defenceless. There was no draught. He looked at Brown who didn't seem to have seen the doll move. Jean didn't acknowledge it.

Nash guided her to a seat, while Brown asked permission to make tea—always bloody tea, always following their formulaic procedures. The grieving family rarely answered her questions about milk and sugar—Jean's world had stopped and he doubted she even knew Brown was there.

'You can't take him away from me.'

'He was a good kid.' Nash had a lump in his throat.

'I only just got him,' she said.

'I know, Jean. It's cruel.'

'He's legally mine. When that adoption came through, I swore to keep him safe. I promised. He was loved, you know? Everybody loved my son. He was like sunshine.'

She didn't speak after that, and she didn't ask questions. This was normal. In his time, Nash had seen every response. The shock was transitioning from a reactionary state to a clinical one and she was shutting down. But that state didn't last. She shook herself out of it. Jean Ross had wilted onto the arm of the sofa, and when she couldn't shriek any more, it turned into a wail until her voice was hoarse.

And in the kitchen, Nash heard Brown tapping a teaspoon on the side of a mug. The budgie—Nash remembered it was blue—was roused from sleep. It chirped from under a plastic cover that was elasticated around the bottom of the cage. The bird was covered for the night already, and it made Nash realise it was dinner time. He knew Jean wouldn't be eating tonight.

He was silent, letting her grieve.

Nash sat with her. When Brown came in, she'd sit further away at the end of the sofa, but she was taking her time, giving Jean space. They were always respectful, even when they wanted to rage against the unfairness. Nash was perched on the edge of an armchair facing the grieving mother, but he didn't touch her. He had no comfort to offer that would make a difference. He was just there—until he faded away. Jean had gone somewhere else, and the detectives ceased to exist. She had to make that initial journey to process the first few minutes of knowing. It was the only way she could come back to the room with a residue of sanity. He went to help Brown bring in the tea, strong and sweet. He put it on the table until Jean was still and had nothing left in the pit of her first wave of grief. Plenty more would come, but for now, while she was quiet, he pressed the cup into her hands.

'Careful, sweetheart. It's hot.'

She tried to push it away.

'Drink it, Jean. It'll help.'

She made a sound like a hissing cat.

'It'll do nothing for the grief, but it might take the sting out of your throat, and you'll need the energy to cope with the pain,' Nash said.

Jean looked at him then. Her head raised and she was wild and momentarily inhuman. She reminded him of an infected zombie from one of the shows Kelvin liked. She looked at him, but he didn't think she saw him until she refocused. And then she did. She saw the man who told her that her son was dead. She stared at him with hatred. The next noise came from the demon of agony inside her. She took the cup and smashed it against the wall on the other side of the room.

Jean had a cat. It could cut its paws, but that was one drama he could save Jean from. He would pick up the pieces, but not yet. He sat with her.

As Noah's mother processed the news, Nash told her some of what they knew so far. The parts that wouldn't add to her pain. He didn't mention the packet of white powder—cocaine?—found on her son. He couldn't give her much, and she wouldn't take it in, but it was words to trample through the agony. The sound of his voice calmed her and she was silent, for now.

After more internal processing, she shook her head and spoke. 'We went through so much foreign policy and red tape when we got him. It took a long time,' Jean said. It was a sentence to fill a silence. Everybody came up with one at times like this, the inane, the sad, and sometimes even the ridiculous. Later, when they heard the news, other people would say, 'But he can't be dead. I only saw him yesterday,' as though their seeing him was a preventative of mortality.

'I know, Jean, and when Noah brought his adoption certificate into the centre, waving it around like a bloody flag, you've never seen a young man more proud. He told me he was going to hang it in his office when he became a member of parliament. He loved you very much.'

Noah had lived with Jean and Harry for five years. First, he was placed with them in a fostering arrangement. Until the evening, over pizza, when they decided they wanted to be a proper family and adopt him. Harry died before Noah became his legal son, but Jean had known the joy of legal motherhood for one month before losing Noah forever. It was tragic.

'My Harry would have been so happy if he'd lived to see it. Do you think they're together?'

Nash thought about his deceased friend, Max, and about Werther's Originals. 'Yes. I believe they are.'

Her loss was too much and she sobbed. He understood. There was no sorrow like it.

'Take me too, God. Let me be with my family.'

There would be probing questions to ask her, but this wasn't the time.

Nash picked up the pieces of broken crockery and Brown called Jean's sister to come.

Brown asked if she could use the bathroom and was gone for a couple of minutes. The silence was awkward but Nash was used to it. When they heard the tap running upstairs, Jean raised her head a fraction of an inch and then dropped it again. Nothing to see here. As Brown came downstairs she bent to straighten the slumped doll on the stairs. As she altered its position the mournful and elongated cry of *Mama* filled the room.

She left it on the stairs and walked away. There was nobody near the doll the second time it cried...

Mama.

Chapter Seven

Paul Gibson said, 'This puts Mum in danger. We can't let them get away with it.'

'Liz, we'll get you protection, and we'll find these people. But we need your cooperation. Can you help us?' Jay said.

Liz was wary. 'I'm scared, Jay. What if they come here? Make them stop.'

Jay was worried about his friend's safety. His work colleagues thought he was a clown, but he'd never felt more grown-up. When crime affected his friends, his job was personal. He was determined to help and prove himself. 'What happened with Andy, and why was he arrested?'

'He saw how frightened I was. He asked what happened, but I just kept saying, "We've got to go. We need to leave." I had to get away from them.'

'Andy didn't say anything to them?'

'Not then. That came after. We hurried into the taxi office to escape, and he had no idea what was wrong with me. I was too scared to tell him. They were following us. It was only a few feet to the taxi rank, but even though I didn't look behind me, I was aware of them coming out of Crystal. The girls from the gang piled into the office and crammed together on the wooden bench opposite where Andy and I sat.

'"Taxi for Anson Street?" The woman behind the security screen announced our road to the room and said our taxi would be there in five minutes. Terror set in. The operator had just told them where we lived, and I had a panic attack. I couldn't breathe and thought I was going to pass out. "What have you done to my wife?" Andy shouted. He was leaning over me and telling me to breathe.'

'Oh, Mum, that's horrible,' Paul said. Liz took another gulp of gin but gagged as it went down. She covered her mouth, trying not to be sick. Paul grabbed the wastebin and held it out to her, but she shook her head.

'All right?' Jay asked.

She nodded and fought for a few seconds to keep the alcohol down. 'The girls weren't scared of Andy. "You'd better keep quiet," one of them said. Then, two men ran into the taxi office and rammed into him, holding him against the wall. The girl behind the screen rang the police.'

Liz said she was aware of the radio operator talking to the police as the first man punched Andy in the stomach. He bent over but came up fighting.

Liz reached for Paul's hand and he rubbed it between his palms to increase the circulation. 'They said terrible things would happen to us if we talked.'

'How many were there?' Jay asked.

'Four girls and two males. The men were attacking Andy. I was screaming but the police weren't there yet. It was only a few seconds, but it seemed to last forever.'

'And they were beating Andy all that time?'

'Yes, but he was fighting back. He didn't just take it. And there were two of them. The fight spilt into the street as they kept hitting each other. I've never seen him like that. Andy was protecting me but was coming off worse against the men. They were vicious. The girls surrounded us and when the men pulled him to the ground they kept kicking him. Two of them held me back and made me watch, but they didn't hit me. We aren't the kind of people that brawl in the street, Jay. I've never been in a fight in my life. And Dad's an IT engineer at the yard. We don't do that. But he fought back. The sound of them hitting each other will give me nightmares for a long time.'

Jay smiled as fond memories came back to him. Since Paul and his sister were born, Liz and Andy had always called themselves Mum and Dad. It re-humanised them. This was a criminal case, but these people were his friends. 'What about street patrols? They're shit hot around town on Saturday nights.'

'Two doormen were running from Crystal to break up the fight and I heard sirens. Their lights came around the corner a few seconds later.'

Liz looked tired. The adrenaline had exploded through her body giving her a frenetic energy until she levelled out, but now she was drunk and sinking into the shock. Jay wanted to get the last details so that Paul could get her to bed. 'Nearly done, Liz,' he said. 'Keep going.'

'It was difficult for the police to know who the bad guys were. Dad has never hurt anybody in his life. The girls let me go when we heard the sirens and they mooched away into the shadows. I wanted to stop them from leaving, but I was too scared. I tried to get to Andy, but somebody held me out of the way. Andy was still trying to protect himself and me. He wouldn't calm down and kept shouting at the police which got him arrested. I couldn't believe it.' She broke down in a fresh flood of tears which happened every time Andy was mentioned. The couple were inseparable and if they had a problem, Liz had always had her husband to lean on.

'Perhaps it was mistaken identity, Mum,' Paul said.

'The fight made it hard for the police to identify the culprits. The men had run away, and Andy was left screaming at one of the girls left behind in the street. It looked bad. He was enraged.'

'Didn't they get any of them?'

'Only two of the girls that didn't manage to run, but they weren't the ringleaders. Just kids, really. Dad lashed out at one of the officers holding him back. But he looked scared when two of them threw him to the ground and slapped him in handcuffs. All the fight left him. He was covered in blood and looked terrible.'

'We'll get him processed and he'll be home in no time. Don't worry. They'll have taken him in partly for his safety. He'll get to tell his side, and as long as he didn't touch any of the girls, he'll be home any time now. You'll see.'

'He didn't touch them. I swear.'

Jay patted her knee. The Gibson's night began with a romantic meal and ended in a full-blown crisis.

'They heard the name of my street at the taxi office, Jay. We wouldn't take much finding. They might come here.'

Jay was out of his depth and was trying to play the big man to impress his friends. Nash would never fling wild promises around but Jay didn't know any better. 'We have protocols for this kind of situation. We can get you into Witness Protection. We'll make sure you're safe. But in the meantime, use your common sense. Lock the doors and windows and keep your phone beside you. Any trouble, call 999. I'll stay in touch, and we won't let anything happen to you,' Jay said.

He rang a taxi, said his goodbyes and left the house in the brisk morning air. The first light pierced what was left of the night, casting a purple glow on the quiet street. The sun was a distant promise on the horizon as it ascended. It was four in the morning, a time when the world slept between the dregs of night and the new day.

With two hours until his shift, Jay waited for his taxi. He wished Nash had been with him, it was the most grown-up thing he'd ever done and even though it was unofficial, it was the first time he'd led a witness interview. He was proud of himself but he was still Jay Bowes, the clown.

He spotted a gnome sitting under a garden table. It was the perfect opportunity for a harmless prank to inject levity into the tense situation. He wanted to make Liz smile and positioned it in the middle of the path near the front door. The gnome had a brilliant expression of exaggerated surprise.

Suppressing a chuckle, Jay admired his handiwork. The gnome looked as though it was guarding the entrance. It occurred to him that Liz might see it as something sinister, so he grabbed the pen he carried out of his jacket pocket and found a scrap of paper. He scribbled over a random girl's phone number and scrawled a quick note. *Nobby here will keep you safe until the leprechauns arrive to guard you. Evil buggers they are. Nobody will get through our defences. Love Jay xxx.*

It didn't occur to him that the note could fly away, or that Liz would have a meltdown before she saw it. She was frightened and traumatised, but Jay didn't think it through or see how inappropriate it was to joke at a time like this. Satisfied with his light-hearted mischief, he tiptoed away from the scene as he saw his taxi pulling up. He left Nobby playing its part in the silent comedy. A touch of humour never hurt, and in dark moments a well-timed prank could make people smile, he thought.

He settled into the back seat and the city stirred around him, the hum of early morning activity replacing the silence.

Chapter Eight

'Listen up, team.'

The Serious Crime team groaned. The boss was in one of his moods. Nash was already talking as he strode into the room with a stack of folders under his arm. He slapped them onto the front table with purpose.

The investigation they'd been working on for months had ramped up a gear and they were liaising with the Greater Manchester Narcotics Team. Nash made his staff sit up, take notice, and not let the side down for the Barrow division.

The incident room buzzed with energy as he surveyed the faces of his team. 'Stop slouching, Lawson. Nature saved you from the invertebrate gene pool for a reason.'

He stood in front of the whiteboard and felt the tension that rained on the room like a sudden storm on a cloudless day. This was a big one. The team would know it from the stick inserted up Nash's arse, to the way his right shoe squeaked when he shifted his weight. He had his best shoes on, ready for his meeting later and they'd never been broken in.

His superior, Chief Superintendent Bronwyn Lewis, liked to attend the first and the final team briefing in any investigation.

She sat at the back of the room and, when he came in, Nash noticed she wore her grey herringbone skirt suit. It was the only one that had a waistcoat, and Nash knew when that went on, combined with black stilettoes rather than small heels, that The Bron was pulling out all the stops. Her nails were scarlet—and even if he wasn't down to attend, he'd have surmised that she had an important meeting with the Manchester team. The tension was high. Nash's squad hadn't worked much top-level narcotics, and they had to get it right.

He pinned three photos to the incident board. Every investigation started with a face. These images captured the frozen moments of young lives lost—three smiles etched with the tragedy of Barrow's recent past. 'These are just kids. They are our children.' His gaze rested on DCS Greg Mason and Seargent Jackie Woods who both had teenagers. 'Cezar Zubkov, fifteen. Emil Bosnjak, fourteen, and Billy Clayton, sixteen.' The room was silent as he left a conspicuous gap and added a fourth photo. 'And this is our most recent victim. Most of you know him, but for those of you who didn't have the pleasure, meet Noah Ross. A charming young man who was going to shake this town up one day.'

'Another junkie, sir?' Greg Mason asked. The tone of derision was clear in his voice and Nash wheeled around on him.

'Get out of my room. You're off the case.'

Bronwyn Lewis frowned, but Nash ignored her.

'What?' Mason asked.

'Is it okay to look down on people because their circumstances don't match yours?' Nash was so mad that he had a tremor in his voice.

'No, sir.'

'Damn right. Now get out, and maybe you'll think about that while you're deskbound for the next few weeks.'

'You're seriously taking me off the case for asking a question?'

'Out of order,' Renshaw said under his breath.

'Something to say, Renshaw?'

'No, sir.'

'What can I do, sir?' Mason asked.

'You can go back two minutes and undo what you said. Now get out before I really lose my patience.'

They waited until Mason had picked up his notes and left the room, slamming the door as much as he dared on his way out. Nash pointed to the fourth image on the board. He waited for them to shut up, and the case settled on the team, along with a bad atmosphere. Nash knew his response was extreme and he'd have to answer to Lewis, but he stood by it. This was a highly sensitive case and it couldn't be run by any team members harbouring preconceived prejudice. The media were all over this and the last thing Barrow needed was bad press.

'This is the fourth young fatality due to drug abuse in this town in as many months. They are made up of three foreign nationals, and one UK citizen. The latest boy, Noah Ross, originates from West Africa.' It was a Western name for an African boy and Nash humanised him for the team. He explained how Noah had sat with his parents and had the pleasure of choosing his own British name when they adopted him. 'He was fifteen. He'd lost his lower leg by stepping on a landmine in Nigeria. Can you imagine what that child went through? He never had a prosthetic limb until he came here when he was nine. When he was thrown in the lake and disposed of like garbage, he lost the shoe from that leg. We've yet to find it. This may not seem relevant to the case, but I want you all to know that Noah cared about this town and the people in it. He wanted to be a politician, and a more driven young man you'd be hard-pressed to find.'

Nash paused for thought, and the room was quiet.

'Hear, hear,' Detective Inspector Molly Brown said. Nash raised his hand to still the team.

'I want to know what makes a young man, hell-bent on a career in government, and with a fierce pride in our town, take a needle and inject narcotics into his body? And why he'd have a bag of coke in his pocket? Most of you knew Noah Ross. He wasn't a so-called junkie, the kid wasn't interested in taking drugs.' He let the words hit home. 'But four dead boys in such a short time, when the norm would be maybe one every couple of years, doesn't make sense. And yet, all four of these teenagers died from a drug overdose.'

'You think they were injected by somebody else?' Renshaw asked.

'We don't know how it was administered. We're assuming self-administration.'

'But it could be another serial killer? That's crazy.'

'We're not ruling anything out, Renshaw. But I think we're dealing with something different. We've had the bloodwork back from the first three deaths and somebody is cutting the town's illegal drug supply with dangerous chemicals. These homicides are the result of a tainted drug trade, not a killer with a pattern. However, which link in the chain is responsible for corrupting the batch is anybody's guess at this stage.'

'The dealers around town are getting younger,' Brown said.

'And the victims. Noah Ross was fifteen. And he was already dead when he was thrown into the lake. The official cause of his death was a narcotic overdose. This is crucial evidence. We need to find out why he had lethal levels in his system, and who is ultimately responsible.'

Brown raised her hand. 'They are all male. Is there any other connection between the victims?'

Nash nodded. 'Good question. We haven't found any familial links, but they all hung around areas with known drug activity, including the Open Arms Refugee and Community Centre.'

'That's dirty,' Lawson said. Aiden, his nephew, worked there and Nash knew Lawson would take this personally.

'We're looking at a contamination of the supply chain, and I want to know who's behind it. Let's continue to hit the streets, talk to informants, and look at every individual hanging around on corners until we get some leads. We stop this, now. Before more lives are lost.'

Nash told them that tasks would be assigned. They'd be working in pairs and checking in regularly.

'We're dealing with a new player in town, a party drug the kids are calling Crystal Chaos. It's a highly addictive, produced chemical compound, a heroin derivative laced with a combination of cocaine and crystal meth. All four victims had large quantities of this lethal substance in their systems.'

'Manny Woods got out of prison a few weeks ago. Could he be involved?' Phil asked.

'It's too early to make wild guesses, but I doubt it. He's small-time. However, in at least one of these victims, it goes against his character which raises questions.'

'Racial?'

'Given that one of the boys was Caucasian, I doubt that too, but the case is throwing up more questions than answers. This is a dangerous escalation, and Crystal Chaos is a scourge. It's tearing through the community and stealing our children, and I take that very personally. Our next move is crucial.'

'Is there any link to the Crystal Club?' Bowes asked.

'We have no reason to think so. The name relates to the meth ingredient. What are you getting at, Bowes?'

'The trouble with my friend's parents. I reported it to you and opened a new case file. That happened in there. The place is rife with drugs.'

'The whole town's infested. I don't think any drinking hole is worse than any other. In fact, we've been keeping particular tabs on The Siren, where known dealers are hanging out. But we'll come to that later,' Nash said.

He collected his thoughts before continuing. 'This is where we are now. But we're going in hard.' A ripple of excitement waved across the team as they sat up straighter, shuffled in their seats and paid attention. 'We'll be working in close collaboration with the Manchester narcotics and vice teams. Our intel suggests that a major source in the supply chain is coming in from a dirty operation in Manchester. The Greater Manchester Narcotics Team opened an undercover operation two years ago. The aim is to apprehend the chemist behind the creation of Crystal Chaos. It's a process, and a climb through the various chain-links and distribution drop-offs to get there. We are a medium-sized town, but millions of pounds worth of collateral comes into it in the form of drugs. The product is sold to produce a huge revenue stream from Barrow's economy, which then leaves the town. We've seen successes, with many low-level dealers apprehended and jailed—like Manny Woods. And as frustrating as it is, we've had orders from above to let several more continue trading to catch the bigger fish. But we need to cut the head off this snake. We know who most of them are, and it's time to take these bastards down.'

Nash let the room absorb the news about a liaison mission and countered their mixed feelings. The collaboration with the Greater Manchester Narcotics Team—GMNT meant a broader scope and access to better surveillance equipment. It was a deep dive into the web of drug trafficking that connected their town to the greater urban network. However, it also meant having more brass to answer to. Nash stressed the importance of coordination and information sharing. The success of their operation relied on the seamless integration of efforts between boroughs.

Nash was excited to be involved in Operation Diamond Light, a sting his team had never heard of until recently, even though GMNT had eyes on Barrow for over two years.

The fight against the infiltrating drug was big, and the collaboration with Manchester was a pivotal step in dismantling the supply chain.

Nash leaned against the edge of the table. The file of their first target, Jerod Mathis was uppermost. When he opened the folder, Mathis' photo smirked at him—arrogant prick. He pinned it to the board on the side they usually allocated to maps, separated from the victims. He didn't want this scum's face anywhere near those kids.

'Jerod Mathis, a data science specialist living a luxurious life on Lake Windermere. But don't be fooled by the pretty boy façade and designer suit, he's filthy. His website says he's a self-made man. With a couple of high-profile, squeaky-clean clients on his books, he keeps his nose out of the mire. After coming up through small-time drug dealing, he made his fortune by selling five-quid domain names for three hundred pounds apiece. That led him to a bigger, and gradually cleaner, operation in the field of data science. But he's running a sizable drug operation out of Barrow and Kendal, and he's the major player in our backwater. We've been tracking him since he took over local operations from Robin Hill nearly two years ago and now we've had clearance from the Diamond Light campaign to make an arrest.'

'Robin Hill the murderer?' Bowes asked. Nash saw Molly Brown wrap her arms around her body. A year ago, she'd been an hour away from being Hill's next victim and it was still raw. 'Sorry, Mol,' Bowes said. He was an oaf, but even he was sensitive enough to pick up on the change in her confidence as she shrank in her chair.

'Yes, but don't get bogged down in the ties to Hill. He's locked away and will be for a long time. Hill was a small-time operator, running fraud scams and some weed and pills. Mathis is our target, and Hill was whitebait in the drug world compared to him.'

'Can we move on, please?' Molly asked.

Nash knew how hard it was for her to hear his name come up in an investigation again, but they had a job to do, and fragile sensitivities had to be put aside. Brown was a worry. She'd come a long way since Hill, and her life was in a great place. He'd keep an eye on her to see that she didn't slip backwards. However, the station would be swarming with the GMNT and the last thing he needed was a flaky officer. He amended his internal thought process to a more inclusive term—an officer with personal mental health issues. He had to set a good example—but hell, Brown was flaky.

'A point of interest, team. Mathis was originally a Barrow lad. He left town under heat years ago, and when Hill was banged up, Barrow was ripe for the taking. Mathis was already established and was one of the big operators in Bolton. He was looking for a new patch to build and had some dubious contacts. With Barrow wide open, he swooped in, took it, but he doesn't shit on his own doorstep and has made a life in Windermere. It's worth noting that Mathis is a recovering addict. He doesn't use the filth he sells on himself. These are animals that we don't want to get mixed up with. Keep it local, and leave the big boys to the Manchester lot.'

Nash looked around his team. 'Are we good?'

'Yes, sir.'

Chapter Nine

Nash contained his annoyance at Kelvin's kids. Imani had visited her dad while Nash was at work and she left a heaviness behind her like a cloying perfume. When Nash got home, he and Kelvin sat in the living room with a new and unspoken tension between them. Unresolved issues lingered and it was affecting their relationship. Nash had broken down some of the barriers with Zola and Taraji but things with Imani showed no signs of improvement. A photograph on the mantelpiece showed Kelvin with his late wife and daughters in memory of happier family times. Kelvin had felt awkward about it being there, but Nash insisted that the photo be displayed. That was Kelvin's life before they met, and Nash didn't want to deny it.

He saw that Kelvin was upset and he poured them both a drink. It wasn't usual practice mid-week but Kelvin was visibly shaken after another argument with Imani. He told Nash that when his eldest daughter had left, slamming the door after another fight, Kelvin had felt helpless and the worry he experienced made Nash protective.

'I don't know how much more of this I can take, Si,' Kelvin muttered, picking up the photograph and lying it face down.

Maybe it wasn't a good idea to have it displayed but Nash felt it was important for the three grown children to see that their deceased mother hadn't been forgotten.

He leaned against the wall and chose his words carefully. 'She's struggling with the change, Kel. We aren't easy for her to accept.' He picked up the photo and put it back in place.

Kelvin swept a cruise brochure off the coffee table and raised his voice, something he rarely did, but it was in frustration rather than anger. 'We've been together for almost two years, and it's seven since we lost her mum. I let her grieve and indulged her and now she's just being a brat. I've spoiled her.'

'I'm saying nothing.' Nash laughed, holding his hands up in front of him. Far be it for him to criticise one of Kelvin's children.

Kelvin laughed and pulled Nash onto the sofa with him. 'She's my daughter. I thought she'd come around by now, but we're drifting further apart.'

The strained relationship between Kelvin and Imani was affecting them all. Nash felt that the other two kids wanted to be closer to their father, and even be friends with Nash, but they held back on Imani's say-so. Kelvin was conflicted between the love for his family and the need to be happy.

'You can't control how she reacts, Kel. You need to be true to yourself and hope that she sees you're happy and comes around.'

Kelvin met his gaze and Nash saw the vulnerability beneath his strength. 'I just want my family to accept us.'

They heard the usual sounds of Walney Island outside—a reminder that there was still a world beyond their conflict.

When somebody knocked on the door, Nash answered it. He ushered Zola, Kelvin's middle child, into the lounge.

'Dad, can I talk to you?'

As they went into the sunroom to talk, Nash stayed in the lounge. Whether the kids liked it or not, he wasn't going anywhere and they were a blended family navigating the complexities of acceptance. How Nash dealt with things would shape the bonds between them, and they could be together, or frayed, depending on his actions. Nash waited to find out what was wrong, and he heard Zola crying, and the worrying word bullying drifted to him.

He took a whiskey to his office to work on the case and closed the door. He spread some papers in front of him, but couldn't concentrate. It had been a long day and the faces of the deceased teenagers floated across his vision—demanding answers—when he closed his eyes and rubbed the tension from his temples.

He felt stifled and opened the window to let some air in. It was late in the year and there were no leaves on the trees in his garden. A wild night was brewing, and he stood by the window taking in the salty air. He lasted thirty seconds before he was freezing and had to slam the window shut. But during the time it'd been open he heard a voice on the wind. 'Row, row, row your boat.' It made him think about the Caribbean, they'd decided on February, and the thought of escaping this bluster appealed to him.

He gave up on work, went to make a coffee, and was sitting at the breakfast bar when the sunroom door opened. Nash watched as they came out and he rose to greet Zola before sitting down. She'd been crying and her eyes were puffy, but she made a feeble attempt to conceal her distress.

'Hi, Si. I'm sorry I didn't say much before. I wasn't being rude, but needed to speak to Dad.'

'Hey, Zola. Great sense of smell. I take it you smelt the coffee?' Nash greeted her holding up his mug and masking his concern with a casual tone. 'Want one?'

She laughed and nodded. 'Yes please, that would be lovely.' Kelvin's children had been brought up with manners. They were extremely polite, and while it was commendable, it highlighted the friction between them and Nash. They hadn't broken out of the ultra-polite stiffness of strangers. He longed for the day they came in without knocking and went straight to the kettle to make their own coffee. That was family. Kelvin's kids always waited to be asked to sit down, but for the first time, Zola pulled out the chair opposite Nash and sat without being asked. It was progress and didn't go unnoticed by either of them. Despite looking worried, Kelvin smiled at Nash over Zola's head.

'It's okay. Don't move, Si. I'll do the honours.' He flicked the switch to re-boil the kettle and Nash guessed that standing with his back to them while it boiled was a purposeful action to take himself out of the conversation for a couple of minutes. Nash knew better than to pry, and they made small talk until two more mugs were put on the breakfast bar and Kelvin sat down.

Zola forced a weak smile, but her eyes betrayed her turmoil.

'Serena's having a tough time at school,' Kelvin said.

'What's the matter?' Nash ventured softly. 'I wasn't listening, but think I heard the word bullying. I hope she's okay.'

Kelvin put his hand over Zola's. 'I hope so, too. A group of kids at her new school have been giving her a hard time,' he said.

Zola's voice shook with emotion. 'It's nothing serious yet, but it's getting to her. Dad thought you could offer some advice. He says you must have come across this sort of thing at work. How do we nip it in the bud?'

Nash hated the idea of Serena suffering. She was a lively kid and always chatted to Nash like a long-lost best friend when they called. He was grateful that, despite their reservations about him, Zola and her husband Greg were aware that little jugs had big ears and didn't discuss the family disputes in front of the children. He'd met the girls a few times, the first in a supermarket with their parents by chance, but he thought they were charming.

'Of course,' he said. 'I'll do whatever I can to help.'

Zola hesitated. 'I appreciate it, Si, but we don't want to make a big deal about it. We're still hoping it'll blow over. I just thought you might have some insight.'

'Children bully those that are weaker or different from themselves. They can be cruel. Pack mentality and peer pressure are often a strong incentive. I wouldn't wait in the hope that it gets better. I think you need to take it up with the school now.'

'I'm loath to do that in case it makes things worse.'

'I get that you don't want to go down an official police route, but maybe I could send one of my officers in to give a talk to Serena's year group about bullying. If it would help, I'd be very happy to go myself, but I wouldn't want to make anything more awkward for her.'

Zola agreed that it was something to put to the headmistress when she made an appointment to speak to the school the next day. She managed a grateful smile before picking up her bag to leave. 'Thanks Si. You've convinced me that speaking to school is the right thing to do. I appreciate your help.' She smiled shyly at him and after hugging her dad, she turned and gave Nash a short, awkward, embrace. It was another small milestone in a difficult climb.

'I hate seeing her like this,' Kelvin said after she left. 'Serena's such a bright kid, and full of life. They've just settled down after moving here and she doesn't deserve this. It's racially orientated, you know?'

Nash had guessed as much. Barrow was still a predominantly white town and children would pounce on anything that set a peer apart. They'd had an unsettled year, with Greg changing his job to work in the IT department of the shipyard. Kelvin had brought his family up in Kendal, but he was living with Nash in Barrow now, and it seemed natural for Zola to bring the children to the same town. They'd bought a nice house and settled the girls into new schools. At least Honey didn't seem to be having any problems.

Nash pulled Kelvin in for a hug. 'We'll figure it out,' he said, though his unease gnawed at him. He knew how important first impressions were at secondary school and how a child could so easily be cast into the role of victim. Once labelled, it was difficult to get away from and could follow the child throughout their school life and beyond. He didn't want that for one of his own.

And while Kelvin's children hadn't fully accepted him, and he had none of his own, Kelvin was his person, so Kel's family were his, too.

Chapter Ten

During the morning briefing, Nash's laser-focus gaze met his task force. 'Team, I'm handing over to Superintendent Mark Turner from Narcotics.'

'Good morning, guys. As you know we've been closing the net on some of the key players around the North West. Jerod Mathis' cover is his data science company, an unusual front for illicit activities.'

Brown raised her hand and waited to be noticed.

'Yes?' Turner asked.

'DI Molly Brown, sir. How does he get away with it? He's been operating for years and we all know it, but he keeps working.'

'Excellent question and I will address it, I promise. But first I want to explain how his pyramid functions. He selects bright kids that stand out to work for him. That's the legitimate side of the coin. However, he's linked to every dark crime you can imagine, gun running, money laundering, trafficking, you name it, he's got a ticket on his back for it. After work hours, he has a glamorous lifestyle that he uses to lure young people in. His parties and glimpses of the high life have them flocking to his place in droves. He's a generous guy. He makes them feel special and doles out a fistful of freebies.'

Turner drew a graph on the whiteboard as he talked, marking off the tiers of Mathis' army. 'The cocaine mountain that covers the surface of a dining table is legendary. We have undercover photos on file of every place setting having a fifty-pound note on a red velvet cushion to snort it with. And we've been told we can't do a damned thing about it, yet. The poor bastards have no idea what's going on until it's too late. One day, they wake up with the mother of all hangovers and are shocked to find that they're hooked on Chaos. From that morning, they are Jerod Mathis' pawns. However, they have a short shelf-life. He takes them and makes them feel like the most special people in the world. Then he calls in the debt and hands them a bill for thousands. They have no way of paying it and no choice but to deal for him to pay it off.'

'Lure them in and then show them that nothing in this world is for free,' Renshaw said.

'You've hit the nail on the head. It's a shrewd business strategy.'

'But if they're fond of the product, don't they steal it, or at least skim off the top?'

'I'm glad you picked that up, Sergeant?'

'Renshaw, sir.'

'Sergeant Renshaw. It's more than their life's worth and they know it. But, that's where the shelf life comes in. He pounces on them when they're hooked but not debilitated by the addiction. When they can't get out of bed without a hit and are caught skimming—and eventually they all do—they're found in an alley with their kneecaps broken. It keeps the others in line. Five years down the road, these bright young people are the ones shambling down the street picking up fag butts. They eat from bins and live under a sheet of cardboard.'

Turner shifted Mathis' mugshot over a couple of inches on the board and circled a location on the map, a beautiful old building on Baker Street. 'Mathis has another game. As well as recruiting his rich party kids, he's realised there's a massive gap at the other end of the spectrum—the immigrants who are desperate to belong.' He pointed to the Open Arms Refugee and Community Centre marked on the map.

Nash glanced at Lawson and saw him straighten in his seat. They'd spoken many times about drugs causing problems in town. But Lawson was particularly interested in it because his nephew, Aiden, helped run the refugee centre. The lad had a troubled homelife, but since working at the centre he'd gained confidence and had flourished in leaps and bounds. It was the making of him, and the thought that the refuge was in jeopardy because of unscrupulous dealers, hurt them all.

'This is the hub for integrating the refugees in this town. It's a good place with good people. The staff have been besieged and are working with us to stop it, but the decay starts here,' Turner said, stabbing his pointing stick at the map as though he could pierce the rot.

Paul Lawson raised his hand and waited for Turner to tell him to proceed. 'PC Lawson, sir. You're right. It is a good place, my nephew works there and he's heartbroken about what's been happening to the kids. He's angry. I want to make it clear that the gang's recruiters don't get inside the building. The grooming is all done on the outside.'

'Don't worry. We know that, PC Lawson. The centre does an excellent job. But these animals wait to see who's going in and out. They target the youngsters, get them onto Crystal Chaos, and when they're snared, and in debt to him and the party lifestyle, he forces them into dealing. It's a vicious circle. He preys on the vulnerable, and turns them into both victim and perpetrator.'

'It's a pyramid scheme, a regular Ponzi,' Bowes said. His face was serious for once. 'Some friends of mine had dealings with a group of kids bragging about killing someone concerned with this drug scene.'

'We're dealing with it, Bowes,' Nash said. 'And I can assure you, it's in hand. I take it Mr and Mrs Gibson haven't had any further trouble?'

'Not yet.'

'Let's keep it that way.'

'They make me sick. Mathis has got henchmen all over town. He's a cocky shit, with more edge than a broken piss pot. We keep getting orders from above to turn a blind eye. And every time we release them with a slap on the wrist, they think they're invincible. Sorry, sir,' he said, showing deference to Turner.

'It's been a process, and sometimes we have to play the long game for the greater good,' Turner said. 'These poor kids are no good to us. And even Jerod Mathis is only a secondary target. We want the head of operations and the chemists. If we take them out, we can halt production.' Turner outlined Mathis' modus operandi. 'He's a puppet master pulling the strings of the network around here. His legitimate company provides the cover to operate in plain sight, while his big house with the private jetty on Lake Windermere serves as a luxurious façade, hiding the darkness going on inside it. His infamous parties are just a mass recruitment drive.'

He pointed to the photos on the board. 'Our job is to expose the local drug operation, dismantle it, and put an end to the destructive cycle. However, to get Mathis, we have to work on the lower tiers. Jerod Mathis likes a manicure and wears Ferragamo shoes. He never gets his hands dirty and mud has never stuck. He thinks it's because he's too clever—but we've been amassing information and we've got established blueprints of his operation.'

Turner pinned other photos. 'These are some of the POIs that we've been tagging. Gloria Burnette, 23, works in the hospital as a radiographer. Barry Barlow, 27, works in the shipyard, and Keeley Norton 29, unemployed but with a big street presence. The first two have responsible jobs and wear designer coats of respectability. Norton flies in our faces and thinks she's untouchable. This one swans around running the street squads. They call her Blight and she rides a powerful Triumph. All three of these guys appeared on the scene a few months ago. Two of them walked into ready-made positions and Blight tried to knock Aleasha Cordon off the number one spot in town.

There's a power struggle going on between them that's as yet unresolved. But Cordon doesn't stand a chance, she's only a kid herself, and Norton's biding her time. Cordon's seventeen and way out of her depth. She calls herself Blue, on account of her blue hair. That's as inventive as their collective brain cells could get. Cordon was Mathis' head dealer until Norton came in punching.'

Bowes gave a low whistle.

'Put your tongue away, Bowes. She'd eat you alive,' Nash said. 'Frivolity aside, apart from the social observation that females seem to make better leads when it comes to drug distribution rackets, what can we pull from this?'

'May I, sir?' Renshaw asked.

Turner nodded.

'Working the streets, we know that something massive is going down. This girl rides into town on her big motorbike and Blue won't move aside to let her in. I've seen Cordon take on men twice her size and come out on top, and when we've brought her in, she fights like a wildcat, so why's she letting this new kid on the block stake a claim? It must be orders from above.'

'Exactly. It's time we shook a few trees to see what falls out,' Nash replied.

Turner briefed them on the opening stages of the operation. They were tasked with arresting the low-level dealers, which would get them off the streets. It made Nash's team proud that they would be instrumental in helping to bring down the top manufacturers, and heads of distribution, in the country.

Turner took his pointer and indicated the board. 'Jerod Mathis might be the face of this operation, but he inherited it from a local kingpin. In the grand scheme of things Hill was a small-time player, but he organised the drug running and scams plaguing the area. Hill and his wife have been taken out of circulation—serving long stretches in Wandsworth and Bronzefield prisons respectively. It's a significant blow to the criminal network, but they have long shadows.'

'And it doesn't end there,' Renshaw said. 'I've been lead on cleaning up after the Hills. One of their three children fled the country. He's believed to be running scams across Spain and the Iberian islands.'

'We need to keep our eyes on the bigger picture,' Turner said. 'This is more than just Barrow and Kendal. It's a linked network, and we're going to dismantle it from the roots.'

Mathis' operation was one branch of an extensive criminal network, and the operation extended beyond their jurisdiction. The fight wasn't about arresting dealers. There was a legacy of criminal influence that had plagued their community for years. The echoes of past crimes intertwined with the urgency of the present and came from outside the borough. Turner told them to brace themselves for trouble from the dealers. Nash thanked him, and after Turner left, he closed the meeting. Nash waited a minute to make sure the big cheese from Manchester was gone.

'Team, listen up. Young people are dying, and I take that personally. GMNT will be stomping all over us. They think we're country hicks, but we're going to show them what Barrow's Serious Crime Team are made of, aren't we?'

'Yes, boss.'

'Are we going to show Turner and his colleagues that we're ready for this?'

'Yes, boss.'

'Dismissed.'

Chapter Eleven

The growl of the powerful engine announced Blight's arrival. She guided her 1,200cc Triumph Tiger to a confident stop near The Siren pub. The machine had a tank that dwarfed the small woman, and it had factory decals in an assertive blue and white. The machine gleamed bright and futuristic under the afternoon sunlight. She swung her leg over the bike, the one-piece leathers clinging to her in all the right places. The material accentuated her waist and curves, and the lines of the outfit conveyed an unapologetic confidence.

With a flourish, she undid the helmet, and her black hair spilled down her back in an unravelling nest of tight braids. It flowed like a rebellious waterfall.

A group of local kids gathered around the bike in awe. They were about twelve and Blight fixed the ringleader in her sights. 'You like it?' she asked, and her voice cut through the afternoon. 'This beauty is my life. I'd sell my mother to protect her. If any of you even think about messing with her, I'll cut your throats and send your dicks home to your mams in a gift box. Got it?' The threat dangled like a low-hanging testicle leaving the kids speechless.

She pulled the heavy bike onto its stand and handed the leader a fiver. 'You. Keep an eye on her for me.' The boy took the money.

'That ain't gonna buy much protection.'

'It might not, but it can secure my respect. You play your cards right and you can come and work for me. Do a good job and you'll find that the note in your hand can buy you a front-row seat to the best show in town. Consider it an investment in your street cred, kid.'

She swaggered along the pavement to The Siren, leaving the boys staring after her, with admiration written across their faces and mid-pubescent erections growing in their jeans. The biker brought a small thrill to an otherwise boring afternoon, and the kids were left with the hope that they might get that job.

She had confidence and walked with a purposeful stride, the leather boots echoing against the pavement like a tribal drum. Her steps resonated with untamed allure.

The atmosphere inside the pub shifted as she walked in. Blight commanded attention. Her presence was as evocative as the scent of rebellion, and the customers knew she'd taken over their pub.

Blight went to the bar, where Cherry greeted her with a nod. 'The usual?' She was already pouring a lemonade. Blight would love a couple of shots of vodka in it, but would never risk her licence. She'd chosen this pub because Cherry and her partner, Louise, hadn't been running it for long. They were settling in and making their mark. Blight liked the layout of the two rooms. She met with her people in the back and always tipped the landlady well for her service. Cherry might not have liked it, but she knew to keep her head down and mind her own business. There was a backroom to fade into the shadows when drugs were passed between people in the pub.

Blight exchanged a few empty words with the landlady, and Cherry hanging glasses up, shot her a warning look. 'No trouble, Blight. You know the drill.' It was lip service, if there was trouble, there was trouble. Cherry could handle herself and knew not to involve the police if a scuffle broke out. It was another reason that Blight had chosen this pub.

Unspoken understanding hung over the bar between them. Blight took her drink and slipped into the back room, her eyes flicking around the pub. She was subtle but took in every person, clocking their position and who they were with. This afternoon there were only two new faces that she hadn't seen before. A middle-aged couple, each with carrier bags of shopping on the floor beside them and a pint of lager on the table. The woman had cankles, and the man was no threat. They weren't police. A quiet acknowledgement of her presence rippled through the few customers standing at the bar.

In the back room, a couple of lads abandoned their game of pool, recognising Blight's subtle gesture, and they joined her at a long table nestled in the corner. It was a strategic place where their conversation wouldn't be overheard and she could monitor people's movements. Originally, there was a camera in that corner, but Blight had suggested to Cherry that she move it in case a flyaway pool ball struck it. The landlady had seen the sense in the advice. Nasty things, pool balls.

Blight leaned against the wall and four young women, including Blue, came in from the main bar to join the lads. Blue cut two lines of coke on a beermat and offered one to Blight. It was polite, but it also said that she was in charge. They did them without trying to hide.

'Oi, you two, pack it in,' Louise shouted from behind the bar.

The group took their usual seats according to rank around the table and created an enclave in the corner of the pub. Blight doubted that many of them were old enough to drink. They were between fifteen and eighteen and she couldn't decide whether to kick their arses when they stepped out of line—or wipe them.

She'd given Blue her head as the leader because it had suited Blight to keep the boat steady and not rock it. But the girl was cocky and making mistakes. It was time to take her down. Blight had been in enough times as Mathis' overseer to make them wary of her. Now it was time to bang some heads.

Blight waited for Blue to sit. 'Move,' she said. 'From today, that's my seat.'

'Piss off,' Blue turned away from the biker and picked up her pint. 'Come back when you can handle more than a lemonade, sweetheart. This is where the big girls sit.'

Blue had balls—and a mouth on her—Blight gave her that. With eleven years on the kid, the takeover was like taking her screen away from her after bedtime. It was too easy.

Blight kicked out fast and toppled the other woman and her chair. As Blue sprawled on her back covered in cider, Blight picked up the chair, swung it around, and sat on it backwards, resting her arms on the back.

Blue came up with her potty mouth working overtime and swung a punch. The stronger woman was ready for her, out-ranking her in height, power, and life. She grabbed Blue's arm and twisted it behind her back before using her momentum to move her to the door where she thrust her into the main bar. 'There's way too many Bs in this equation,' she said. 'One of us has to go.'

Blight didn't give her another second of her time and went back to the table. Blue could have jumped her when her back was turned, they all carried weapons, but she knew Blue wouldn't have the guts.

'Deal with her,' she said to Blue's second.

He looked shifty, weighed up his options of alliance—and nodded.

Her eyes scanned the eight faces. Theirs was a squad forged in the shadows. Their loyalty was as trustworthy as a nest of snakes. Confrontation was held at bay with an understanding of hierarchy. Blue had control. Blight took it from her, and the standoff between them was electric. The order was established but still contested.

The pub's regulars turned back to their business and drank. The flow of conversations and the clink of glasses served as the backdrop to the rest of the meeting.

Chapter Twelve

Blue's people were a crew of petty criminals and kids who didn't know any better than following the wave of their peers. They discussed matters away from the ears of the bar hoppers.

Blight leaned in, her gaze hard, and locked onto each face. 'You messed up.'

'It was Shelly's fault,' the second in command said.

'What's your name?'

'Dave Roberts.'

'Well, David Roberts. You messed up.'

Nobody spoke. Blight's words hung between them like a threat. Another kid had died from an overdose and it brought unwanted attention. Roberts picked up his pint and masked his nervousness with a long slug, but Blight saw the glass shake. 'Why isn't Shelly here?'

'She's scared,' he said. 'She was panicking and wanted to hand herself in after her customer died, said she was going to grass on us. But we can keep her in line. We've delivered a message.'

Blight assessed his resolve. 'You mean you knocked the living shit out of her. Are you sure you can handle it?'

The challenge was made, and she slapped her glass on the table. The gang watched the cross-play as Roberts met her scrutiny. He held her stare but he was on edge. 'I'll keep her quiet, but if she doesn't settle down, we might have to silence her.'

'You messed up with Shelly. She was weak—not right for the job. And I've heard there was a witness at the Crystal Club. That was sloppy. Did you think I wouldn't hear about it? Know this, little boy. I hear everything. You're out of your depth. Do you think we can let that slide?'

'Are you challenging me? You aren't the boss around here. Scorch calls the shots.' He rose from his seat, his stance aggressive and his fists balled, but Blight stayed seated across the table.

'We can take this outside right now, sweetheart.' She had the knife in her hand and open before they realised what was happening. They didn't see her go for the butterfly knife. She was on her feet and manipulated the Balisong blade, twirling the ivory handles so fast that they blurred. She repeatedly sent the safe edge of the razor-sharp blade to knock against the back of her knuckles in a three-twist movement before lunging forward and stopping with the point of the knife at his Adam's apple. She had the advantage and he glared at her to save face in front of the others, but Blight knew she could make him piss his pants in seconds.

'So, what are we going to do about it?' Blight closed the knife and returned it to her boot. She looked around the group, waiting for a challenge. These kids didn't have a set of balls to shave between them. The room had the intensity of a storm gathering in the fading afternoon light.

One of the boys was the first to speak. 'I know where the Gibsons live. We'll send a friendly message to keep their mouths shut.'

Blight weighed him up. Silencing people with threats of violence both outright and implied was a dance she had grown up learning in the realms they inhabited. She'd dragged herself up tough, without a family dynamic, and was above the rabble in this backwards town.

The subtle orchestration of messages, delivered with intimidation and veiled threats, was a language they spoke fluently. An agreement settled over the table without another word being spoken. The Gibsons would be dealt with.

Blight had a message of her own to send on that score. She needed to get a warning across regarding the Gibsons and Shelly Myers.

'Anything else?' Blight said.

Nervous glances were exchanged, hinting at more trouble lingering in the background.

'Spill,' Blight said to Roberts.

He hesitated. His eyes met hers before shifting away. He lowered his voice and bent his head from the rest of the room. 'Another customer's overdosed on Chaos.'

'When?'

'A few days ago, but it's okay. Nothing to worry about. We cleaned up.'

'Define "cleaned up" for me, sweetheart.' The endearment was as menacing as the knife she'd held to his throat.

'We disposed of the body.'

'Where is it, David?'

'We threw it in the lake,' Roberts said.

'And you made sure it wasn't going to rise like bloody Jesus on the third day?'

One of the girls giggled. Her nerves had got the better of her. Blight's head turned like an owl spotting prey. 'You. Speak.'

The girl didn't answer and put her head down, fiddling with the label on a beer bottle with her pink gel nails.

'Hardly. The water's only five feet deep. He was found on Friday. The kid only had one leg and wasn't working out, so it's no biggie' Dave said.

'And you think we need that kind of publicity? A disabled kid?'

The realisation that they were being verbally battered intensified and Blight worked through the ramifications. Crystal Chaos had claimed another victim and she was furious. 'Why are these kids dropping like flies?'

'It's not our fault. We only deliver what we're given.' One of the girls had found her voice and Blight saw the way she glanced at Roberts and blushed. He ignored her, and Blight knew he hadn't shagged her yet.

The choice was clear, deal with the consequences or risk being found out and locked up for a long time. Their next move would determine whether they could protect the operation. Blight needed to speak to the boss.

The new batch of Chaos was cutting a deadly swathe through the town like a poisonous cloud. Roberts defended the gang. 'Distribution came through Gloria Burnette. Our people told us the batch was clean. They said the cook sorted the issue, and we wouldn't have any problems with this delivery.'

'Let me get this straight. You're saying the new batch that came in last week is contaminated? Are you sure none of you are stamping on it?'

'You know Scorch would kill us if we cut it. Look, lady. It comes in, Burnette bags it, and we sell it as it comes. We don't add anything to bulk it out.'

Unease settled over them as Blight's fury erupted. Damn, those poor dead kids. 'We can't afford the heat. The profits are going to drop. We won't survive a police investigation.'

'It's okay. The police around here are clueless. We're always ten steps ahead of them.' He laughed and the phlegmy noise made Blight want to punch him in the throat.

'We don't get a lot of heat.' Another of Roberts' female groupies backed him up.

'You'd better hope this dies down and goes away fast. The potential fallout from this is massive. It's a domino effect. The flack will float upstream, not down.'

'Does Scorch want a recall on the product?' Roberts asked.

'God, no,' Blight said. 'Just keep the deals clean and tidy up any mess on the way. My boss, his boss, and the ones at the top will be breathing on us. And you bastards had better be ready for that. I'm not putting my neck on the block for you. I can promise you that.'

The profit margin was precarious in the face of the consequences but they had too much invested in the new batch to recall it.

Blight got that Roberts couldn't roll over and give in to her completely. And she needed him on board to deal with Blue and run operations. She let him have a moment of power. He was fuelled by defiance and stood up to her. 'Who are you, anyway?

You come in here, taking over, making accusations, and asking questions about an operation that was doing fine until you turned up. The kids were alive in this town until you got here.'

'Sit down. You don't know what you're talking about.'

'You don't call the shots. We had a good thing going before you came in, and now everything's falling apart. Maybe you're the problem.'

Blight's expression was impassive, but the tension thickened.

'Come on then, big shot. What's our next move? Do you want the hot seat? You've got it. It takes the heat off my pretty ass.'

Roberts tried to save face in front of his toadies. 'We do what we've always done. The kids on the streets do their thing, and we keep our heads down.'

'Jesus Christ. That's what you've got? We're saved, folks. Hallelujah. All we needed was the gospel according to Dave Roberts,' Blight said.

'You can take the piss, but I know plenty. Word on the street is the feds are coming from out of town. The last thing we need to do is panic,' Roberts said.

'What was that about not getting much heat and being on top of it?' She slammed her fist on the table, 'I've got news for you, sunshine. They're already here. You're talking big words but not saying anything. Are you ready to listen now?'

'Suppose,' Dave said and the others nodded, any allegiance to Blue was out of the window.

'We need a new product. But to do that we have to get to the source. Our contact is Scorch Mathis—we need to bypass him and go higher. One way or another, I'll get to the top of the ladder and speak to the big boys directly. Stick with me, and I'll bring you all up with me. And that's a promise.'

'Are you nuts? We don't go up. The consignment comes in, and Scorch has it delivered through Burnette and Barlow. And now there's another guy who's even higher than Scorch. Look, we just do what we're told. But I know something else as well.'

'Go on, Einstein.'

'Burnett and Barlow's boss has come to Barrow to keep an eye on things. And he's your boss, too.'

'Is that right?'

'Yeah, and you have to answer to him, so you're not all that.'

'Okay, smart arse, wind your neck in. We all have to answer to somebody. But what I'm saying is, we need to find out where the supply comes from.'

'I know the cook's name.' He grew three inches and Blight had to catch herself not to react.

'I doubt that very much.'

'I heard two of the drivers talking. They call him Acetone.'

Blight doubted his information was correct. He was talking about the actual creator of Chaos. Roberts was a scroat who didn't even dangle on the end of the fishing line. He was the shit in the worm's stomach. But she was willing to play along with him. 'Well, aren't you the main man? What else have you got?'

'I've got more than you have.' Roberts rolled up his hoody sleeve to show off a tattoo of a syringe with the word acetone running through it. Blight laughed in his face. 'Are you trying to say, you're the cook?'

'No,' he went red. 'But he's the man, bruv. It's a holdage to him isn't it?'

She laughed in his face. 'You mean homage. No, dick brain, I'm not talking about your man-crush. Do you know anything else?'

'Never needed to. We do the exchange every Thursday night, regular as clockwork and there's never been a problem until kids started dying.'

'What's your driver's name?'

'Don't you even know that?' Roberts sneered.

'Of course I do. I want to know if you do.'

'Course.'

'Come on, then?'

'He's Jimmy the Gent, innit. And sometimes Bobby the Rob.'

This kid had a lot to learn. Even Blue would never have been so loose-lipped about operations. And those names, somebody was pulling this dick's chain.

'Stick your tongue out.'

'Why?'

'Tongue. Out.'

Roberts looked nervous but did as he was told, and then waggled it in a lewd manner. Some of his cronies laughed.

Blight was like lightning. She reached forward and grabbed his tongue. In a second she had her knife pressed against it, making Roberts scream. 'The next time you wag that. I'll cut it out. Do you hear me? You ever spill names again, and yours will be the next body they fish out of the lake.'

Blight had spent months establishing herself in a position of power within the group. Contrary to the word she'd put around to give her provenance, she didn't meet with Jerod Mathis. He wasn't her point of contact—and, for personal reasons, she'd wanted to keep it that way. Until now.

Blight had transferred from the Bolton dealers. And Big Steve from Bolton had talked to Steppenwolf from Accrington, who'd talked to Stanley from Preston, who spoke to Jerod. That was the interview process to move base. There was too much heat in Bolton. The drug squad was raiding. She'd been arrested there more than once and her face was known. The story was that the establishment decided it was time for a shift of personnel and a shake-up. But if this scroat had been listening to the drivers' loose talk, she'd gained some valid information that she could use to get where she needed to be.

'I want in on the next drop,' she said.

Chapter Thirteen

Nash watched from the doorway, and anybody with the time to look at his expression would have seen pride on his face. He was outside the investigation room, checking on his Serious Crime Team working inside the busy office. Three years earlier, he'd hand-picked them with DCS Lewis, and had chosen well. A good mix of skill sets was standard—but Nash had taken his closest members for their character as well as their abilities. They were a cohesive unit and would have each other's backs in a crisis.

It was after six, and some of the team were wrapping up for the day. The hum of electronic devices and the staccato rhythm of keyboards made it difficult to hear any individual voice. The general buzz of activity created a familiar vibrato of investigative effort. Nash never got sick of hearing it. Eighteen computer desks lined the space, with officers scouring databases, answering phones, and putting together often conflicting pieces of evidence as they came in.

Molly Brown was leaning over a desk explaining protocol to a colleague. She had an air of authority and it was obvious which outranked the other. The room crackled with purpose as officers navigated the internet and relevant police databases with the eyes of skilled hunters. Sometimes they got to work in the field, but mostly, this was what detection came down to—ball-breaking, repetitive computer grafting and endless lists of names.

Bowes paused his conversation with Lawson and took his life in his hands. With a mischievous glint in his eye, he aimed an elastic band at Brown's backside. The incongruent act brought a momentary pause to the otherwise intense atmosphere.

Nash's first word was laced with stern authority and cut through the ambient surface noise. 'Bowes.'

The tone of admonishment shifted the dynamics in the room and activity stilled as the team looked at Nash.

Brown spun around, her eyes narrowed on Bowes. 'Bowes, I swear to God. You're such an arsehole. This is a serious investigation, not a playground.' Her voice cut through the hum of activity. After her stern reprimand, she grinned. 'Dickhead.'

Bowes straightened up and looked sheepish at being caught by Nash. The sexist moment gave way to a serious acknowledgement of the professional setting they were in, but only when he saw Nash leaning against the doorjamb. Busted, Nash thought.

Detective Nash nodded at the room and beckoned Bowes out. As they stepped into the corridor he ran his hand through his hair. He was tired and could do without having to deliver more bad news. 'Bowes, come on. I need you at the hospital. There's been a development in the Gibson case.' A sense of urgency underlaid his words with the hand he placed on Bowes' shoulder.

Nash briefed him on the way to the car park—a call had come in saying that Andy Gibson had been stabbed and badly beaten. Nash was on his way there to secure a witness statement. The matter concerned the Gibsons, and as a courtesy, Nash told Bowes that he'd be the accompanying officer. He'd reported the matter regarding his friends, and as there was no conflict of interest involved, Nash felt he deserved to see it through.

A new mystery had opened up in the case, but Nash didn't feel the need to share it with Bowes. As he'd gone to get his coat after the call about Andy Gibson came in, he saw a note on his desk. It was internal. One of their own had left it. It warned that Shelly Myers was in danger.

Nash had sent officers to have her taken out of her house. They'd strongly advise that she leave town and stay with relatives. If she had nobody she could stay with, she'd be put in a hotel away from here until they could make better arrangements for her safety.

The note also said that the Gibsons were in danger. He'd seen it too late where the Gibsons were concerned. But was relieved when he had word that Shelly Myers was unharmed and packing to stay with a relative in Wales.

'What the hell happened?' Bowes jolted him out of his thoughts.

'Andy Gibson was jumped on his way home from work by the men who threatened him on the night of the trouble. They waited for him to leave the yard and ambushed him in the car park as he opened his car door.'

'Christ. Is he okay?'

'He's had surgery for a punctured lung. His pretty face is a mess, by all accounts, but nothing too serious. But there's more. While Mrs Gibson was at the hospital with her husband, they had a break-in.'

'Poor Liz. She was terrified they would come for her,' Jay said.

'They were out to make a statement. They kicked the door open and didn't try to hide it. They were finished and gone by the time a neighbour ran out to confront them.'

'Thank God Liz wasn't there.'

They ransacked the house in minutes, but the living room was the epicentre of the chaos. Furniture was overturned, cushions ripped open, and family photographs pulled off the wall and stamped underfoot. The thieves had no regard for the sanctity of the Gibson's property. It was a fast and frenzied home invasion meant to cause maximum damage. They wanted to make an impact on the family.

'Did they get away with much?'

'Enough, but it was more about sending a message. In the kitchen, cabinets were emptied with everything thrown across the floor. Shattered crockery and glass highlighted the brutality because the family dog was in there and cut his paws. The police found him trapped in the kitchen.'

'Poor Finn, he must have been terrified.'

'The son's taken him. But the criminals went right through the house. In the bedrooms, clothes were scattered around the floor, and personal items were pilfered. It was efficient and ruthless. They were methodical and took small items that they could move on fast. They stole a laptop, Liz's jewellery, money, and other easily transportable items. The neighbour said they had rucksacks. He gave chase, but they ran.'

'Description?'

'Three males, jeans, hoodies, trainers. No CCTV.'

'So basically, it could have been anybody?'

'Pretty much.'

Nash told Bowes that Liz had spent a tense night at the hospital. It was early morning when she went home to get some sleep, and she stepped into the second nightmare.

The police had boarded up the front door, but it would have to be replaced. The wreckage was a violation of their home. In her witness statement, Liz said she didn't care about the burglary, she was too worried about Andy. The stolen items were nothing in comparison to the loss of their security, and she was frightened by the degree of malice.

They walked to the police car and Nash threw Bowes the keys to drive. Bowes had unease etched across his features, and as he pushed the car into gear, Nash had to remind him that it wasn't the vehicle's fault. The news of Andy Gibson's brutal assault stilled their usual banter.

'I promised we'd keep them safe,' Bowes said.

'This isn't your fault.'

'Tell them that.'

At the hospital, they saw Andy lying in bed with multiple injuries. He had enough bruised swelling to make him almost unrecognisable. The contusions on his face drew an image of the attack, and he had defence wounds on his hands where he'd been kicked. Liz had seen too much that night in the Crystal Club. The consequences of speaking out were evidenced in the brutality Andy had suffered. A message had been delivered.

And Nash was furious.

Chapter Fourteen

Nash stood at the door and shouted. 'Brown and Lawson. Stake-out. Now.'

Brown groaned but stood up from her desk and packed her electronic device into her bag.

Lawson finished typing a paragraph and hit save. He called Nash over. 'Do you want me to leave this? You told me to check the PND records and cross-match for vehicles leaving Mathis' property. And then I've got two interviews in the diary.'

'Okay, Lawson. Finish up here and then come and relieve me.'

'It'll be a few hours.'

'Dammit. Brown, you're with me.'

'Hope this means you're buying lunch, boss,' Brown said.

They sat in the unmarked police car and were positioned in an alley adjacent to the Open Arms Refugee Community Centre. Their vantage point gave a clear view of the side entrance, where they could monitor the door. The unmarked old banger, chosen to blend in, faded well in the urban backdrop.

Brown had her camera focused and poked the long lens through the window every time a new pair of kids came out of the centre, and picked up their bicycles from the rack at the side of the building.

The rapid click of the camera captured each moment for further scrutiny at the station. The importance of detail was everything, and the photographs might hold clues to the broader narrative.

Every kid coming out of the centre had a new mountain bike. It was the first red flag. These children didn't have parents who could afford shiny new wheels, but they all had one.

Brown wrote on her device, *10:07, Two youths, both male, approx 12 and 14. Came out of the centre.* She described the two boys in detail. They were both European. She took note of each of the pairs as they came out.

'Look at this, boss. They come out in twos. At first, I thought it was just boys but see here, the third set is a boy and girl—but always a pair. They go straight to their bikes and ride away together.'

'I was wondering when you'd see it. I've been watching the time frame, they leave every ten minutes or so. It's unnatural, and it's more than two friends flying off for fun on their bikes.'

They were getting some good results as the photographic evidence accumulated. It formed a mosaic of connections to be deciphered back at the station.

Max Jones' nephew, Sebastian, Aiden Lawson, and the older staff were at a loss about how to do more than keep drugs out of the centre. The law allowed for searches under certain circumstances, such as ensuring the safety and security of customers and maintaining order within the facility. The staff were compliant because employees could be charged if drugs were found on the premises and the staff were seen to be turning a blind eye.

Kids were searched going in, a horrible, invasive decision that nobody enjoyed. It went against the feeling of freedom the centre aimed to instil in its service users. Although there was no legal requirement, it had been Seb's idea to get the parents and guardians on board with the searches. He said there would be less obstruction if parents were informed and made part of the process.

Their surveillance continued, and Nash noted that it was often an older and younger kid leaving together. The age differences were odd. It was an important clue that stood out to him. In his experience, older teenagers didn't hang around with young ones. It wasn't done.

The hum of the urban environment was intended to cloak the kids' activity, but it was strange behaviour to anybody taking the time to watch. Nash was put in mind of drone bees leaving the nest to collect nectar. It didn't take much guesswork to hit on what these kids were collecting.

The answers concealed in the activity at the refugee centre were there. All it took to pin down some suspects was man hours and donkey work. The nuts and bolts of community policing, regardless of whether they were special ops or uniforms, were in the detail. Detective work came down to the time-consuming art of gathering evidence. They were like every other cop in every department.

The unmarked car was ready to leave with the next paired departures on bikes.

'What could look more innocent than kids riding bikes?' Nash said.

'This crock of shit, Nash. That's what. It stinks.'

After two hours of meticulous observation, they had some good intel. The kids rode around the corner, where they met other teens in an alley. They swapped their empty water bottles for full ones. Nash and Brown had put names to half a dozen that had been through the station already and had records. And they had twenty more that were unknown to them.

The repeated cycle of the same kids leaving and returning less than an hour later exposed a repetitive pattern. But a subtle anomaly caught Nash's attention. The stream of newcomers had dwindled, leaving a space in the routine.

Nash told Brown to follow at a discreet distance. Two kids pedalled away from the centre, and Brown slid behind them like a silent shadow.

They stopped at the park gates behind the leisure centre. Brown guided the unmarked car into the car park, positioning it among other vehicles to maintain their cover. The leisure centre was a large enough building to give the kids discretion.

They stopped and leaned on their bikes. They were away from the concrete shield of the building and out of range of its cameras.

They'd chosen to follow a pair with mismatched ages. They were both boys, the youngest was twelve at most and of foreign nationality. Nash thought about the dead kids and his anger spiked. The friend was about fifteen, with hairs sprouting from the exposed inches of his legs where trousers, that were too short for him, had ridden up. Nash smiled, growth spurt. Even well-off parents struggled to keep up with that. The kid had stubble on his chin.

The unsuspecting boys continued their activities with nonchalant carelessness. The older one looked around every so often but didn't have the gumption to notice that the dark car in the fifth parking bay hadn't dislodged its passenger. He was oblivious to the scrutiny of the undercover detectives. The kid's lack of caution showed a level of cockiness off the scale and highlighted their inexperience. They thought their illicit endeavours were hidden in plain sight.

They set up shop and the transactions opened. The eldest kid was constantly on his phone making many calls lasting less than a minute. The younger one seemed bored and shifted his weight often as he sat across his saddle learning how to deal from the older lad. They drew a mix of people—adults mostly, but some older teenagers seeking the produce offered by the entrepreneurs on their bikes. And they weren't selling homemade cupcakes in a bake sale.

Brown remarked on the simplicity of the operation as she watched them digging in their opaque white water bottles and pulling out small packages. The camera clicked with every transaction. And once, when an adult couple pulled in opposite the detectives and bothered to check the car park, Nash took Brown in his arms and she buried her face in his neck.

'Even if you suspected them of dealing, and stop-searched them, you'd never think of looking in the water bottles, would you?' Brown said. Nash acknowledged the cleverness of the concealment. The innocuous water bottles hid the sinister reality beneath their intended purpose.

Since they'd pulled in, Nash had been tetchy. Every time Molly spoke, he snapped at her but couldn't stop himself. He was furious. These were kids. In some cases, they were selling drugs to other kids, and he couldn't do a damned thing about it. His hands had been tied from above for the duration of this case.

They had to turn a blind eye to the small-time dealers for now so that they could catch the big fish. And he had to sit back and watch. It went so far against the grain that it took every ounce of his strength not to jump out of the car and apprehend them.

The kids ran a brazen operation, and Brown captured the events with the camera. However, their approach had to be cautious. The location had been chosen with care, and Nash knew that the choice wasn't down to the young boy. Although they'd ridden fast through the car park, they were careful not to use the leisure centre property to operate from. They were on a narrow tract of land between the swimming pool and the park where they couldn't be seen and weren't guilty of trespass. The kids were blissfully unaware of their discovery or that they were the focus of the lens. However, some of the adults entering the car park displayed a level of street smarts that demanded circumspect surveillance. The youngsters with the drugs were putting themselves at risk. The likelihood of somebody reporting them was one thing but that faded into insignificance next to the physical danger they were putting themselves in from adults collecting their gear. They were selling to desperate addicts far bigger than they were. The risk to them was massive and, for that reason, they only carried a handful of baggies in their bottle before going back to exchange the money they'd collected for more drugs. It was a dangerous position to be in.

Brown swapped to a shorter lens and captured images without arousing suspicion. The adults had an inert wariness coming from experience. They scanned their surroundings with shifty glances.

They'd been there half an hour when they struck gold. A female rider on a powerful motorbike roared into the car park.

The growl of the engine resonated in the air as she circled the space with daring confidence before leaving.

'Blight,' Brown said.

'Bingo.'

Brown grabbed a snapshot of the woman as she rode away. Her silhouette in tight biker leathers conveyed an aura of power. Dozens of tight braids cascaded down her back, adding to the allure of the rider.'We are honoured indeed. Jerod Mathis' rottweiler doing the rounds to check on their investment,' Nash said.

'Should we follow her?'

'No. We're under orders not to. She's made us. If we hadn't been here, she'd have collected the kids' takings, and would have done another drop with them.'

'How long are we going to let them get away with this?' Molly asked.

Nash punched the dashboard in frustration. 'Put it this way, I don't think she'll be free for church on Sunday. And that's classified.'

'There's going to be a raid? I'm in,' Brown said. 'I want to be there when we take that arrogant bitch down.'

She clicked to enlarge the image on the camera's digital viewer and the woman's presence mocked them from the frame, a fleeting addition to the gallery they'd compiled. 'It's only three thirty and the light's fading already,' Nash said.

'I hate winter. Bring on the daffodils,' Brown agreed.

They watched as the kid answered his phone. He scanned the parked cars and his cold stare stopped on the unmarked police vehicle.

'Damn, Blight's warned them. No point in hanging around any longer.' Nash turned off his device and put it in his pocket.

The kid punched his mate on the shoulder and said something. As they screwed the lids back on their bottles, the younger one fumbled in his haste. They pulled their hoods down their faces and drew the cords tight. And the two boys rode out of the car park as if the devil was on their tail. The older kid gave them the finger as he rode past and stared in the passenger window to leer at them.

The car park was mottled with dancing shadows and secrets. The kids looked cold. Nash had seen the younger boy trembling as the damp evening air drew in and the temperature dropped. He looked miserable and scared.

'Poor kid. I wish I could take him home to his mother,' Brown said. Any fool could see he wasn't enjoying what he was doing—but that didn't mean he was being coerced or forced into anything against his will. They needed to gather more evidence to prove that. 'Maybe they aren't allowed to call it a day until they've sold out.'

The woman on the motorbike left an imprint on the investigation and Nash was itching to disobey orders and trawl the streets looking for her.

'I hate what's happening.' Brown let loose with a string of expletives. Her voice was like hot gun-metal. Nash didn't approve of her foul mouth, but he couldn't deny the sentiment.

Chapter Fifteen

Two days later, Nash's phone pierced the air in his office with an urgency that shifted his focus. He was in a bad mood after attending Noah Ross' funeral that morning, and he was still sitting in his stiff black suit feeling uncomfortable.

An incident at the Star Select supermarket had been called in, and the desk sergeant thought Nash might want to take it. He explained that a fight between the security guard and a customer had caused a disturbance in the supermarket car park.

'What's that got to do with our case?' Nash asked.

'Maybe nothing, sir, but you asked to be told about any drug-related incidents coming in. And Lance Taylor, one of the town's most prolific users, is implicated in the call out.'

'I doubt it's of any relevance to us. Taylor's small time and about as far down the road of addiction as you can get, but I have to go home and get changed, so I'll take it on the way.' He turned to Bowes. 'Bowes, grab your coat, we're going out.'

Lance Taylor was a man teetering on the brink of life. If Nash had to express an opinion about whether he was more alive than dead, he wouldn't be able to call it. A long-time drug abuser, he was a regular figure begging around town and shoplifting from any store he could sneak into. None of them would let him in willingly.

'He was in some of my classes at school,' Bowes said. 'He was that kid that all the girls creamed their knickers for.'

'All right, Bowes. That's an image I can live without, thanks.' Nash pulled a face.

Bowes laughed, then blushed. 'I always bung him a couple of quid when I see him around town. The thing is, he was okay. You know. It's sad. He even hung around with us for a while. Me and the lads tried to help him out, but he wouldn't have it. A couple of us wanted to be in the force, so we had to cut him loose.'

'Not your fault.'

'I've never stopped feeling bad. What if we could have done more?'

'You couldn't.' Nash was seeing more of this caring side to Bowes, and he liked it. It had always been there but was covered by wisecracks in the incident room.

Taylor was a nuisance who'd never worked a day in his life. He'd started out dealing and was into some serious crime when he had more than two thriving brain cells to rub together. These days, he was just a pest, a curse on the town. He was like the seagulls, but more annoying. However, take your eyes off him for a second and he'd still steal your chips. He had no purpose, other than begging for cigarettes and money. People crossed the road to avoid him and it wouldn't be long before death came for him.

He could get nasty when he was begging, and the beat bobbies were always being called out to him around the cash points.

Nash was shocked that he looked even worse than the last time he'd seen him. He wouldn't have thought that was possible until the day he'd stare at his corpse on the slab—and at least then he'd be cleaner.

The man was a skeleton with a shock of dirty blond hair, in the true sense of the description, and stumps of rotten teeth. His face was covered in breakouts and the sores were wet and filled with blood-discoloured pus. His clothes were so dirty that the filth gave them a layer of fortitude to stop them from falling away from his body in a decaying corruption of old cloth. His trainers were held together by elastic bands, with both soles flapping. Nash saw the sores on his bare black feet through the holes. He was surprised that the addict could still walk.

Lance hadn't spoken for years, not much, just the odd grunt as he held his hands out for change, and tremors ravaged his body, a seizure never far away.

Nash spoke to constable Miller who was already on the scene. Miller had already put a customer in his police car with the door open and the suspect's feet on the ground. He hadn't been arrested yet but had been told to sit still and calm down. A security guard stood by the supermarket door holding a damp tea towel covered in blood against his nose. Nash heard him refuse an ambulance and watched to make sure Miller made a note of it. A woman, presumably the puncher's wife, was talking to Sergeant Patel, her voice was raised and shrill as the details unfolded. The couple were embroiled in a moral dilemma. They'd seen the desperate man on their way into the supermarket.

The woman, torn between compassion and pragmatism, explained that she hesitated to offer money. She was aware of the potential repercussions. She said she felt awful just smiling and walking past him like hundreds of people before her. She was happy to tell Nash her story again and said she couldn't get the beggar out of her head. She intended to buy him some hot food. It was something she could do to provide sustenance without giving him the means to buy drugs or sell something to obtain them.

Her husband, Grant, had told her to ignore him. He'd stalked ahead into the shop, leaving her to trail behind. 'You can't give them anything, Carole. It just encourages them.'

'He's a human being,' she'd said.

She told Nash the emotional strain of the encounter upset her and left her grappling with the conflict between empathy for the man and not fighting with her husband.

Nash was accustomed to navigating the complexities of human nature and listened. Societal dilemmas had played out against the backdrop of the supermarket before, and tempers often boiled to breaking point. While things had increased like a stressed fault line lately, it was an age-old problem and Nash would never be able to rid the town of a curse as old as nature. The new wave of chemicals coming in was a different brand of warfare. It was emblematic of the struggles faced with the influx of more drugs being brought into town and the trouble that came with them. The end product spat out people like Lance Taylor who barely survived on the fringes of society.

The couple's argument had continued in the aisles of Star Select. Grant Milton, was staunch in his perspective and contended that he worked hard to provide for his family. He questioned why he should bear the burden of a stranger's meal when he had his own children to feed. His rationale echoed the sentiments of fiscal responsibility and self-preservation.

Carole, propelled by compassion, argued for empathy and humanity in the face of somebody else's suffering. Things were heated in the store, and one of the security members kept an eye on them from the cameras, while another guard watched from the end of the aisle in case he had to intervene. The tension between them simmered, creating an undercurrent that spread down the aisle like spilt milk.

Unable to reconcile their differing principles, Carole stormed off, leaving Grant to fight with the trolley and get their shopping out.

Carole went to the hot food counter and bought a warm sausage roll, some chicken wings, and a cake from a stand positioned by the checkout. She paid for the begging man's meal. Her compassion made her the aggressor in their fight. After checking out, Grant abandoned his trolley and stormed to the car to wait for her.

When Carole followed, she looked for the addict but he was gone. She spoke to a security guard who had trailed her from the store. She explained that she had food for the man. According to her account of the events, the security guard was rude and told her that he'd moved the man on. 'I don't want filth like him outside my store.'

Nash didn't need to be there for what was essentially a domestic. Bowes laughed when he spouted his rank. 'What are you laughing at me for?' Nash said. 'I've got better things to do than deal with this.'

'Maybe just a tad pompous there, sir. I get it, this is beneath your pay grade, but we're here now. Let's do it and get out of here.'

Nash had never been told off by the PC before. 'Bugger me. We'll make a decent cop of you, yet.'

'Do I have to, sir? It isn't in my job description.'

Nash laughed, 'Spoke too soon. Come on, let's wrap this up.'

Carole said she'd held out the food and asked the security guard to give it to the man when he returned.

The guard was nasty and shouted at her, accusing her of encouraging the beggar. Instead of understanding and humanity, she was met with hostility. He told her they were sick of driving Lance Taylor away. He yelled that they didn't tolerate panhandlers outside their store. Carole told the guard he was rude and that she'd like to see the manager. He unleashed a torrent of hostility. His tone was aggressive, and he shouted at her again.

Grant was waiting in the car but when he saw his wife subjected to the security guard's aggressive tirade he sprinted across the car park. Nobody shouted at his wife except him.

Grant confronted the employee, and the exchange got out of hand, creating a disturbance that caught the attention of bystanders.

The commotion had reached a tipping point, prompting a customer to call the police. In response to the situation, the head of security, a calmer man called Barbosa, ran over to diffuse the tension before the police arrived.

The husband was furious in defence of his wife. He lunged at the younger man, took a flying swing at him, and punched the guard in the face. His nose burst sending a cascade of blood down his uniform.

Barbosa had tried to mediate the conflict but it was still heated when officers turned up.

After being removed from the premises, Patel had rounded up Lance Taylor as he lurked outside the gates waiting for his opportunity to slink back in. Nash allowed the wife to give him the food she'd bought while her husband and the initial member of security glared at them.

He remembered when Taylor had been a good-looking young scally. Always on the short side, he'd make up for his lack of stature by being the Cock of the North. He wore his blond hair long and was popular with the lads, while girls followed him wherever he went. Nash felt the same sadness as Bowes. He had been the first cop to lift him when the kid was fifteen and caught shoplifting from Asda. He remembered his strong white teeth and disarming smile. With his bent posture, tremors, and shambling gait, he was the most pathetic human being Nash had ever seen.

The kid had shagged half the girls in town in his heyday—and then the drugs had shagged him in return.

Nash helped calm the scene and moved shoppers away from the area. He returned an errant trolley to its bay. The busted husband had been issued a warning and it would be up to the young security guard to decide if he wanted to press charges.

'Bowes, let's go.'

Chapter Sixteen

Bowes dropped Nash off at home. He was met with another tense atmosphere that signalled trouble as he walked through the front door to change his funeral clothes.

Kelvin was rushing around pushing one arm into his coat. At the same time, he was fighting his way into his shoes by the front door without bending down—they were less than cooperative. And with his other hand, he grabbed his keys from the key holder. Nash held his coat for him to get the second arm in.

'Cheers, Si. Sorry. Gotta go,' Kelvin said. He kissed Nash, aiming for his lips, but his shoes distracted him, and the kiss landed on Nash's chin.

'What's going on?' Nash asked.

'It's Serena. She's had another run-in with the bullies. Honey was with her.'

Nash's gut twisted. The thought of her enduring more torment made him furious. 'What happened?' His voice was sharper than he intended.

Kelvin's shoulders rose with the worry. 'I don't know the details yet, but she was walking home from school with Honey when some kids cornered her in the park. They taunted her, calling her names and pushing her around.' He was burdened with sadness. 'They spat on her, Si. They spat on her.'

'Did they hurt her?'

'Physically, she's okay, but emotionally? I don't know. She's been through a lot of crap.'

Nash's jaw clenched with anger. He couldn't bear to think of any child being bullied, let alone Kelvin's granddaughter.

'This needs to stop.'

Kelvin nodded. 'Zola's at home with the girls. She's in a mess, and I need to go over and see they're okay.'

'I'll drive,' Nash said. 'Let's go.'

'What about work?'

'There's nothing that can't wait an hour. This is more important.'

He couldn't shake the image of Kelvin's granddaughters walking through the park where Noah's body was pulled out of the lake a couple of weeks earlier. He imagined their dark faces paling with fear as their tormentors closed around them.

After they got in the car, he clenched his fists on the steering wheel. He wanted to arrest the thugs who did this and would go to any lengths to protect Kelvin's family. He hoped Serena and Honey were strong enough to deal with the racial intolerance.

It was quiet when they went into Zola's house. The family's tears had dried, but the atmosphere was tense. Greg hugged his father-in-law and shook hands with Nash. 'Thank you for coming,' he said. He asked what everybody would like to drink and left the room to make coffee.

Zola sat on the couch, her eyes red and swollen from crying, and started again the second she saw Kelvin. 'Oh, Dad.' She ran into his arms and hugged him with tears streaking her cheeks. 'Do you know what they called my beautiful girls?'

'There's no need to repeat it. I know exactly what they said.' Kelvin tightened his arms around her.

Their words hit Nash like a punch, and he could only imagine the rage that Kelvin felt.

He didn't know if he should be there, but he put his hand on Zola's shoulder as he went to sit with the children. She raised her head from Kelvin's chest and smiled at him. This wasn't about him, but for the first time, he felt welcome.

Serena and Honey huddled on the sofa. They were freshly bathed and Nash sat down. He smiled at them and was close enough to smell their apple shampoo. Another vision hit him as he imagined them walking home with phlegm hanging from their hair.

Honey slithered off the sofa and climbed onto Nash's knee. She snuggled into his side and sucked her thumb. He stroked her tight braids and muttered soothing words. Not to be outdone, Serena sat on the edge of his seat and put her arms around his neck. The girls were building a bridge for the adults to cross. Her hair was loose and he imagined the awful image again. Her tight halo of curls was clean now—it was his job as Kelvin's boyfriend to keep her that way. While Kelvin comforted his daughter, Nash took care of the girls. He had a place here. He was useful.

Kelvin got Zola to sit down and knelt in front of the sisters. 'Are you okay?'

Serena nodded. 'We're fine, Grandad,' she replied, her eyes brimming with tears, 'But they were mean.' Both girls flung themselves into Kelvin's arms and he carried them back to the sofa and sat between them.

'I can't get my head around this,' Greg said putting coffee mugs down. 'Why?' It was a rhetorical question that nobody had an answer to.

'We won't let them hurt you again. I promise,' Kelvin said to the girls, and Nash wished he hadn't made a promise that they might not be able to keep. This could be a long process. He knew from cases he'd dealt with at work that bullying was a disease that took hold of both parties. It destroyed the victim and the person inflicting the pain.

Nash saw the toll it had taken on a family that, if he was allowed, he wanted to call his own, and felt a fierce resolve to stop it. He stepped up. 'Do you know their names? I'll make a house call and put the fear of God into them.'

'No, don't do that.' Serena pulled herself out of Kelvin's arms and looked terrified. 'They said they'd kill us if we told.'

'I'm not sure we want to go in all guns blazing at this stage,' Greg said. 'We don't know what kind of families they come from, or if it would do any good.'

'I'd make it do some good,' Nash said.

'Is there anything else we can do first?' Zola asked.

Nash saw that he was upsetting the girls. This wasn't his call or decision to make. 'Of course. I'm sorry. What have the school said?'

'They told me there's nothing they can do if it happened outside the school gates.'

'That's rubbish,' he told her. 'Head teachers have the legal power to make pupils behave outside the school premises. It's part of their duty of care and I won't have you fobbed off to make their lives easier. It's laziness on the school's part.'

'Not in my backyard,' Kelvin said.

'Exactly. They're shirking their responsibility.'

'Because we're black?' Serena said.

There was a shocked silence and Greg was the first to recover. He held her by the upper arms and put his face level so that they were eye-to-eye. 'No, sweetheart. Don't ever think that. It's not true. We're all the same. Everybody.'

'But you're white, Daddy. You don't understand.'

Nash was gut-punched again. To hear something so profound coming from the mouth of an innocent eleven-year-old was awful. She'd already discovered that her white friends had an easier life than they did.

'We need to stand up to these bullies and show them we won't back down,' Zola said. Despite her fears, she was strong and determined to protect her daughters.

'No one messes with my family and gets away with it,' Honey lisped, taking her thumb out of her mouth, and they all laughed. She was a nine-year-old ready to fight for her family.

'The next thing to do is gather evidence,' Nash said. 'You need to start a journal and document every instance of bullying. That includes every hurtful word and cruel act. I mean everything, no matter how insignificant or petty it seems. It all builds a picture. If you can, take photographs and videos. But, remember, it's not a good idea for the girls to get their phones out in front of them.'

Kelvin nodded in agreement. 'And we'll ensure the school takes this seriously,' he added. 'They need to take decisive action to protect our girls.'

The door burst open and Imani blew in like a sirocco. She ran over to her sister and put her arms around her, gesturing for the girls to come into the hug as well.

'My poor nieces,' she said. 'I'll kill these white *Buulu* for their insolence.' She saw Nash and her hatred encompassed him in her fury. 'What's he doing here?'

'I invited him,' Zola said, which wasn't exactly true.

'This is family business. He has no place here.' Imani was rigid with anger.

'Not in front of the children,' Kelvin hissed. 'Keep your feelings to yourself.'

Imani shot Nash a dirty look, but she had the grace to look ashamed of speaking out of turn in front of the girls.

'They've seen enough prejudice without facing it in their home,' Greg said.

Not wanting to make the situation worse, Nash stood up and used the excuse of having some calls to make in the car. The last thing he wanted was another run-in with Imani. He said his goodbyes and got hugs from both of the children. He told Kelvin to take his time.

As the days passed, Nash kept in touch with the family to help them. Zola and Greg were immersed in meetings with school officials. They advocated for their daughters against the bureaucracy that the school shielded themselves behind. Greg demanded action to address the bullying. He was united with Zola and refused to back down. They were determined to hold the school accountable for ensuring the safety and well-being of Serena.

Honey wasn't at that school yet, but it still affected her when they played out on the way home. Greg and Zola organised their schedules to take their children to school and pick them up. Kelvin helped where he could and Nash was humbled the day Zola rang, saying she was held up in traffic and would he be able to pick up the girls. She'd already rung her husband and Kelvin and said Nash was her last hope. He was happy to be any hope.

When Kelvin had moved in with Nash and opened a new branch of his practice in Barrow, Imani, and Kelvin's son Taraji, were settled and had their lives mapped out. They opted to stay in Kendal partly due to work commitments. Taraji worked in the path lab at Lancaster Royal Infirmary and Imani worked in her dad's practice having passed the bar five years earlier. Since Kelvin had moved to Barrow, Imani had been promoted to the second solicitor in the Kendal branch of Jones & Deacon Solicitors. It was another bone of contention for her that her father and his partner, Wesley Deacon didn't feel she had the experience to make her a partner in the firm. Kelvin had worked for his position, nothing was handed to him on a plate and he wanted the same drive and independence for his daughter.

As the school implemented programs to help, Nash was glad that Zola's perseverance made a difference, but they were vigilant, knowing the fight wasn't over.

Serena and Honey showed remarkable courage. The following Monday, Serena stood up in a special assembly and spoke to her year group with dignity about the effects bullying had on them.

Nash had been worried about her speaking out and the backlash it might cause. But Serena insisted. The kid took after her grandad. She had Kelvin's resilience.

Chapter Seventeen

A week later, Nash and Brown arrived at another filthy crime scene, surrounded by the acrid stench of decay. The low-rent tenement flat was Lance Taylor's final dwelling.

The detectives were confronted with a grim sight in the cramped living space. Rot and waste covered every surface including the floor. Hamburger wrappers littered the place with other half-eaten food. And bottles, filled with a brown-yellow substance that would prove to be urine were beside the filthy armchair. Nash had seen this many times before. Addicts were so strung out that they either couldn't move or were too lazy to get up and walk the few paces to their bathrooms often situated on the same level as the living room with a kitchenette and attached bedroom. Rat droppings topped every pile of rubbish and clothing, and the smell of ammonia and weed was unbearable.

Lance was twenty-four years old and died snared by his addiction. He was in the bathtub with his glassy eyes staring at the wall after death took him. The porcelain was ingrained with filth and Nash could tell this was the first time the tub had seen water in years. The long yellow limescale stain from the tap to the drain gave the impression that the bath had been unused until now.

Like everything in this hovel, it bore the grimy residue of neglect and the pervasive decay that had claimed the space. There was little room for the man who had made the mess.

The flat was a microcosm of Lance's problems. It painted a portrait of desolation. Along with the accumulated dirt and countless diseases, more dangerous weapons waited to stick Nash and Brown. Discarded syringes littered the floor like macabre confetti, an indicator of personal battles fought and lost. Nash refused to believe that anybody would set out to become a smackhead. They all had it under control and could stop any time they liked. The naked lightbulb barely illuminated the grime and faeces that streaked the walls, hiding despair and closing in on every side.

Foul-smelling blankets, thick with the odour of mould and substances long abused, were strewn across a piss-stained mattress in the corner of the bedroom. The kitchen, a mockery of its intended purpose, harboured unwashed dishes and an assortment of spoiled food, creating a breeding ground for the rancid scent that clung to the air.

After an initial sweep to check the flat was empty, they didn't want to return to the bathroom, but it couldn't be avoided. The place where Lance met his tragic end was a mosaic of filth. Black mould crept up the walls, a deadly invader, and the stench of uncleanliness hovered in the cramped space.

'Hell, Nash. The smell's alive. It's crawling into my hair and building a nest,' Brown said.

The bathtub cradled the lifeless body of the young man, still fully clothed and lost for eternity to the grip of his addiction.

They navigated the nauseating environment, confronted by the reality of Lance's existence. 'This is grim,' Brown said. 'I feel like dragging him out of there and punching him in the face for ruining his life like that.'

'It could happen to any of us, it's easy to judge from the outside, Brown.'

'I'm not judging. I'm angry at the waste.'

She picked up Lance Taylor's extensive pile of mail as they went back into the living room and flicked through it, bills, court summonses, flyers. They'd all been ignored. They were waiting for Bill Robinson to arrive, and when they were disturbed, they thought it was the coroner.

They were startled when a skinny man, reminiscent of a weasel shuffled in and cowered at the bedsit door as though he expected to be beaten. He'd taken them by surprise and it was a moment before Nash's blood pressure returned to normal. But he recognised Skinner, one of Lance's acquaintances—another denizen of the shadows, drawn by the insidious lure of addiction. The individual, known to the police from his extensive record, slinked across the threshold, his demeanour marked by fear, but he got no further. One of the coppers blocked his path but he was held in place by his terror and didn't need telling to stay back. He was skin and bone, spotty, with rotten teeth and filthy clothing and nails. But he wasn't as close to death as Lance had been. It made no difference, they were all one bad hit away from where Lance was now.

The coroner arrived and Brown took Skinner aside to interview him. Nash told her to read his rights and said he'd be there in a second. He shook hands with Bill who didn't attempt to hide his distaste of the squalor. The seasoned coroner cast a discerning eye over the scene. 'The body's been in the bath for at least three days.' Bill looked from Lance to Skinner in the corner of the hall outside the flat and shook his head. Skinner was the living corpse of the two, snivelling and frightened. He was the reality of lives entangled in their sordid world.

Skinner could wait a few minutes—it would do him no harm to stew. The detectives continued their examination of the body, looking for clues to unravel the mystery surrounding Lance's death. Skinner was on the periphery of the investigation, and whether he liked it or not, he was an unwitting participant in the unfolding tragedy.

Nash got an initial verbal report from Bill, shook hands again and left him to bag and tag when SOCO arrived. Nash went over to Skinner.

'Got any money? I need it bad, man.'

Nash noticed that although he didn't attempt to go in, Skinner's eyes kept darting to the bathroom. The door was ajar, but from where they stood, they couldn't see the body.

'You know what's in there.' Nash said.

Skinner nodded.

'Tell me what happened.'

'I need some stuff first.'

Brown grabbed the only other seat in the flat, a basic dining room chair, and dragged it into the hall. Skinner winced as it made a noise like chalk on a board. She spun it around in front of Skinner and pushed him into it hard, without showing an iota of sympathy. 'Talk,' she said.

When he didn't answer she laid into him with a barrage of questions.

Skinner's squeaky voice cut through the squalid air. 'It was bad Chaos. One minute he was flying, and the next he was shaking about on the floor like a dog with rabies.'

'Why didn't you report it?'

Visibly shaken, Skinner stammered through his response, revealing the depths of his paranoia.

He admitted withholding information out of fear of repercussions. These people existed in a state of perpetual vigilance, waiting for trouble to knock on the door, always with tabs owed and debts outstanding that would signify their reckoning. Skinner was terrified of grassing but was hopeful that if he gave chapter and verse now, they'd see him right with some money for his next hit. Nash had to admire his unfaltering optimism.

'What happened?' Brown asked.

'I don't know.'

'You do. You were there.'

'I was out of it man.'

'Did you drown him in the bath?'

'Yeah. No. I mean, we put him in there to try and make him breathe, but I think he was already dead.'

'Who's we?'

'Give me some money and I'll tell you. I need it, man.'

'Give me their names or so help me God, I'll beat it out of you.'

'Tucker and Stan.'

Nash had arrested them both in the past.

Skinner looked from Brown to Nash in terror, and Nash put his hand on her shoulder to warn her to ease off.

They listened to his story and Nash called it. It wouldn't serve anybody going through with his arrest. He was de-arrested on the spot. They could set him up in a hostel for the night but he wouldn't stay. The kid would be on the streets and begging again in an hour.

Although he'd been present at Lance's death, they didn't need to hold him. He wasn't going anywhere, apart from back to the depths of hell with his next hit. He didn't want help—only drugs.

When Skinner started talking, the words came fast. He'd been hiding since Lance died five days before. The sight of police cars converging around the decrepit flat had shattered his resolve to lay low. He'd hoped that the horror would go away if he ignored it. Faced with the suspicion that law enforcement would throw at him, he'd succumbed to his paranoia. The fear of arrest, exacerbated by his anxiety, had driven him to give himself up.

Brown continued the interrogation, and Skinner's story was pitiful. In the dishevelled room, the detectives worked behind them, looking for evidence of Lance's final hours, and the tendrils of fear wove through Skinner's ability to sit still.

Brown's rebuke echoed in the confines of the hallway, cutting the air with a harshness that Nash thought was unnecessary. 'Ease up, detective. He's told us what he knows.'

Brown was unyielding and direct, and she held Skinner accountable for the delay in getting help for Lance Taylor.

Nash, put his hand on her shoulder and squeezed. He stepped forward, acknowledging the man's fear and lack of choices. Nash had spoken to Bill and decided to put Skinner out of his misery. There was no case to answer, and holding the kid there in terror was like a cat toying with its prey. He pointed out that coming forward sooner wouldn't have altered the grim outcome. Bill Robinson's findings ascertained that Lance was dead before his body was submerged in a futile attempt to revive him by his three cronies.

Nash asked for the addresses of the other two, though they wouldn't have to look further than this warren of stinking flats. Skinner refused. Then he saw a new opening to try some blackmail and was prepared to rat his friends out again for a tenner. It fell on stony ground.

'It's your choice, mate. We can do it here or at the station. Which would you prefer?' Brown said. 'We have every right to keep you for seventy-two hours, by which time you'll be rolling around in the height of withdrawal.'

'Detective, please go and wait in the car,' Nash said.

Brown held her hands up in submission and backed away from Skinner but she didn't leave.

Nash's compassionate approach humanised the victim. They were all victims in those flats. The complex interplay of fear defined the lives of the addicts. A tragedy unfolded in the decrepit apartment, and the detectives investigated Lance's death and the intricacies of a world where lives hung in the balance every day. They were caught between the grip of substance abuse and the consequences that followed.

Skinner spilt the fragmented narrative about the drug-induced episode. 'Four of us shot up in the living room. We were out of it for hours.' Skinner was shaken awake by Tucker who was coming down and noticed that something was wrong with Lance. He was grey—and still—and had white foam dripping from his dead mouth onto the greasy threadbare carpet. Their futile attempts to revive him escalated from a drug-induced stupor to dragging him into the bathroom. 'We filled the tub with cold water and pushed him in the bath.' It was winter. However misguided their attempts were, they had tried to help him. It spoke about the community that permeated their dismal lives.

Nash was calm throughout and listened to Skinner's account. Despite the gravity of the situation, he assessed that the young man posed no immediate threat. Recognising the proximity of his flat in the nearby block, Nash made a judgment call—he was letting him go. They'd need to talk to him again and his friends, Tucker and Stan, but there was no flight risk. This poor sod wouldn't get to the end of the road, never mind out of town. Brown had been harsh when she was interrogating him. Nash got it, she was getting information and sometimes it called for a hard approach. When they had all he knew, her soft nature took over. She brought him a cup of black tea. There was no milk. He was shivering and she took off her jacket and put it around his shoulders. She'd been tough on him to try and get an honest story, but her compassion was apparent in the way she put her hands on his to stop them shaking. She helped him to drink and spoke gently to him, telling him that his life would be better when he got clean. They both knew that was never going to happen.

Nash conveyed authority and understanding. He said he'd accompany Skinner back to his flat, and they went via the bakery on the corner where he said they did an excellent meat pie.

Chapter Eighteen

That Friday night, Renshaw, a detective in the middle of the mass of officers, felt the riot vest pressing against his chest. He had his bullet-proof visor pulled over his face, wore a Kevlar vest, and held a riot shield. He wasn't armed, but the men from GMNT behind him were. They used vehicles as their shields and some of the snipers were on one knee. A couple of them lay on their stomachs to get better rooftop shots and Renshaw was in awe of them. He'd shot sub-machine guns along with self-loading rifles and browning pistols on the range as part of his training, but he'd never carried an SMG in the field yet. He felt a kick of adrenaline. This was playing with the big boys.

It was the biggest nighttime police raid his town had seen. It was an orchestrated sting that incorporated a specialised team from Greater Manchester. The convoy of police vehicles had their flashing lights turned off and the reinforced navy blue vans were filled with teams in riot gear. They rumbled through the streets like an approaching storm on a moody horizon.

As three clocks—the Church Walk tower, Barrow Town Hall, and its counterpart in Dalton—struck ten, the synchronised raid unfolded with a precision that left no room for error. Thirteen houses across Barrow, Dalton, and Ulverston were the targets of the sweeping operation and Renshaw was the senior officer for the Ulverston team. They closed in on their target, a residence on The Crafters estate in Ulverston cloaked in shadows and dark secrets.

Paul Lawson had argued his case to be put on the Ulverston team, but Nash had called it and put him on the Barrow squad instead. He said he wanted him on the same raid as him to have his back, but it was more that he didn't want him involved in the raids on Ulverston. You don't crap on your own doorstep—and by the same token, you don't clean up other people's if they live next door.

Lawson was young and keen. He lived in Ulverston, on the same estate that was being raided. His sister and her husband were both involved in the drug scene and had been in and out of trouble all of their adult lives. Paul had taken his nephew under his wing the year before when his mum was admitted to Dale View mental health facility. The kid had stayed with his uncle Paul, and even though at twenty-five Paul wasn't much older than Aiden, it had been the making of both of them. It made Lawson grow up fast, and Nash had seen him joining in with Bowes' daft jokes less as his serious side emerged. Lawson wanted a promotion and was working hard towards it. He felt strongly about protecting his town, but Nash put him out of the way. It was too close to home and could jeopardise future court cases if anybody shouted about his conflict of interest.

Nash was pleased that his sister's house wasn't one of the ones being raided. No intel had been put forward for them. It saved Lawson from any embarrassment.

The door, a barrier into the unknown, yielded to the battering ram's single assault. The resounding crash filled the night, announcing the intrusion of authority into the familial home. Three houses were hit on that estate and Renshaw felt proud when he heard similar doors in similar houses disturbing the night in similar streets nearby.

The comfortable silence around the low hum of the television was shattered, and replaced by the frenzied thump of fight or flight reactions.

The family's fear was palpable as the weight of law enforcement surged over the threshold. DCI Bold from Manchester was aptly named and second in command under Turner. The GMNT squad led the entry and Renshaw and his men followed their orders. Bold navigated the chaos with practised resolve and cleared each room with method. They honed in on the target—a seventeen-year-old, caught in the network of dealing. He was the embodiment of misguided choices and lay on a bed in his boxers, frozen in the glare of police flashlights. The porn running on his tablet added a guttural soundtrack to the proceedings.

The family, caught in the crossfire of their son's reckoning, displayed a spectrum of emotions—fear etched their faces like a tribal tattoo. After the arrest was made, Alan Cropper was in cuffs and causing no problems. Renshaw went to speak to the family in the living room. These were innocent people caught in something insidious and evil—even Alan was a victim. Once the bad guys got hold of you, they didn't let go. Renshaw noticed the TV on the wall, one of the biggest models. As a police sergeant, with a small mortgage and a car on finance, he only dreamt of being able to afford one like it. He gave up all hope of the finer things in life when he got a wife and two kids.

The suspect's sisters, both under eight, were caught in the madness and were terrified by the pounding feet and shouts of the strangers that swarmed through their house. They didn't understand what was going on and huddled under duvets in their beds, crying with terror. One of the officers stayed with them, taking off his riot helmet to show the girls his face.

Renshaw looked in and gave the officer the thumbs up. He stayed in the doorway until a WPC came into the room. Renshaw had an eight-year-old son with disabilities and it made him protective of any child, regardless of whether they were in trouble. He joined the force to protect kids like these two little girls in their dirty nightclothes and lying in a cold room that smelt of urine. They tore at his heart.

The shouts of officers and the screaming family, the clatter of boots on linoleum floors, and the creaking protest of doors forced open, mingled in a cacophony of noise that rattled through the house.

Renshaw executed his duty to the letter and with unwavering determination. The responsibility of representing his team pressed down on him. After the arrest, he made time to be sensitive to the exposure of a fractured family. To the out-of-town dealers, they were collateral damage in a filthy but lucrative business. To Renshaw, they were just people getting by. They were like him but with a better TV. The raid was conducted in the underworld of a community that bore the scars of the drugs reality.

Chapter Nineteen

At the same time, in Barrow, the foggy air clung low to the pavements outside The Siren. The old pub had been turned into flats a few years before, but it reverted to a pub when the locals were up in arms at its loss. A muted orange glow fractured in a blur from the faint streetlights, casting elongated shadows that played hide-and-seek with the corners where anybody could be lurking. The hum of traffic further away on Duke Street made a steady soundtrack to the unfolding drama.

A tightly coordinated operation unfolded as two police cars and three riot vans circled the pub like a steel corset. A week of meticulous surveillance had culminated in this moment—Nash knew Blight and nine lower-ranking members of the Barrow gang were inside and they didn't suspect a thing.

Inside, the pub would be a hub of illicit activity, buzzing with the exchange of goods and the murky transactions of the underworld. It had always been a pub with shades of grey.

In the old days, the landlord ran a tight ship and had a good relationship with the police. But he'd always been one to turn a blind eye to the odd character coming in with a bag of hot CDs, or a sneaky side of beef and pouches of foreign tobacco that were sold in dingy corners. And in turn, the police let him be. He kept any trouble contained and dealt with it in-house. It had been an excellent pub in those days, run in the old ways, with a cracking landlord at the helm.

It was different now, and it wasn't the landlady's fault. When a gang took over a local pub, there was little that the landlords could do about it. Cherry and Louise came in as managers under a London-based brewery. They didn't want trouble. They were starry-eyed and ambitious. Cherry barred the big characters on day one at the first sign of illegal activity. The following day, the pub was the target of petrol bombs through the letterbox and the windows were smashed. They fought the corruption, but eventually, they had no choice but to live with Blue and her gang and they turned their blind eyes to far worse than the previous landlord ever did. They were corrupted over time. They'd wanted a clean pub but when that didn't happen they accepted the backhanders and bungs as their rightful due.

The seasoned leader of the Greater Manchester Narcotics Team, forty-eight-year-old Superintendent Mark Turner, was leading the Barrow strike from the command centre. Superintendent Carter had been drafted in from Manchester to run this arm of the strike, putting Nash's nose out of joint. Carter's weathered face bore the lines of countless operations, each written into his skin as a badge of experience. Some of his scars were metaphorical, others real, and ragged, giving him a mean look. Beside him, Detective Nash was better looking, softer in approach and seconding Carter as the local lead whose area knowledge lent invaluable insights into the operation. Carter had experience in narcotic arrests, but Nash knew his town and the people.

The streets were draped in the cloak of night but soon harboured curious onlookers—shadows peering from behind curtains. Their eyes glinted with morbid curiosity. The officers, in the anonymity of riot gear, melted into the urban backdrop and were hidden by darkness as they took their strategic positions.

In the loaded silence, Carter raised his hand, a non-verbal signal to be ready. The team watched as though it held the sword of Damocles. They waited for the command to go. The moment lingered, pregnant with anticipation, until Turner, at the command centre, shouted through his headset.

'Go. Go. Go.'

On his command, the officers surged forward, a synchronised force of pounding boots converging on The Siren. The darkness shuddered with the collective movement of black uniforms as they stormed the bar. They fanned out, taking offensive positions as they barked orders at the patrons. The team was familiar with the layout and covered both rooms, with an officer levelling a gun at the staff behind the bar.

The Siren crackled with tension, a volatile mix of fear and defiance as the police raid sent shockwaves through the two public rooms. Chaos erupted like a storm unleashed on the customers. It was as if a spotlight shone in the murky spaces and their world of shadows and secrecy was laid bare.

The initial attempt at escape by some of them through the back door was futile as officers were positioned outside to intercept them. The night transformed into a blare of sirens wailing in the distance.

In the dim back room, the melee intensified. Desperation fuelled resistance as a male dealer brandished a pool cue in a feeble attempt to repel the advancing police clad in riot gear.

The impact of the makeshift weapon against reinforced shields echoed through the pub, a futile rebellion drowned out by the authoritative commands of law enforcement.

Nash was shielded by his men, looking for Blight.

'Stand clear of the tables with your hands above your heads,' Carter shouted.

The scene devolved into a cacophony of shattering glass, overturned tables, and the cries of people caught in the crossfire. The air buzzed with tension, the smell of spilt drinks mingling with the metallic tang of pepper spray. In the bedlam, Cherry and her partner, Louise, fought to salvage what remained of their pub, shouting protests through the wreckage.

The officers, seasoned in the art of controlling chaos, moved through the commotion, apprehending individuals involved in the criminal underbelly of Barrow. The pub was a battleground of conflicting interests, a microcosm of a larger war waged between law and disorder.

Blight stood up and screamed a torrent of abuse. Grabbing the girl nearest her, the lower-level accomplice became an unwitting pawn in her survival. Blight seized her around the throat, broke a bottle on the edge of the table and pressed the jagged glass against the skin of the younger girl's neck. The tense standoff unfolded like a morbid tableau, frozen in the whirlwind of the raid.

The experienced officers, immune to such theatrics, closed in with calculated precision. Blight's attempt to use a human shield crumbled as the weight of law bore down on her. The broken bottle clattered to the floor, a useless weapon abandoned in the face of overwhelming force when she was taken to the floor. She was cuffed and arrested.

Outside, the screech of more vehicles joined the chaos, marking the advance of law enforcement determined to quell the rebellion. The pub yielded as the arrests piled up, filling the riot vans with raging thugs. It was a battleground where order triumphed over disorder at the cost of damaged limbs. Shattered glass and the clinking sound of handcuffs sealed the fate of the apprehended.

***

Jay Bowes was in front of Nash. He knew he had to prove himself and was determined to show he was a capable team member. He saw a boy coming at them with a pool cue and if ever there was a good time to channel his Bruce Lee, it was now.

In the second he had to think, he considered dropping to the floor and rolling, but the carpet didn't look like it had been cleaned in years. And anyway, there were people and tables in the way. He glanced at Nash. He had two choices. He could get out of the way and prevent his skull from being split like a boiled egg, or he could save his boss. While Bowes was reaching out for him, Nash thrust him to one side and then pushed the boy out of the way. Another kid was behind the first and he had a knife in his hand. Nash went for him and a second later, he had the attacker's arm bent up his back and screamed, 'Drop it or I'll break your fingers.'

Bowes made do with grappling with the wiry young kid to wrestle the cue from him. He resisted the urge to yell, 'Aiy-ya!' but only just. He was on fire. When he had the cue in his hands, he tried to break it over his knee, found it didn't yield, and glanced around to see if anybody had noticed. He threw the cue out of the way. The kid was screaming abuse at him as he restrained the gang member with an unyielding grip, his fingers working to fasten the handcuffs behind the thug's back.

The arrested lad was unrepentant and seized the opportunity to boast about his role in the assault on Andy Gibson. A smug grin played across his mouth and Jay wanted to punch his smarmy face but lifted his knee into the back of the kid's leg to drop him.

The boy's leg buckled and he staggered but didn't fall. Bowes rammed him face-first against the wall. 'Name?' he shouted.

'Mickey Mouse.'

'Original. Remind me to buy you a joke book for your fifth birthday, kid' Bowes grunted as he pushed him onto his knees. He wanted to avenge the beating Andy had taken and drove his knee into the dealer's back harder than necessary. It was just a nudge to show him that the balance of power had shifted. Nash would have done the same. The impact forced the air out of the loud-mouthed yob, transforming his bravado into a pained howl.

Jay was unfazed by the cries of discomfort and cinched the handcuffs further than usual. The ratchet noise of them tightening sealed the gravity of the arrest and was a physical manifestation of justice tightening its grip on the criminals. The boy felt the cuffs digging into him as a consequence of his actions.

Jay Bowes knew he was a force to be reckoned with for anybody who trampled over the law. He might be a humble PC, but he had a lot of physical strength and was learning fast. He didn't often get to take a bad guy down, and the fact that this streak of bacon probably weighed about 80lb, wet through, was irrelevant. He'd been flinging a dangerous weapon about. It was Bowes' collar and he was proud of it. He moved on to the next one and thought about his first promotion.

***

Nash's breath was laboured from the adrenaline-fuelled madness. He guided another arrested boy in cuffs to the van, then joined Carter. The raid was under control but the night was jacked with residual tension and the wail of sirens.

'That was successful,' Nash said.

Carter looked at him without much expression. 'It was your intel, you should take the credit.'

Nash surveyed the scene. 'They won't go down without a fight. This is just the beginning.'

Carter's gaze was steady. 'You have our support on this. Barrow might be your turf, but the drug operation extends far beyond the area.'

Nash pulled his car keys out of his pocket and noticed that his hand was bleeding. 'We need to cut off the supply at its source. Barrow's just another town on the route up the country.'

Collaboration between local and regional forces was imperative against the criminal underbelly eating away at their communities.

'The cleanup won't be easy,' Nash said.

Carter smiled. 'Easy was never the goal. Between us, we'll dismantle the damn operation.'

In the aftermath of the raid, with collective responsibility hanging in the air, Nash and Carter understood that this only marked their first victory.

Carter looked at Nash's hand. 'You want to get that seen to,' he said.

Chapter Twenty

After the success of the raids the night before, Nash got to work early. The custody staff had suffered a difficult shift as they attended to the fourteen arrested suspects from three towns in the area. Most of them were acting out, some of them were high, and the staff had left them to sober and calm down. When they were released and screamed the injustice from the rafters, turning the heat on Mathis and his boss might lead them to make mistakes.

Nash had put in a day of interviews. He was exhausted and wanted to get home for a shower and a hot meal. Most of the arrested gang members had already been processed and screened. Apart from small amounts for personal usage, nobody from the pub had been found with much in the way of illegal substances on them. Not enough to justify holding them on remand. There were a few minor assaults to add to the rap sheet, but again, nothing to detain them on, apart from Blight. At best, they had some minor charges and more paperwork than the raid warranted.

She'd been taken in for her initial interview, and to have her case presented. It was mainly so that she couldn't say they'd left her to rot, but a deeper investigation was pending and they were holding her. She wasn't talking and would be held over.

They'd started by interviewing the low-level tiers and the ones most likely to spill their guts. The strategy was to leave Blight, as the new boss around town, to stew in her juices for a while. Nash figured it would do her no harm to sit and lose some of her arrogant edge. Roberts had been a pain in the backside and was charged and released with the rest of the gang, pending court appearances.

Blight was the last to be spoken to. Her second interview would be carried over until the next day. It was fine—she'd interview better tired. When he'd left, she was still hammering on the cell door and verbally abusing the staff. She'd spent the night trying to rile her cronies in the holding cells and rotated between inciting them to play up and threatening them to keep their mouths shut. When she heard people passing, she would look up at the camera with her middle finger extended. 'Filthy pigs. Get me out of here,' she shouted. Nash could tell she'd been arrested before. Different station, different cot—but she knew the drill. She was going to be trouble, and when he went down to the holding block, he'd been torn between doing the second interview that night to get it over with and leaving it until the next day. But she was still pounding on the door and screaming like a wildcat, so to hell with her. A second night on the hard bunk might chill her soup by morning.

Some of the backroom team had been collating evidence to put before her during her second interview. Nash wanted an airtight case. Taking a hostage, and threatening her combined with assault with a broken bottle, had ensured that. They had enough on her, and Blight would almost certainly be remanded in custody until her trial.

He was tired too.

The light in his office cast shadows on the leather furniture as he went in to grab his jacket. There was a knock on his door and he cursed.

Conrad Snow poked his head around the door. His floppy mop of blond hair was the first thing Nash noticed, followed by his t-shirt with the slogan *I'm Not a Detective, I Just Look Like One*. 'Got a minute, Si?'

Nash would normally be pleased to see him. They'd become friends outside work and their meetings could break the monotony of usual police procedures. But he'd almost got away from work and he suppressed a groan. 'I was just leaving. Can it wait?'

'It's urgent.' He tapped his temple to indicate that he had a psychic report to make.

Nash had learnt that when Snow had something to say it was wise to listen. He motioned the psychic medium to come in and take a seat and managed to smile as Snow sat across from him. Nash had always been sceptical about involving a psychic in police work, but Snow's abilities had proved invaluable.

'I'll get straight to it. I've had a kid coming through to me all day. I'll type up my report for the team, but I've made some notes in the interim, in case I can't get him back. Let's see if I can make contact.' Snow closed his eyes, and his face relaxed. All expressions disappeared. The atmosphere in the room changed. He slowed his breathing and counted his meditative mala beads for a few minutes. Nash suppressed a sigh and looked at the wall clock. The shift in the air was subtle but seemed charged with a different energy. Snow's voice was soft.

'He's here, but it's not a strong connection. His name is Noah and he's waiting in a shadow realm.'

'Noah Ross? Are you sure it's him?'

'He's tethered to the chaos that claimed him.'

Nash sat forward and worked to keep the excitement out of his voice. Snow hadn't been brought into this case. However, Noah's death was all over the press, and he could have linked the word 'chaos' enigmatically to the boy from the news. But Nash knew that Snow didn't use cheap gimmicks. His reputation for being a clean shooter was too important to him.

'Chaos?'

'That's what he said. He's telling me his story. He was jumped and dragged onto the waste ground by the docks. There were four of them. He's very specific that I tell you, they injected him with Chaos.' Snow thrashed his head and sweat broke out on his brow.

A shiver ran down Nash's spine as Snow's voice changed, embodying a younger essence.

It's taking effect. They're holding me down to stop me from running, Noah said using Conrad as a vessel.

'Jesus, Nash, I can feel this kid's terror.' Snow experienced the drug's effects and told it through Noah's eyes then jumped back into his own skin to relay images and feelings. He started retching and Nash grabbed his wastepaper basket in alarm, but Snow kept his gorge down.

'Who used Chaos on Noah?' Nash asked.

'I don't know, they're indistinct, but he was injected against his will.'

They said they'd kill me if I went to the police.

'The threat of exposing him after he'd been forced to take drugs coerced him into dealing.'

They said I'm a criminal now and I'd be deported if I didn't sell the packets of Chaos.

'The poor kid's so ashamed, Si.'

Nash listened as Snow reassured the dead boy. His tone was soothing. Nash's jaw clenched. The bastards had caught Noah in a web of manipulation and bound him with terror.

'Can Noah guide us to the evidence, Conrad? Ask him if he can give us anything to expose the criminals.'

'He can only show me disconnected glimpses of things he's seen. A woman's ankle with a trailing flower tattoo. They're all wearing hoodies but he can't give us much more. They use this place a lot. I can see multiple syringes in the grass, DNA, maybe? He says the truth will reveal itself.'

Snow spoke about a twisted path and nothing else made sense as he talked. He told Nash that Noah had been taken a second time. They took him to a squalid flat. Snow described a series of graffiti tags and Nash put a pen and paper in front of him to reproduce them. Peculiar tags and patterns emerged and Nash recognised many of them. He'd seen them around town, but specifically in the concrete stairwells of the awful apartment blocks. They led him through the labyrinth of Barrow's underbelly.

As he talked, Snow was lost in desolate alleys, following the spectral trail left by Noah's spirit. He said the symbols painted on brick walls glowed in the darkness and he scribbled as he talked.

'Is the refugee centre involved? Yes, he's taking me there now,' Snow said. 'They're recruiting kids from there. I'm in a corridor. I'm stopping by a picture on the wall. It's the path he spoke about, twisting through How Tun wood. He's telling me that's where they go. Sometimes they pick up drugs there.'

This was a vital piece of new information. Nash's mind buzzed with new lines of enquiry as he followed the spectral breadcrumbs left by Noah Ross. The cryptic symbols, guided by Snow's connection, led him to several places including the tenement flats where Lance Taylor died. They were in a grim part of town.

Nash scribbled a new method of attack and wrote down some points to follow. He wanted to examine the screening forms on entry for identifying tattoos on the suspects. Nash had things to do and felt anxious as the loud tick of the clock taunted him with lost time. His chest was tight and he wanted to close the meeting, but Snow wasn't finished.

His voice changed. His eyes rolled back into his head and his body slumped in the chair. A new tone of urgency gripped him. 'Max is here.'

Max Jones visited the liminal space between life and death. He spoke through Conrad Snow and Nash picked up on an increased sense of anxiety.

The night's obsidian colours made the room oppressive. Nash got up and, thinking it would help, he turned on the overhead light. He rarely used it, preferring the muted glow from his lamp. The sudden brightness didn't ease his turmoil and Snow motioned for him to turn it off. He did.

Making contact was difficult because they only had a low telepathic connection. Conrad was a conduit between the living and the departed but he struggled to maintain contact with Max who compelled them to strike hard in the new case.

Guided by Snow's spirit connection, he took Nash into the heart of town. Snow was standing across a divide and on a plane where the living and the dead met. He etched symbols. Nash pushed the pad in front of him again and had to put the pencil in his hand because Conrad Snow was in a trance.

Snow drew random shapes and scribbled circles to strengthen the connection and form energy lines between himself and Max on the paper. Without lifting the pen from the pad, he drew an image. It was a van. He said the word, 'Red.' The van was outside a burnt house. Next, he drew in other houses, a Chinese Takeaway on the corner, and a small piece of green waste ground the size of a postage stamp for children to play on. Nash recognised the area.

Max said, *Nikki's in the van. Help her, she's scared*.

Before Snow finished, Nash was already putting his coat on. Conrad came out of his trance and Nash could see him struggling to come to full wakefulness. He put his head in his hands and ran his fingers through his hair. 'I'm coming with you,' he said.

Nash didn't stop to tell him yes or no. He didn't inform anybody where he was going but tore out of the station in a hurry. Conrad Snow ran to catch up with him. He had his hand on the passenger side door handle when Nash pushed his fob to unlock the car. He started the engine, but before pulling out, he keyed his police radio.

'All units. All units. Possible 10-54. Marsh Street. Approach with caution.' He had no idea if the kid was alive or dead—if there was a kid. But he had to get some backup to her fast.

They were there in minutes, and Nash screeched to a halt leaving the car door open as he ran to the red van parked along the side of the road. As he approached it, a chill permeated the air, accentuating the gravity of Max's message.

The small rear window had been smashed, and he used his sleeve to cover his hand and try the door. It was unlocked. Lamenting the fact that he'd worn his best shoes, a mist of cement dust fell from the van as he opened one of the two rear doors and looked inside. It was filled with scorched rubbish from the burnt house. There were a lot of black bin bags. Children playing on the grass gave up their football to come over and Conrad told them to stay back. But trying to hold a growing crowd of chattering kids wasn't as easy as it looked on the television.

'What's he doing?'

'Ugh, he's a skip-rat.'

'Shut up, Daniel. Maybe he's hungry.'

'Doesn't look it. And he's a copper. Billy Platt told us to keep away from his van or he'd chop our balls off.'

'Shut up, Daniel.'

Despite the gravity of the situation, Snow laughed and then apologised to Nash. He said it was at the thought of Nash scrambling into a load of rubbish bags for his dinner and Nash glared at him. He heard sirens. Thank God backup was on its way. Snow was a great clairvoyant but was pants at holding back a crowd. It was growing by the second and a man coming out of the Chinese takeaway was prepared to let his meal go cold to stick around and watch.

'Give us a chip, Steve,' one of the kids said.

Nash shut everybody out and concentrated on protocol.

Look first.

He took out his phone and snapped some initial photos of the van. He found a long piece of wood towards the top of the rubbish and used it to sift through burnt memories – a tattered journal, a weathered photograph, and a doll with no head that once held sentimental value.

He didn't like the position of a coat. It was spread out and unnatural amongst the rest of the crap that had been thrown in. He used the stick to poke it aside and saw a girl's foot.

This didn't belong to any doll.

He ran back to his car and called it in. 'All units. Confirm 10-54. Confirm 10-54.'

Chapter Twenty-One

Nash and Turner stepped into the interview room, and after being held for two nights, Blight's perfume was still detectable on the air, though it was stale and had an acrid underbelly to the fragrance. A perfume that dressed a wrist for three days didn't come cheap, Nash thought. She'd washed in the cell's tiny sink and he recognised the scent of prison-issue soap over the perfume. Blight was a white woman of British heritage but had her hair braided in tight corn rows. It didn't need any brushing but, without being oiled, a fly-away halo of fluffy strands covered her head.

The fluorescent lights buzzed in the silence and cast harsh shadows across the VCT flooring. Keeley Norton, alias Blight, lounged in her chair, her long black hair falling over the backrest as she propped her feet on the interview table.

Her posture radiated confidence and her lips curled into a smirk as her piercing gaze locked onto Nash. She oozed arrogance with a palpable aura of defiance emanating from her and she seemed at ease, as if the interrogation was a trivial inconvenience in her grand scheme.

'I need out of here, Daddio,' she said as Nash and Turner arranged their evidence and settled in plastic chairs opposite Blight and her solicitor.

Nash felt a surge of irritation but he schooled his features into an expression of cool professionalism. Her provocations wouldn't rattle him.

After a subtle nod from Turner, Nash signalled his readiness to take the lead. As the local detective, he knew that maintaining control of the interrogation was paramount, but Turner was the commanding officer during the Diamond Light Operation and Nash had to ask permission to proceed. It stuck in his craw. He settled his features and focussed on professionalism. Petty jealousy over Turner peeing up his tree wasn't important. He aimed to be unreadable. Their cards would be dealt, sequenced, like a magician with a folding petunia.

Blight's smirk widened, a challenge in the curve of her lips. She revelled in the tension and her green eyes were astute as she waited for the opening salvo of the tennis match.

The room shrank around them, the walls closing in as Nash prepared to confront her. Every detail of the scene played to him in real time—the creak of the chair, the buzz of the light and the lingering scent of furniture polish.

He sat erect and squared his shoulders. Despite her outward bravado, he could sense uncertainty in Blight's demeanour.

Small tells gave her away. She steepled her fingers, an indicator of being in control. The gesture suggested power, and having the upper hand, but under Nash's direct stare she couldn't maintain the posture and her fingers crumbled into an interlaced submission. She wrapped her arms around her body. Closed. Not so cock sure. That was all right, for now, he wanted her cautious.

There was a defined chink in her armour hinting at vulnerabilities that she was well versed in hiding.

'Good Morning. I am Detective Chief Inspector Nash, and this is Superintendent Mark Turner of the Greater Manchester Narcotics Team. This interview will be recorded and a copy will be made available to you and your counsel. Please take your feet off my table.'

'Way to go, Daddio. My, aren't we the forceful one. No softly-softly rapport building to make us best buddies before you start? Where's the five minutes of cosy chat about our families and combined hobbies? Cutting the crap and taking the direct approach. Manly. I like it.'

She knew some interviewing techniques, a lot of them did, but as the tension ramped up, and questions were more awkward, they tended to forget. In a show of defiance, she put her left foot on her right knee—the barrier posture. In effect, it said, this is private property, keep out.

'You've been watching too much TV, Ms Norton.' Nash watched her take her time lowering her feet to the floor. She took a piece of chewing gum, that her brief had given her, from her mouth and stuck it to the underside of the table. Nash didn't rise to it but had an incredible urge to tell her to grow up. He bit it back and considered speaking to the solicitor about giving her contraband. She wasn't a suicide risk, but standards were slipping around here. Blight's razor-sharp eyebrow with the unnatural curve rose and Nash saw her pupil trying to focus on his pad to see what he was writing. He turned it over.

'Nice ankle tattoo, by the way. Is there some significance to the trailing rose?' Nash suppressed a grin as she glanced down at her trouser-clad leg. Got you. Tiny hit points now made for a better score later.

'You can't see my ankle.'

'I've seen your admittance photos.'

'Perv.'

Nash stared at her stony-eyed.

'Is there some relevance to my tattoo?'

'Not at the moment. A colleague mentioned it in passing. Just shooting the breeze, but you never know what we'll uncover.'

She glanced down. Her shoulders tensed and then she caught herself and slumped again. Nash counted the body language tells. Rising from his seat, his movements were deliberate as he retrieved two fresh cassette tapes from the nearby shelf. He unwrapped the Cellophane and inserted them into the recorder, his fingers navigating the controls as he set the device to record. They did it the old-fashioned way, but the interview was on secondary equipment and recorded digitally from the control room behind the two-way mirror. As the red light flickered to life, signalling the start of the recording, Nash and Turner introduced themselves for the tape and Nash turned his attention to the suspect.

'Ms Norton,' he began, his voice authoritative, 'For the record, please state your name.'

'You can call me Blight.'

'May I remind you, this is a serious police interview? I need your correct and full name.'

'Keeley Norton, your honour.'

Nash wasn't playing and looked at her solicitor.

'Roland Purvis, LLB Hons,' he said.

Blight snorted. 'Purvis the pervert. I bet you go down a treat at kids' parties.' Nobody responded to her.

'Before we get started, I'd just like to check that you have been well looked after. And with that in mind, that you were given fresh regulation clothing and relevant toiletries.'

'Yeah, but I didn't like the green tutu. However, this seasonal grey slob suit is ready for the Primarny runway. I assume I'll be getting out of this hellhole at some point today?'

'That very much remains to be seen.'

With the recording underway, every nuance of the interrogation was captured. The internal recording, fed into the viewing room, had audio and video monitoring so the behavioural psychologist could read the suspect's body language. Nash didn't need a degree in psychiatry to read this madam. She was sharper than a chainsaw. But she was rattled.

'Let's see if you're going to play ball. What do you know about Crystal Chaos?' He asked.

Blight's eyes narrowed as she watched Nash with renewed interest. He'd come in with a direct approach to throw her.

'What's that? A new goth shop in the precinct?'

Nash pressed on. 'You're connected to a criminal organisation operating within our jurisdiction, and I intend to find out how. How do the consignments come in?'

'You've got nothing on me. Think again, big man.'

Nash opened a folder and put photographs of the dead teenagers in front of her.'

She flinched—but recovered fast. 'These your kids? Cute. Invite me for a BBQ sometime.'

'You aren't that callous, Ms Norton. I think you're playing a game. Who are you really?'

She held her nerve and it didn't surprise him. Turner shifted in his seat. So far, Blight's solicitor hadn't said anything. Turner interrupted. 'Your connection to Jerod Mathis? Talk.'

'Never heard of him.' Blight picked up the photos and handed them back to Nash. He didn't take them, so she put them face down in front of him. He was getting under her skin. It was all part of the game, a psychological battle of wills.

Nash settled in his chair, his gaze locked on Keeley Norton, who lounged in her seat and picked her fingernails. Turner's expression was stony as he watched the exchange, while Blight's solicitor was ready to intervene if they stepped out of line. Nash was an experienced officer and rarely did.

'I've seen a thousand young people like you. You think the world owes you. You're entitled and spoiled. Putting on your hard attitude, all for show. I could cut you down and make you cry in a heartbeat.'

Purvis seemed glad to have a reason to earn his salary. He leaned forward and made a note on his pad. 'Intimidation, inspector. You're threatening my client. Please stick to questions and make them relevant to the charges.'

'Okay, let's cut to the chase. You're here because you've been implicated in several serious crimes, not least assault, and taking a hostage by force with a dangerous weapon. You're also charged with drug trafficking, possession with intent to supply, and association with known criminals. Do you deny these allegations?'

'I wouldn't say deny,' she replied, her voice laced with sarcasm. 'But I admit nothing, and it's your job to produce evidence to support your wild allegations.'

'Is that what you call flooding our streets with dangerous narcotics—a wild allegation? You contributed to the deaths of countless people, including several teenagers.'

Blight shrugged nonchalantly. 'It's a tough river to swim out there. I'm just a nice person, going through life like a glittering rainbow and making people happy. Can't fault me for that, can you?'

Nash's nostrils flared. 'Noah Ross? Do you deny involvement in his death?'

'I think I heard about him. Maybe I saw it on the socials. Poor kid. Tragic, but I can't be held responsible for every lad who experiments with stuff he shouldn't.'

Turner's jaw clenched, his knuckles white. He slammed his fist on the table. His anger had come from nowhere. Sudden. Out of character. 'You're an animal. You'll go down for a long time. You make my skin crawl. You have no regard for human life. No one is above the law. We'll stop at nothing to bring you to justice. I'll see to it that you're put away for life.' His voice was low and dangerous. Nash was surprised. The barrage of short staccato sentences showed that Turner was rattled—or playing a part. They sounded unnatural. Nash didn't like it and was glad when he let Nash take back control. Going off like that would get them nowhere. Turner's flash of temper subsided as fast as it came.

Blight's lips curled into a sardonic smile as she leaned back in her chair unfazed by Turner's threat. 'Human life? Spare me the moral lecture. We both know the only thing that matters in this world is power and money. You're governed by it as much as I am.'

Nash had somewhere to be and wanted to get this over with. 'As you are aware, the officers attending your arrest wore body-cams. We have some irrefutable footage of you smashing a bottle and holding it to a minor's throat. I'd like to see you wriggle out of that one.'

'No comment.'

Blight's sudden laughter was a chilling sound that sent shivers down Nash's spine. 'Bring it all on me, Daddio. You won't make anything stick. I've faced worse than you and come out on top every time. I'm playing to win.'

'You're delusional.'

Blight leaned forward and spread her hands across to Nash as though she wanted him to take them. 'I promise you this, chief inspector. I will be out of this room today and you'll be left catching flies. You can close your mouth now.'

Turner shot Blight a look that could put out the flames of hell. 'Shut your filthy mouth.'

'Chill your soup, man. I'm just playing.' She retrieved her chewing gum from under the table and put it in her mouth. Working it for a few seconds until it was pliable, she blew a bubble and let it burst against her lips.

Nash's frustration boiled. He threw the photos in front of Keeley again but kept his tone neutral. *Always keep your tone flat, Nasher.* Max calmed him. 'Look at them,' He said to Blight. His head was thick with emotion but his voice didn't alter. 'These are the young lives lost because of your poison. Did you directly supply these children, or know who did?'

'No comment.'

'Names? Now?'

'No comment.'

'Look, Keely. You can save yourself. I'll do what I can to help you. We're not interested in you. You're nothing to us. I can get you a lighter sentence by saying you saw the error of your ways and cooperated. But you have to give us something. Tell us the names of the chemists.'

'No comment.'

Going any further would be futile. Once they got into the no-comment loop, you'd had it and had no choice but to call it off and let them stew in the cells. He made a note to have the heating turned down to the minimum temperature allowed by law. But he wasn't giving up without another try. 'Look at the children, Keeley. I know there's a human being in there. You don't want the world to see you as a monster do you?' He used the Ried Method. *Appeal to her better nature*, he heard Max say in his head. *Give her the chance to put her side forward and make her admit to a lesser charge. Nice man. Number fifty in the interviewer's handbook.* He was hearing Max's voice more. Too often.

Blight glanced at the photos before meeting Nash's gaze. 'Don't look at me like that. I didn't force them to take anything. People make their own choices. Nothing to do with me.'

'Who's your supplier, Keeley? Who's pulling the strings?'

'Nobody pulls my strings.'

Nash exchanged a glance with Turner. 'You're protecting criminals who don't give a damn about you.'

Turner cleared his throat. 'We have evidence linking you to the distribution of Chaos. You can either cooperate and help us bring down the house of cards, or you can face the consequences alone.'

Nash stabbed one of the photos with his forefinger. 'Help us stop this,' he said.

But she was silent. It was clear she wasn't budging. They were fighting a losing battle against a woman determined to protect her interests at any cost.

Nash pressed Keeley for information for another forty minutes, but her response didn't waver. 'No comment.' Her bored monotone grated, and despite his efforts to rattle her, Blight was cool and mocking.

He glanced at the clock, realising that time was running out. They had her on the assault and taking a hostage. On a good day, she'd go down for three years, maybe five. But with a good defence team, she'd walk. They could only keep her for another day without proof of distribution. The photographic evidence of her at the leisure centre was circumstantial. She didn't engage with the young dealers. Blight rode in on her motorbike and rode out again. That wasn't against the law. A good defence would deny it was even her. And linking the numberplate back to her didn't mean she was the rider, even though a blind man could identify her distinctive appearance in a line-up. He exchanged a frustrated glance with Turner, acknowledging the futility of their efforts.

Blight's solicitor intervened, reminding Nash and Turner about their legal obligations and advising his client to exercise her right to remain silent.

Nash mentally regrouped as he approached the interrogation from a different angle. Dragging information from someone as obstinate as Blight required a strategic approach. 'Don't you want to help the children?'

'No comment.'

Nash had no time for this young woman. 'Okay, Keeley, we're getting nowhere. Let's get you back to your cell. You'll be remanded in custody until further notice and I'm sure we'll speak to you again later. Perhaps you'll be more forthcoming after time to reflect. Interview terminated at ten thirty-two a.m.' He shut off the recording, extracted the cassettes and put them in their protective cases. Taking a roll of red tape from his drawer he sealed the boxes and gave one to her solicitor. He collected the photographs and put the tape and evidence on the files.

He had better places to be and a scared child to talk to.

Chapter Twenty-Two

As Nash approached the front door of Nikki Moor's house, déjà vu attacked him. He'd been here before, different house, different kid, but he was here after another child had fallen victim to the terrible scourge of Crystal Chaos. He remembered having to tell Noah Ross's mother about his death. The house, in a suburban Barrow street, housed a typical family.

The building was modest, with a whitewashed façade, a well-tended garden and a teal green door. There were two window boxes and two hanging baskets. The symmetry gave the house the appearance of a face wearing makeup, but Nash didn't feel like smiling. He hesitated before knocking. The sound reverberated through the stillness of the neighbourhood, echoing the sense of solemnity. A curious child on a new mountain bike stopped a few doors down to watch him.

After a moment, the door creaked open, revealing a woman with tired eyes and a weary expression. Sandra Moor's face was etched with lines of anxiety. Nash saw the weight pressing on her shoulders.

'They said you'd be coming. Please come in,' Sandra said, her voice strained but polite as she stepped aside to let Nash pass.

As he crossed the threshold, he was greeted by the warmth of the family home. The living room was cosy and filled with modern furniture. Like Noah's house, family photographs hung on the walls. A sense of lived-in comfort softened the space, giving him a glimpse into the lives of the Moors. He read the room. Middle income. They had a holiday in June and saved for the rest of the year to afford it. Dad had the only armchair, and though he was at work, his presence always surrounded it.

A black cockapoo ran in from the kitchen with his teddy in his mouth to show Nash. The detective made a fuss of the friendly dog, who just about wagged himself double in excitement.

Sandra motioned for Nash to sit on the fabric sofa, her movements deliberate as if wary of the outcome of his visit. He sank into the cushions and had to sit on the edge to avoid further sinkage. The sofa was built for comfort over posture.

Sandra Moor waited, the silence punctuated by the hum of passing cars and the tick of the wall clock. 'Get down, Bailey,' she said to the dog, and the girl on the sofa laughed.

Nikki sat quietly. Her attention was absorbed by the glowing screen of her tablet. She appeared detached as if retreating into the digital world of Roblox offered comfort from harsh realities. She was here from the brink of death. A lucky girl. But a terrified child scared of what they'd do to her next. Nash ached at the sight of her fragility. Her brother ran in holding a football and was sent to his room.

Nash offered a sympathetic smile. Sandra returned the gesture with a nod. It was clear that she'd been through hell. Nobody expects their child to be hooked up to machines in a hospital after a drug overdose. Nash wanted to tell her that Nikki was one of the lucky ones—but he didn't. Uncovering the truth behind

Nikki's ordeal needed patience. Nash showed her his recording device and let her be the one to turn it on when she was ready. She put her tablet to one side but found it difficult to make eye contact with Nash. She looked terrified.

'You aren't in trouble, Nikki. We're just glad you're safe. But we do need to know what happened. There's no rush. You can take your time and tell me in your own words.'

Nash broached the subject gently, probing for answers without overwhelming her fragile state. Nikki barely looked up and answered in a monotone. In another child, it might be seen as rude belligerence, but he recognised that Nikki was traumatised and struggling to hold it together. The conversation was had with halting pauses and hesitant confessions, each revelation peeling back the layers of what she'd been through.

Nikki had hardly started to speak when Sandra interrupted and recounted the events leading up to her daughter's disappearance. She struggled with her emotions as she relived the harrowing uncertainty and fear when she got the call to say Nikki had been found.

Nash probed Nikki to speak about her ordeal, but the story was told in jagged fragments. She spoke of her tormentors, faceless shadows that she refused to name lurking in the background. She admitted that it was older kids at her school. They'd been bullying her and forcing her to do things for months.

'I knew something was wrong. But whenever we asked her, she just clammed up.' As Sandra told Nash about the bullying, he felt the familiar surge of anger.

Nikki's survival was a testament to the strength of the human spirit, it had been touch and go regarding whether she'd pull through.

'I need you to be really brave, sweetheart. We can't help you if we don't have all the facts. You need to tell me everything.'

The fourteen-year-old was pale and recovering from her ordeal. Despite her youth, the weariness around her eyes spoke of experiences beyond her understanding. Sandra sat next to Nash, desperate for answers. She said there was a lot that Nikki hadn't been able to talk about.

He probed Nikki for details about her overdose, allowing her the space to share at her own pace.

Her fingers fidgeted in her lap and kept touching the edge of her tablet as though they had a mind of their own. She struggled to find the words to articulate the horrors she'd endured.

'It's okay, Nikki. Start at the beginning.'

'It was when I moved up to the third year.'

'Go on, love,' Sandra said.

'Some of the fifth years—it's a gang—they make you do stuff.'

'What kind of stuff, Nikki?' Nash asked.

'They'll get me if I tell. They'll kill me next time.'

'No, they won't. I'm here to keep you safe but you've got to be brave so that I can help you.'

Nikki's voice trembled as she recounted the horrifying ordeal of being forced to take drugs by her tormentors. She described how they had threatened to expose her as a drug user to her parents and the police if she didn't comply with their demands. When he came to Nash through Conrad Snow, Noah Ross said his murderers had used the same threat. Thank God she'd only been forced to swallow the drugs twice and had never been injected with Chaos. That's how they coerced her into delivering personal-use packets to customers around town. What could be less suspicious than a child in a school uniform walking home?

Her fear was palpable as she relived feeling utterly trapped with no way out.

Two days ago, overwhelmed after taking the drugs and desperate to escape her tormentors, Nikki had managed to get away from them. She'd heard their feet pounding the pavements behind her and their shouts of 'Get her. Don't let her escape.' She'd run through the darkness as she looked for somewhere to hide and saw the van. A man was loading it with bags of rubbish from the burnt-out house, and when he went back in for more, Nikki had broken a window to open the door. She crawled inside out of options and needed sanctuary from her captors and what was happening to her body.

'Why didn't you tell the man when he came back out?' Nash asked.

'I didn't dare. And he threw more rubbish on top of me and a piece of wood hit me on the head. But I had to be quiet. Then he locked me in and went away. I heard him calling the police about the broken window and I thought I was going to get into trouble. The drugs made me feel strange. I was frightened, and then I was sick all over myself. I was scared that he was going to drive away with me and that I'd be arrested. And there were all these swirling colours around me, and the rubbish was moving with hands that could grab me.' She started to cry. 'I don't remember anything after that.'

Nash was horrified. As she'd huddled in the shadows of the van with the stinking rubbish on top of her, the drugs had dragged her into the nightmare abyss of unconsciousness. As Nikki spoke, her voice quivered with emotion, the memory of it too fresh in her mind. It was a scene from a horror movie. The age-old twisted tale of innocence lost and evil triumphant.

During Nikki's hesitant retelling, Sandra's protective instincts shielded her daughter, but Nash needed her to let Nikki talk.

The revelation of bullying at school struck a chord, and the connection to Serena's situation was undeniable. The girls attended the same school as Serena, a splinter group was attacking weaker pupils, and the worst of the trouble happened after the school day ended. He made a note to follow up on the lead and the possibilities for intervention and support.

'You said they made you do stuff you didn't want to do?' Nash went in very gently. 'What things?'

'Bad things.' She started to cry and her mother jumped out of her seat to put her arm around her daughter. 'They made me deliver the drugs.'

Nash was careful not to let any expression of shock show and he kept his body language relaxed. 'Who to, sweetheart?'

'People. Houses in town.'

'Can you remember which houses?'

Nikki nodded. 'Some of them. There were a lot.'

The thought of innocent children being coerced into such dangerous situations made him feel ill. Is this what was happening to Serena?

'Nikki, I promise, we'll do everything in our power to stop what's happened to you. You've shown incredible courage coming forward, and I won't let you down.'

It took time to gain her trust, but she reluctantly gave him the names of the children governing the school. 'Will I have to go to court and tell on them?'

'Perhaps, but if you do, you won't have to face them. You'll give your evidence in a nice room with a lady dressed in normal clothes and it will just be you talking into a camera.'

Nikki nodded, but her expression was troubled. 'What if they come after me?' she whispered.

'You won't face this alone. We'll be with you every step of the way.'

Sandra's grip tightened on Nikki's hand. 'You keep her safe.'

'We'll work with the school to make sure Nikki is supported.'

Nash rose from his seat and said goodbye. Nikki had already picked up her tablet and her eyes were fixed on the screen. Still sitting on the sofa, she had left this broken town.

Chapter Twenty-Three

Nash was furious. He was white hot mad and could feel his temper rising as what he would say turned on a hamster wheel in his mind. His footsteps were hollow in the corridor of the station. He passed a unit with several piles of informative leaflets and swept his arm across them. He felt an instant of satisfaction as they fluttered to the floor, but then he thought about Hayley, the station cleaner, having to pick them up and how irresponsible and uncontrolled his behaviour was. Nash thought about the example he was setting the lower ranks and lost vital minutes stooping to pick the leaflets up.

He clenched and unclenched his fists, the tension in his muscles mirroring the turmoil in his mind.

Turner had let Keeley Norton go. He couldn't believe it. They had her, and he just opened her cage to let her fly away. Blight's release gnawed at him like a beaver making a dam of his ankle. She was the answer to unlocking this mess, but they'd given her a golden key to her cell. It was another reminder of the uphill battle they faced in the fight against a drug epidemic.

As he got close to Turner's office, the muffled sound of voices seeped through the closed door, amplifying Nash's sense of urgency. He paused, his hand hovering over the doorknob, steeling himself for a confrontation.

The way he pushed the door and strode into the room without knocking showed his superior officer that he meant business. His gaze fixed on Turner, who sat behind his desk with a weariness that matched Nash's.

'Would you like to explain to me why you've let Keeley Norton go?'

Turner looked at the receiver in his hand and addressed the person on the other end. 'Forgive me. I'm afraid something's come up and I'll have to call you back.'

Turner looked up, and while he was nowhere near as angry as Nash, the interruption rankled. 'I could have been on the phone to anybody. I'll thank you not to burst into my office without knocking. Try that trick again, and I'll have you on a charge for screaming station business around at the top of your voice.'

'This is my station, Turner, and my operation. I didn't sign off on her release.'

'No. Lewis did. And I think, if you check the letters on the brass plate attached to her door you'll find that this is her station, not yours.'

This was ridiculous, they were engaged in a pissing competition that any five-year-old would be proud of. 'Keeley Norton?' Nash said.

'We didn't have enough to hold her.'

Nash's jaw clenched, his fists tightening at his sides as he struggled to contain his anger. 'That's a load of bollocks, and you know it.' Nash never swore at senior officers. He calmed himself. 'She attacked a civilian with a broken bottle and held them hostage. That alone is enough to put her away for at least five years.'

Turner leaned back in his chair, pinching the bridge of his nose. 'We're not interested in putting her away, Nash,' he said. His voice was calm despite the mounting tension in the room. 'She's small fry. We need to find out what she knows about the drug saturation in this town. You know the score better than anybody. I shouldn't have to explain it to you.'

Nash understood the need to gather information, but they'd let a dangerous criminal slip through their fingers. 'And what if she disappears before leading us to anybody? She's not from around here. She turned up out of the blue one day and could just as easily press the ignition button on that motorbike of hers and leave the same way.'

'We're keeping an eye on her. Round-the-clock surveillance. We won't let her out of our sight until we know what she's involved in.'

'And you don't think she'll make the undercover team in three seconds flat? You're delusional.' With a frustrated growl, Nash turned on his heel and stormed out of Turner's office slamming the door. His mind was awash with questions and fears. They couldn't afford to let Blight slip through the cracks when so much was at stake.

They were playing a dangerous game and walking a fine line between justice and unacceptable compromise. Keeley Norton should never have been released.

As he reached his office, Nash slumped into his chair reeling from the confrontation with Turner. He couldn't let anger cloud his judgment, but the injustice of it bit him.

Why had Turner let her go? It didn't make sense. He pushed his next thought away and grabbed a pile of paperwork to take his mind off it. The words got up from the page and danced in front of his eyes. He couldn't concentrate and didn't see any of them until the ballet of consonants morphed into that niggling question.

Was Turner in the cartel's pocket?

His thoughts went back to the streets of town, where the fight against drugs raged on. So much was at stake.

Nash reached for his phone, his fingers flying over the keys as he dialled a familiar number. He needed to regroup and come up with a new plan. And for that, he needed a special kind of help—Conrad Snow.

However, the call hadn't connected when there was a tap on his door.

'Come in.'

Too late, Bronwyn Lewis was already halfway across his office. She had The Look on her face and Nash knew he was in trouble. He tensed at her arrival, bracing himself for the impending lecture.

'We could hear you right down to the bullpen. What's got into you, and which part of "Get along with GMNT" didn't you understand?' She didn't give him time to answer. 'Any problems in this station, you come to me. Me, do you hear? You don't go off being a half-cocked maverick. I'm shocked. You're acting like a green rookie having a dick-waving contest with your seniors.'

Nash bristled as he met her gaze. 'Have you finished?'

'No. It's not good enough, Nash. You know we're trying to make a good impression on GMNT.'

'And you're good with that? Even if it's at the expense of solid policework? Shame on you, Bronwyn. Turner let Keeley Norton go.' Nash's tone was laden with accusation. 'After everything she did, he let her walk. How is that right?'

'You know why we decided to release her.'

'He claims there wasn't enough evidence to hold her. And we both know that isn't true. The bottle attack alone was enough to put her away for years.'

'Turner presented the evidence to me,' she admitted. 'And I agreed that we needed to focus on the bigger picture.'

'You went along with it? You willingly signed off on letting a violent drug dealer go?'

'It's done, Nash.'

'But did you believe in what you did, or were you just following orders?' His voice was tinged with scepticism and he stood up to pace the room.

'I don't know,' she admitted, her voice barely above a whisper. 'But Turner presides over all of us, and as much as I may disagree with his decisions, I have to abide by them.'

'No, Bronwyn. You still have the final sign-off with any decisions regarding this station. You could have said no. Something isn't right. It's like we're just cogs in a machine. When did we start taking orders without questioning what was moral?' He sat down.

Bronwyn grasped his hand across the desk. 'I know it's tough, but we have to trust that Turner knows what he's doing. They're a specialised branch with experience in high-level narcotics. Hang in there, Nash. We'll get through this, together.'

Nash nodded, 'Sure, but this feels like walking a tightrope over a pit of alligators.'

Chapter Twenty-Four

While he was talking to Bronwyn, Nash's mobile buzzed in his pocket, interrupting their tense exchange. He shot an apologetic glance at his boss. 'Sorry, I need to take this. It's Kel and he doesn't call me at work unless it's urgent.' Nash stood up to step out of the room, but Bronwyn motioned him back into his seat and pointed to the door. She smiled at him as she left.

'Kelvin? What's going on?' Nash's voice was tight with concern as he answered the phone.

'It's Zola,' Kelvin's voice crackled through the line. 'There's been more trouble and this time, it's a police matter.'

'What happened?'

'Serena's been threatened and Imani's car has been vandalised.'

'I'll be right there.'

'Si, I know you can't get involved in an official capacity. Zola's ringing the station to report it through the normal channels now. I just wanted to hear your voice because this is getting out of hand.'

Nash gritted his teeth, knowing that Kelvin was right. As much as he wanted to jump into action, he couldn't risk compromising his career or the investigation. 'Tell Zola I'm bringing Brown. I'll bum a ride with her as your partner, and I'll keep out of the investigation. We can still handle this together.'

Nash ended the call and hurried back into the office to grab his jacket. Turner shot him a questioning look as he rushed past, but Nash didn't explain as he left the station.

'Brown, you're with me. I'll fill you in on the way.'

'Boss,' Brown said. When Nash issued an order like that, you didn't waste time asking questions. She saved the file she was working on, logged out of her terminal and didn't even wait for the blue circle of doom to finish doing its stuff and show the black shut-down screen.

As they drove to Zola's house, Nash explained everything regarding Serena and Honey.

'What do you think happened? Did Kelvin say?' she asked. Brown was driving and cursed as the lights turned red ahead. She went through the gearbox, came to a stop, wound the window down and reached for her vape.

'Must you?' Nash said as the car filled with a blackcurrant-scented mist. Brown grinned an apology and put it in the driving console.

'I don't know all the details yet. Imani's car has been damaged. And Serena's had some kind of attack from the bullies.

'Poor Serena, I can't help feeling pleased about Imani though. She needs taking down a peg or two.'

'If the devil himself damaged her car, I doubt it would stop her coming out swinging,' Nash said.

As they pulled up, Nash took in the scene using his policeman's eye, rather than wearing his boyfriend hat. He walked up the drive and his heart sank at the sight of the hidden shards of glass sticking out of the gravel, and the deflated tyres. It was a deliberate act of sabotage, a cruel reminder of the lengths the bullies were willing to take to intimidate and harm Kelvin's family.

He looked at the bonnet of Imani's car. Presumably, the gang had mistaken it for Zola's, though her Peugeot was more modest than Imani's sleek Mercedes-Benz AMG Premium. The words *Black Bitch* were scratched deep into the elite finish. Nash winced.

They were invited in and after passing a few preliminary words with Brown, the girls were sent upstairs to play. Serena had been hit by a stone and the bruise was livid on her cheek. It hadn't required hospital attention, but Brown said she'd need to take photographs of it to be put forward as evidence. Kelvin met Nash at the living room door and kissed him. They'd heard Imani ranting as they waited for the door to be answered. For once, Nash wasn't the subject of her verbal paintballing, but she still managed to curl her lip in disgust when she saw him. Nash and Kelvin sat out of the way in the window seat while Zola and Imani were interviewed by Brown. They were still in the room but kept out of the way to let her do her job.

'I told you not to move to Barrow,' Imani was off with one of her favourite tirades. 'It's your fault, Dad. You started this by coming to this drug-riddled town. You live in that monstrous house, but eat toast-based meals on trays in front of the TV. Doesn't he have a dining table? And I don't know what you expect me to do while my car's being fixed.'

Nash tried to tell her that she'd be provided with a courtesy car by the insurance company, but she cut him off and wouldn't entertain him. 'Are you going to catch them?' She asked, speaking to him directly for the first time.

'We'll do everything we can,' he said, but she jumped down his throat again before he could say anymore.

'Not we. You. What are you personally going to do to catch these thugs? You're some big honcho in Barrow, aren't you? This would never have happened if you'd stayed in Kendal, Dad.'

Brown had heard enough. 'Actually, one of the kingpins of the drug problem in the area, runs out of Kendal. The supply hits them before it filters down to us in Barrow. Do you think there's no problem there, that Kendal is better than Barrow? They had twice as many drug and hate crimes as Barrow last year.'

'Well, I wouldn't want to live here. There's far too much tacky stone cladding and too many potholes for my liking,' Imani had to have the last word.

Nash's frustration simmered beneath the surface as he listened to Zola recount her day leading up to the attack. She'd had another meeting with the school that morning, and the headteacher said that three of the girls bullying Serena were to be suspended. The vandalism to the car happened from the fallout of the suspension. And the girls never made it home without being attacked by the same group. Serena had come home after being struck in the face with a stone. The bullies had bayed like wolves at the direct hit and it added fuel to their fire. They had stepped up their harassment to the next level.

Brown's expression was grim. 'I'll need statements from everyone involved. And we'll need to document the damage to the car.'

Nash watched as Brown gathered evidence and interviewed witnesses—Kelvin's family. It was outrageous. As he watched her documenting the scene, he vowed to make sure justice was served.

As they drove away from Zola's house, Serena's subdued demeanour during her part of the interview raised questions. Nash glanced at Brown with concern. 'Do you think she's hiding something?' He asked moving her sweet wrappers in the passenger's footwell with his shoe.

'It's hard to say. She's been through a lot, but there was something very guarded about her reaction.'

'That's what I thought,' Nash said. 'It doesn't sit right with me.'

'There's more to this than meets the eye, and we owe it to those little girls to get to the bottom of it. That Imani's got tickets on herself, though, hasn't she? I wouldn't blame them if they went after her.' Brown swerved into the path of an oncoming vehicle and then lurched back into her side of the road making Nash reach for the handle above the passenger side window.

'Brown, watch your mouth. Nobody deserved to be racially abused.'

Brown grinned. 'Sorry, boss. She's right about the potholes, though.'

Chapter Twenty-Five

Nash stood at the front of the room. He collected his thoughts and straightened up from the papers he was shuffling on the briefing room table.

'People. There's a lot of not happening happening today. We need to step it up. I want every one of you on top of your game. There's too much slacking and lip-wobbling, not enough doing.'

He was shattered after another long day of interviews and interrogations the day before, but they'd progressed, and Nash rubbed the back of his neck before sharing their findings.

His voice commanded attention as he spoke to the room. 'We've made some significant headway, thanks to your hard work. Now we strike hot and hit the next tier. Here's what we've uncovered so far.' He gestured to the whiteboard behind him, where three key points were outlined in bold.

'First, during the interviews, we've learned that the drug operation we're dealing with has deep roots. The lower tier threw out some names we weren't expecting to hear. We already have eyes on the higher rankers in question, but as well as having big mouths, little dealers have big ears. Small-tier nobody in Barrow shouldn't have heard about a couple of the politicians and government members in Diamond Light's pocket. They should be warning their transporters to keep their mouths shut. The street-shufflers may be nothing, but they are cunning buggers and were willing to shout "Grandma" for an easier time in court. There's a large network at play, with connections that reach higher than you can imagine.'

A murmur of surprise rippled through the room, and Nash watched the gears turning as they processed the implications.

'Secondly,' he continued, 'we've received multiple reports of coercion and intimidation tactics being used to force individuals into compliance. This includes threats of violence, bullying, blackmail, and physical force. In extreme cases, children as young as ten are having drugs forced on them to make the frightened child complicit. We're dealing with a dangerous and ruthless organisation.'

The tension in the room increased as Nash delivered his brief. It was nothing they didn't already know, given the recent body count and people affected, but still chilling to hear in cold terms.

'We've uncovered evidence linking the drug operation to incidents of violence and intimidation in our community. This isn't just about drugs anymore; it's about protecting the safety and well-being of our town –and especially our children. 'He thought about Serena and Honey and hoped to God they weren't mixed up in this. Nikki Moor, same school, same age, same bullies. She'd been forced into selling drugs around town, why would he think that Serena and Honey were treated differently? Given Serena's furtive manner when they spoke to her yesterday, Nash had suspicions and needed to talk to Kelvin about it before worrying Zola and Greg.

As he finished speaking, he scanned the room, taking in his team's reactions. He could tell which of them were ready to press forward with renewed vigour, and the ones that were daunted by the magnitude of the task. Aptitude didn't always come down to rank. Sometimes it was about courage. He made a mental note of three officers who needed individual one-on-one time to encourage their potential.

Nash was drawn to the back of the room, where Turner sat beside Bronwyn Lewis. Their heads were bent together in conversation and judging by the way Bronwyn jerked upright and looked shocked, Turner had just told her something that Nash wasn't privy to. He didn't like that and couldn't shake the unease settling in his stomach as he watched them. Something was off about their closeness.

Nash kept an eye on Turner. He didn't trust him. There was something about his behaviour that didn't sit right. If he stepped out of line, Nash might not have a gun on issue like him but he'd be right behind Turner with his nightstick at the ready.

He was pulled from his thoughts as the door banged open. It slammed against the wall hard enough for the handle to indent the plaster behind it. Heads snapped up, startled, as a figure in sleek black leggings, a bike helmet, and sturdy boots strode into the room. Nash noticed the gun belt beneath her jacket and hated that he wasn't permitted to carry a firearm unless they were directly involved in a Special Op.

'Get down. She's armed,' he screamed.

All eyes followed the biker's progress down the centre aisle. She used it as her runway and swaggered like a bad-bitch sassy model.

Bowes let out a 'Woah,' before dropping into a brace position in his seat, but Nash couldn't determine if it came from a place of admiration or fear.

With a fluid motion, Blight removed her helmet, revealing a Valkyrie's mane. Each braid held an assorted number of wooden beads in bright colours. They shone with an oiled intensity that matched the fire in her gaze as she surveyed the room with a cool, unwavering stare.

'Hello, everybody. You can sit up. You look like bloody idiots,' she announced, her voice cutting through the silence with a sharpened edge.

The room pulsed with energy and seasoned police officers were silenced by the power of her presence. This wasn't an ordinary newcomer to the party, but someone who commanded attention wherever she went.

Nash's eyes narrowed as she held the room in a stupor. Renshaw was the first to react. 'Get on the floor with your arms behind your back.' His voice turned into a shout far louder than necessary in a room with excellent acoustics. 'Get down. Now.'

Blight was dressed in black leather and held her blue striped bike helmet under her arm. She put it on the table and her sturdy boots clicked against the floor. She owned the space like a force of nature. All eyes fixed on her as an unexpected disruptor during their morning brief.

'Put down your weapon,' Nash screamed.

Blight shrugged. She reached across her body and took a browning pistol from the shoulder holster. Her jacket was open for effect. She'd wanted them to see it as she made her entrance.

'Slowly. No sudden movements. Put it on the table where I can see it.'

She lifted it in front of her face with the Muzzle pointing at the ceiling. Her movements were rapid and accomplished as she showcased making the gun safe before laying it down on the table and taking two steps away from it. Nash was left in no doubt that her weapon was as familiar to her as her right arm and that she'd be just as good when it came to shooting it. Nash motioned to Renshaw who jumped up and took it.

Blight smiled at the sergeant, displaying her perfect teeth. 'You can get a hard-on from holding it, sweet boy, but I want it back when this pantomime's done.'

Chapter Twenty-Six

'What's the meaning of this?'

Nash's voice sliced through the room, tinged with a sharp edge of disbelief. His stare bore into the intruder's. His jaw clenched in frustration.

He seethed with indignation. It was obvious why she'd been set free. And as hard as it was to get his head around it, she was rubbing their noses in the smell of her crap. His pulse quickened with a surge of protection for his unit. His irritation felt like a fire inside him. This was his turf, and badge or no badge, he wouldn't stand for anyone trampling it. She must feel that her position made her above the law. For the first time, Nash wondered if he was dealing with a psychopath. None of the indicators had been present in her arrest interview, but they could mask body language and suppress their tells. She couldn't be one of them.

Turner stretched his legs out, crossing his ankles with an air of casual confidence. His arms folded across his chest as he leaned back in his chair, a smug smirk playing at the corners of his lips. 'Showtime, this should be good,' he said. Nash picked up on a note of humour, and, was that anticipation in his tone?

In thirty seconds, Nash had lost control of his room and the world had gone mad. He exchanged a furious glare with Lewis, looking for answers. His expression showed his betrayal. 'Did you know about this?' he asked.

Bronwyn spread her hands in a placating gesture and her brow furrowed with concern. 'Nash, I've only just been told,' she replied.

Blight seized the marker pen he held from his grasp, her action dripping with audacity.

'Bold move,' Bowes muttered, with awe in his voice. He didn't dare say it very loud, and he covered his mouth, leaning towards Patel, but Nash heard him. Now that the risk of being shot had passed, Bowes was a kid staring at the villain and waiting to shout, 'She's behind you.'

Nash looked at his empty hand and felt like a fool. Norton was wiping the floor with him. He watched her stride to the wall, pick up the eraser and wipe the board clean of his presentation. Fury knotted his chest. This couldn't be real.

She scrawled some words in a large, cursive hand on the board. *Superintendent Keeley Norton/AKA Blight. You will address me as your superior officer and use the term ma'am in the incident room.*

Nash's incredulity deepened. He was speechless as his mind processed the implications. Superintendent Norton. Not even a low rank—a bloody Superintendent. This was ridiculous, a superintendent should be involved in planning and overseeing special operations. It was rare for them to work directly in undercover activities because of their responsibilities and the risks involved. But here she was, breaking the rules and flaunting her feathers. He hadn't read many public records of police superintendents in the UK going undercover in special operations, but he knew it had happened. She had bigger balls than most men of her rank.

He'd seen her smash a bottle on the rim of a table and hold it against an innocent girl's throat. It didn't make sense. But she was one of them.

She faced him and her gaze locked onto his with confidence. Nash felt indignation rise inside him like bile. Who did she think she was, waltzing in and commandeering his briefing? The nerve of asserting her authority in such a brazen manner was beyond belief.

'Is this a joke?' Nash's voice came out sharper than intended. He couldn't fathom how the criminal could expect him to accept her assertion. 'Ma'am,' Norton said. 'What? Lawson, get her out of here.'

'Let's start as we mean to go on shall we, Inspector Nash? What you mean to say is, "Is this a joke, Ma'am." I realise we're in a town where people still count in hay bales and chickens, but I don't want to repeat myself.' On the word, ma'am, her tone rose. Nash's gaze hardened as he met her challenge. If she thought she could intimidate him with her arrogant attitude, she was wrong. He wouldn't let her undermine his authority. He looked at Lewis who stood up to speak.

'Team, please welcome our newest member, Superintendent Keeley Norton, who will be joining us for the time being as part of our GMNT contingent. Due to the sensitive nature of the case and the utmost need for discretion, I've only been updated on this matter in the last five minutes, myself. But I'm sure we'll all do our best to welcome her and make her feel at home.' Her gaze was directed at Nash.

He was flabbergasted and had to gain control of the room. They were reacting to the new chain of command and the noise was a babble, shattering the order of his meeting. Blight slotted into her position immediately after Turner and Bold, it seemed. She was above anybody in the Barrow Station—including him. His mind tried to make sense of the absurdity. Blight had barged into the briefing room with an authority that defied logic. And she was asserting her superiority over everyone present except Turner.

The room buzzed with murmurs, the officers exchanging glances as they processed the new twist in the case. Blight's audacious claim had thrown them for a loop, and Nash felt the anticipation mounting. Trees were shaken to see what fell out.

To regain control, Nash searched for the words to assert his authority without escalating the confrontation. But before he could formulate a coherent response, Blight turned on him. Her expression challenged him to challenge her.

He should have thought more about his next statement but the words were out of his mouth before he could stop them. 'My God, you look about twelve,' he said. Once the words slipped past his lips there was no sucking them back in and he realised how petulant he sounded. It was too late to soften it with a welcoming smile. He winced, cursing himself for his lack of tact, but the damage was done. Blight's eyebrow shot up in surprise, her lips twisting with amusement.

'And you look like my dad. Pretty hot for a silver fox, though.'

The room exploded in laughter and Nash was incensed to see that even Mark Turner was laughing.

Norton was still talking, damn her. She should take her points while she was ahead, rather than making a sworn enemy of him.

'The difference between us, though, is that I'm not a misogynistic old bastard,' she said.

'How dare you talk to a colleague like that. If that's what you are.'

Bronwyn rose from her seat, but Turner put a hand on her arm. Nash realised that it was like opening a box and introducing a new cockerel into the house. A working score had to be settled. And at this moment Nash's money was on Blight.

He braced himself for her next onslaught, but to his surprise, it didn't come. The instant change in her demeanour was remarkable as her body language relaxed and softened. She smiled at Nash and it transformed her face. 'I'm sorry, DCI Nash. The ongoing charade is necessary, but it's good to be myself for a minute to say hi. She held out her hand for him to shake and Nash stared at it as though it might explode in his face. Her expression was warm and open and Nash was confused at the sudden change. All soft and cuddly, she was like a different person. Nash didn't understand the rules of the game, or what new line of trickery this was. She was talking to him but addressing the room at the same time.

'Forgive the theatrics, guys, but it was necessary. I am Superintendent Keeley Norton, but most of the time you will know me as Blight. This is the only time you will see me like this, so, before I pick up my coat of thorns, let me say hello as Keeley, and I'm looking forward to having a drink with you all at the after-case party when the job is finished.'

The room buzzed with conversation and she gave them a minute before holding up her hand. 'But it won't be before then. If I ever meet any of you outside it will be from opposing sides of the fence. Don't give me a wave in the supermarket because you'll get a mouth full of abuse. I'll probably have been shoplifting.'

This time the laughter was awkward, not sure if she was serious.

'I'll do whatever is necessary to be a member of that gang. My loyalties will appear to be with them and there may be times when you doubt me. I'm good at what I do and intend to rise to the top and infiltrate Mathis' fortress. However, to stand out, I have to fit in. My role means never coming out of character. Not for a second. I've just done it for the first time in over six months and it will not happen again for the duration of this case. And that's it from Keeley, I'll sign out and hand the baton over to Blight.'

The room broke into a round of applause which was customary when welcoming a new member to the team but this time it was more enthusiastic, especially among the younger male members. It was led by Bowes who accompanied it with whooping like a coyote in the rutting season.

Nash was about to tell them to pack it in, but Blight beat him to it. 'All right you pathetic collection of losers, stop clapping like fools or I'll throw you a fish.'

Even Nash couldn't suppress a grin at her response. He would have to get used to the idea, albeit with reluctance, but she was certainly going to shake things up around here. Brown had a face like thunder and he saw trouble coming from that direction head-on.

Whatever Blight's strategy was, he'd play along. Her brazen display of authority had thrown the meeting into disarray. With a curt nod, Nash said. 'We all agree, that was quite an entrance.

But Westend performances aside, I am still taking this meeting, so if you'd like to take a seat, Officer Norton, I'll continue.'

Blight grinned, winked at him and went to sit down. 'Officer Norton,' Nash said and he inclined his head to indicate the helmet sitting on his pile of paperwork. Blight went back to the table and picked it up. 'You got it going on, Daddio.'

The room was in chaos, and any concentration they'd had was gone. Nash had little choice but to bring the meeting to a premature close.

As he passed Lewis and Turner, he halted, his expression thunderous. 'I need to speak to both of you. I will see you in DCS Lewis' office in five minutes.'

'Make it ten, Nash. Get a coffee and calm down,' Bronwyn said. It seemed they all had some hierarchy to reestablish.

Chapter Twenty-Seven

Nash stormed through the station to Lewis' office. He rapped on the door before barging in without waiting for a response.

Lewis looked up from her conversation with Turner, startled by his abrupt entrance. Her brow furrowed as she recognised the anger simmering in his eyes.

'I told you to calm down before coming in here, DCI Nash.'

Unlike the sterile atmosphere of the station corridors, Lewis's office was warm, with a thick rug underfoot and tall potted plants bringing the corners into the room. It did nothing to align Nash's shattered Zen.

Turner sat in one of the three chairs opposite Lewis' desk. His posture was relaxed but his eyes alert as he watched Nash's entrance. Nash sensed the squall of underlying tension between them.

Lewis looked at Nash and Turner as she tried to defuse the situation before it became heated. 'It wasn't my decision, Nash. However, while I don't appreciate being kept in the dark, I endorse Superintendent Norton being brought in. I think she's the right person for the job. Superintendent Turner has been telling me about the groundwork she's put in to gain people's trust. Norton had to make many personal sacrifices that has affected her health. This operation has been a long time in preparation and we have to consider the bigger picture.'

Nash's frustration boiled over, his voice rising with each word. 'Bigger picture? What bigger picture could justify letting her go after what she did?'

Turner leaned forward, his voice calm as he attempted to placate Nash. 'It was imperative that the suspects accepted her as one of them. The girl she took and threatened was one of the kids who wanted out. She was primed beforehand, and while she didn't know what to expect, she had our word that she wouldn't be hurt,' he explained, his tone measured.

'She was in on it? But she looked terrified.'

'She was. She didn't know what Norton was going to do. But she came to us to get her out and was helping us. You could say she was an unofficial informant. By letting that happen we kept her safe so her cronies wouldn't be suspicious.'

'It all seems convoluted to me, and highly dangerous exposing a young girl like that. I wouldn't have allowed it.'

'With respect, Nash. That's the reason you weren't in the loop. Sometimes Special Ops do things—differently,' Turner said.

Sensing ruffled feathers, Bronwyn stepped in. 'Norton's going to be a great help. She's already got them eating out of her hand.'

Nash scoffed, his fists clenched at his sides. 'Help us? She nearly killed a girl with a broken bottle.'

Lewis held up her hand and was sympathetic but resolute. 'I understand your frustration. But we have to make tough decisions and Norton is one of them.'

'A decision from Manchester, that we had no say in.'

Lewis dropped her head and he saw her face colour. He didn't mean to put her down, but he was furious at being sidelined and kept out of the loop. This was his station. He ran operations and managed the team, but he was being treated like one of the lower-ranking officers. He turned back to Turner, who met his glare with a cool attitude.

'We can't let people like Keeley Norton get away with this,' Nash insisted, his voice tinged with desperation.

'I agree,' Lewis said. 'But sacrifices have to be made to achieve our goals.'

With a frustrated sigh, Nash ran a hand through his hair. Petulance would get him nowhere. 'Fine. But don't expect me to approve of your methods while she walks free.'

'I wouldn't expect anything less than total commitment from you.'

He looked at the plush rug underfoot and the vibrant greenery that breathed life into Bronwyn's office. She said it was an extension of her home and she needed it to be a calming oasis to work in. It was all that and sometimes resembled the Amazon when the umbrella plant wasn't tamed, but the tranquil atmosphere clashed with the storm brewing, amplifying his frustration.

'It wasn't my decision, Nash, but I did endorse it. Superintendent Turner presented the evidence, and we made a collaborative decision based on getting the cooks. I need you on board as my second and my friend. Certain aspects of Keeley's role will be difficult to hide, and your tact and leadership will be imperative in keeping the team in order.'

Nash remembered Brown's face after Norton's showdown but his jaw clenched at the mention of Turner's involvement. He struggled to contain his anger as he demanded answers.

'What could justify letting her go? And you let her waltz in claiming she's a cop. That lot in Manchester have a funny way of policing.' He shot a look at Turner who outranked him. He should have shown him respect, but Nash was old school, and in his book that still had to be earned. Lewis raised her sculptured eyebrow in a warning that he was stepping out of line.

Turner grinned. It seemed he didn't hold a grudge and Nash had to admit it was big of him. 'We're all on the same side, Nash. Keeley Norton is a valuable asset to the operation. She's one of our top agents, and quite frankly, I'd choose her to have my back any day. Wait until you see her in action. She's remarkable.'

'I'll take your word for it. The girl's uncouth. She behaves like a criminal, for God's sake. And are we conveniently forgetting that she's been involved in selling drugs? In what parallel universe is that okay?'

Lewis tried to mollify Nash's anger. He was struggling to accept their decision. 'From here on in, we won't be keeping anything from you. And you will get your say in all decision-making.'

He clenched his fists. Lewis was right. They could bring in who they liked, but it didn't make it easier to take.

There was a rap on the door. Nash's bad mood hadn't abated and it irritated him some more that the idiot tapped out a stupid tune in their knock. Bronwyn Lewis looked up and tutted. 'Come in.'

Keeley Norton strode in. She was confident and her demeanour oozed swagger. She wore her Blight persona like a second skin with every movement exuding defiance.

Nash watched her theatrical entrance. 'Oh, for goodness sake,' he muttered under his breath unable to contain his exasperation.

'My ears were burning, so I thought I'd come and see what you lot were saying.' Blight grinned and blew a chewing gum bubble until it exploded.

'Do you mind?' Nash said. He knew he was being an arse but he couldn't stop himself.

Bronwyn shot him a warning glance to keep his cool. With tensions running high, the last thing they needed was a confrontation.

Keeley smirked at Nash's reaction, jumping on the opportunity to rile him. 'What's the matter, Detective Nash? Not happy to see me?'

Nash ground his teeth and wondered if they heard her raucous voice in Blackpool. He wanted to put Keeley in her place, but losing his temper would play into her hands. He thought about what Max would do and suppressed a grin. No, that was a bad idea. He thought about what Kelvin would do and took some breaths.

Bronwyn stepped in, her voice calm as she addressed Keeley. 'In this office, you can relax, Superintendent Norton. I don't think we need your alter ego.'

'Lady, this is me. Get used to it because I 'aint changing for no ho.'

Nash stood up and slammed his fist on the table. 'How dare you speak to DCS Lewis like that.'

Keeley's smirk widened into a grin. 'You think I want to do this? I have to eat, sleep, think and crap as this girl. Do you have any idea how hot this leather is? And believe me, if I could, I'd be the first in line to knock her out. But this little girl, with the tight braids and the smart mouth, might have to save your bacon, sometime, Daddio.'

'I doubt that very much.'

'Do you know what will cause this op to fail faster than your blood pressure's rising?'

Nash didn't answer.

'One tiny slip is all it would take. I wouldn't expect it from you, but I don't trust some of your rookies. They see me in the street and give me the police officer's nod. That could be enough to get us all killed. So I'll snort their coke and slap their backs, and I'll even stroke their dicks if I have to. I'll massage their stupid egos as much as they like until we have enough to take them down.'

He was horrified but didn't show it.

Blight went on, 'And when that day comes, I hope you'll be as proud to join me in a drink as I will be to sup with you.'

'That's quite a speech.'

'Yeah, well don't get used to it. I'm not nice very often.' She spat on her palm and held it out to Nash. Lewis picked the cuticle on her thumbnail and Turner was grinning like an idiot. Nash looked at the outstretched hand, made a comical show of screwing his face up, and shook it with reluctance. Then he took a tissue out of his pocket and wiped his hand making Lewis roll her eyes. Blight grinned.

It broke the tension for now and they laughed, but Nash was faking it. Go on, he thought. Laugh it up. I'll take your joke at my expense but don't make the mistake of underestimating me. Having this loud-mouthed upstart in his station upset the apple cart and he'd be watching for any slip to get her out. These weren't his methods, and he couldn't condone them. He knew Norton was playing games, but she wouldn't get the better of him.

Bronwyn had her work cut out. 'You've made a truce for now, but you two are like dry wood and accelerant. The last time I saw you this fired up about somebody was when we had Max Jones under investigation for murder. Norton reminds me a lot of him.'

'Who?' Norton asked.

Nash was about to rage that Keeley Norton wasn't fit to walk on the same pavement as Max when he stopped and looked at her. For a split second, the sunlight distorted the room and Max's face was superimposed over Norton's features. He tried to convince himself that it was a trick of the light, that's all. But it threw him. He saw it. Blight was exactly like Max Jones. 'Those would be big shoes to fill,' he said, but it was almost a whisper.

Blight said, 'Oh, shut it, grandad,' but Nash saw she'd picked up on his reaction. She looked at Lewis for an answer—but Bronwyn had nothing else to say.

Blight's words cut through Nash's thoughts, her insolence dripping from every syllable. And he smiled at the disrespectful remark, his jaw clenched as he fought to maintain his composure. To deal with Norton's insubordination, all he had to do was remember how Max had treated him at first. They were peas in a pod.

Bronwyn shot Blight a reproachful look. But Blight was unfazed.

Ignoring her taunts, Turner brought the meeting back to order. 'What's the status on the operation, Blight? Any updates?'

She smirked and swivelled in her chair. 'Mathis has heard about my big balls act, and he's having a soiree, as he calls it, in Windermere on Friday night. And guess who scored an invite?' She blew on her fingernails and rubbed them on her shoulder.

'You jammy devil,' Turner said. 'Who did you screw to manage that?'

'Charm and beauty, sweetheart. No screwing necessary.'

Nash was appalled at their unprofessional exchange, but arguing was getting him nowhere so he tutted but kept silent.

Blight saw the look of disgust on his face. 'I got in by personal invitation from the man himself. Beat that, Nasher.'

Nash almost fell out of his seat. 'What did you call me?'

'I called you Nash. It's your name, isn't it? Have you got a problem with it? I can call you sweet cheeks if you prefer. Get over yourself. I'm not going to kowtow to you every time I need you to jump. I say jump, and you ask how high. Got it?'

Nash didn't answer. Max was here. He'd seen his face and now he heard him calling him Nasher. It was his voice coming out of Norton's mouth, but the others didn't hear it. He had to pull himself together. Turner was talking and he brought himself back into the conversation.

Turner spoke to fill the awkward silence. 'Well done, Blight. I thought it would take longer for you to get in. But you're going to have to watch yourself. We can't risk putting a wire on you, and we can't get anywhere near that place. It's like a fortress. You'll be flying solo.'

'Are you out of your mind? It's far too dangerous to send her into a situation like that,' Nash said.

'Inspector. Superintendent Norton is a highly trained Special Ops officer who has spent the last two years infiltrating the ranks of this organisation. Your Jerod Mathis and his cronies are small fry to her,' Turner said. Blight swivelled in her chair making two complete revolutions as Nash tutted.

She grinned at him and blew a chewing gum bubble. 'It's on, Daddio.'

Chapter Twenty-Eight

Blight arrived at the Mathis mansion on the shores of Lake Windermere as the sun dipped to float on top of the water. The ride had been exhilarating and it was a pleasant change watching the beautiful countryside zip by rather than looking down filthy alleys for criminals and cronies. The motorbike roared down the Newby Bridge road and her kneepad lightly grazed the floor as she banked to take the tight corners. It wasn't her bike. She wasn't risking her Tiger being locked behind those gates if she couldn't get to it. She'd insisted Turner hire a replica, same model, same colour, same wear and she put her plates on it. Mathis would know her bike as well as he knew his mother. It would pass muster—but it wasn't hers. It was several grams heavier, and she felt it. Her legs hugged the tank, but there were a few millimetres difference. But her bike was safe at the station.

The ride was a welcome blowout to give her time to breathe and rebalance for the evening. She felt a twinge of apprehension. If she was made, this could be the last ride she'd ever take. Blight took her fear and twirled it around like candy floss on a stick. It morphed and resettled into a new feeling—cock-sure ballsyness. She could do this.

Faced with the grandeur of the imposing mansion gates, she squealed the tiger to a bilateral stop. Putting her feet down to steady the bike, she removed her helmet, shaking her braids, to let them fall loose. After half an hour of bending over her handlebars, she straightened her spine and looked into the fisheye lens. She blew a gum bubble and let it pop. The intercom on the gate was the golden key between her and a night that could go either way. She pressed the call button feeling the weight of unseen eyes scrutinising her through the camera mounted at eye level. With a final cud-chew, she took her gum out, rolled it into a ball, and stuck it onto the camera's all-seeing eye. 'Take that, morons,' she muttered loud enough for the security guards to hear her as the connection was made. Damn, she hated gum.

Before she could announce her arrival and give them her name, the gate buzzed open and she moved her helmet up her arm, wicker basket style. She revved her bike, easing it through the fifteen-foot-high gates and onto the winding driveway.

Manicured hedges lined the path, there for aesthetic purposes. They hid the imposing fencing, with a barbed wire top, keeping intruders out—and unwitting guests in.

The grounds were immaculate, a nod to wealth and the meticulous care of hired help. Flowerbeds were psychedelic with colour, a mash of reds, yellows, and purples that contrasted with the green of the lawn. Established, forty-foot-high old oak trees provided pockets of shade and added to the secluded luxury.

The mansion was a sprawling Georgian pile. Its façade was as imposing as Scafell Pike butting against the landscape, and the bleached stonework of the house gleamed in the waning light.

Tall windows framed with lead shutters punctuated the walls like a score of musical notes. They reflected the colours of the sunset and Blight wondered how many eyes watched from them. She caught the glint of metal in two top-storey windows at opposite ends of the main building and hoped she looked good in the crosshairs. Ivy clung to the stone, adding a touch of wild charm, but she only saw it as a ladder offering a potential escape from the upper floors. The entrance—two guards—both armed—was flanked by alabaster columns. Their surfaces were polished to a high sheen, supporting a portico that beckoned visitors with promise of luxury and excess. In a shootout, the pillars would offer coverage.

Blight parked her bike near the entrance, her boots crunching as she dismounted. She put her helmet into a pannier and though she made a show of locking it, she left it unfastened in case she had to vamoose fast. The air was filled with the scent of flowers and cut grass, but lying over it, there was no mistaking the earthy tang of the lake.

The doormen stood sentinel on either side of the entrance, their expressions impassive. Dressed in sharp black suits, they wore earpieces, and sunglasses despite the sinking light. Beneath the refinement, this was a house of danger and power.

Blight straightened her jacket. She couldn't afford to be intimidated. When she approached the doormen, her steps were confident. She had a part to play, and her swagger was impressive.

The men's efficiency was eerie against their silence. One of them stepped forward with the face of a waxwork. He didn't ask for permission before putting his hands on her.

Blight spread her arms and legs, a smirk insolent on her lips. 'Is this how you get your thrills, big boy? I wouldn't touch what you can't afford.' Her voice dripped sarcasm.

The doorman ignored her. His hands moved over every inch of her body, checking for concealed weapons and wires. He patted her legs and felt the knife holstered against her hip. With a practised fluidity, he drew the blade and held it up to the light. 'Nice try. You can have this back when you leave,' he said.

'I will, and your tiny little balls will be impaled on the end of it.'

The doorman finished his search, and the other guard opened the heavy front door. Blight's smirk widened. She felt the reassuring weight of her second blade, a thin stiletto, hidden in a special pocket sewn into her other boot. They'd missed it, just as she intended. Shoddy workforce, Scorch. Amateurs.

The doormen stood aside like the King's Guard and allowed her into the entrance hall. Blight's confidence grew as she crossed the threshold, so far so good.

The building was the blueprint of modern luxury, incorporating sleek lines and expansive glass panels offering breathtaking views of Lake Windermere. The sun was almost set, reflecting off the ripples of the lake.

A sweeping staircase curved to the upper floors, where she knew there were ten lavish bedrooms and Mathis' penthouse suite. Turner had obtained schematics of the mansion and its grounds. They'd been signed in as evidence, and, before coming, Blight had scrutinised every inch down to the high society woodworm and rat holes.

The floors were polished marble and the walls hung with contemporary art. Through the floor-to-ceiling glass walls, she could see the private jetty extending into the lake, its wood shimmering with blue algae. She imagined a body crashing through the glass, falling backwards, arms outstretched and freefalling into the freezing water. She noted a similar jetty on the other side of the lake. Mathis' escape route if heat came to the door. It was another detail she filed away, just in case.

The party was in full swing even though it was only tea time. Music thumped through the house, a heavy bassline that drummed in her chest. Guests milled about in designer clothes. Young people. Most of them were under twenty. Full of life and self-entitled attitude. Their laughter created a buzz that filled the ground floor.

Waiting staff in crisp uniforms circulated with trays of champagne and canapés, ensuring no one was left without. She waved one away. The scent of expensive perfume and cologne mixed in the air, with the sweet smell of cannabis creating an intoxicating atmosphere.

Blight moved through the crowd, her eyes taking in every detail. The living area was dominated by massive, L-shaped sofas in white leather, surrounded by glass coffee tables with drinks and hors d'oeuvres. A DJ played music recorded on a giant screen, while recessed lighting and dry ice blowing from the ceiling cast an ambient fugue over the room.

A table was filled with the notorious gift bags, each one a designer label and undoubtedly filled with luxury items for the guests to take home—and drugs. They were the bloody chalice of entrapment.

At the other side of the room, another table was deadly: a mountain of cocaine sat in the centre, flanked by fifty-pound notes to use for sniffing the powder. Guests crowded around it, indulging in the drugs with a casualness that spoke volumes about the world.

The dining area, off the living room, featured a glass-topped table set for a feast. Plates of food were artfully arranged, and a chandelier cast sparkling light over the spread. Beyond that, sliding glass doors led to a heated indoor swimming pool and spa. Then a terrace with an infinity pool that merged with the fairy-lighted lake. Drug-ravaged youngsters had stripped down to their swimwear and were splashing in the water. People lounged by the indoor pool, drinking. They wore micro-costumes or were naked.

Chapter Twenty-Nine

Blight spotted Mathis at the centre of the action. He was holding court among his guests. A tall man with effortless charisma and a lot of tattoos, he was dressed in a tailored suit that screamed money. His dyed black hair was slicked back, and a diamond-studded watch glittered on his wrist. He laughed at something one of his sycophants said, his veneers flashing white in the dim light.

Blight was intercepted by a young woman offering a drink. She accepted a glass of champagne for pretence but didn't touch it. Before long she'd have to drink and take drugs, but the longer she remained sharp-witted the better. She could still control her beast.

Scanning the room, her trained eye logged eleven discreet security cameras, their lenses hidden among the décor. Guards were positioned around the room, their eyes roving over the guests.

She didn't make a beeline for him. Blight ran to no man, but when she went to walk past Mathis with a confident stride, her gait was feline. Her presence drew the attention of everybody nearby. She never intended to blend into the background like your average undercover agent. Mathis looked up and smiled as she neared, his recognition apparent in the grill.

'Blight. Glad you could make it, babe. I see you dressed for the occasion.' So Mathis had seen her picture. He greeted her with his arms outstretched and kissed her on each cheek. 'Well, well, what a surprise, my lovely' he said into her ear emphasising the last two words. The song reference wasn't lost on her.

'I wouldn't miss it for the world, Scorch. All those sweet drugs for free.'

Mathis chuckled, clinking his glass against hers. 'Only the best for my friends. But please, call me Jerod. I outgrew my nickname years ago, but they won't let it die on the streets.'

Blight let her gaze wander over the guests. 'Your friends seem to be enjoying themselves.'

'I make sure of it.'

Blight's eyes went to the table laden with cocaine, then back to Mathis. 'And you know how to keep them happy.'

'All part of being the perfect host.'

Blight took another sip of her champagne, her mind racing. She was in the heart of the beast's lair, surrounded by luxury and decadence. But beneath the surface, she knew there was a world of danger. She had to keep her wits about her, but sobriety wasn't an option. It was a given that most of the guests would stay the night. The bedrooms were reserved for Mathis' special guests and the rest of the partygoers would take one of the dozens of camp beds set out in the ballroom. Blight would choose her cot, but she had no intention of staying. She'd leave by whatever means necessary, and if she had to abandon the bike, sobeit. It was difficult running in her heavy bike boots but she'd done it before. She had a route in her head through woodland and around the edge of the lake to a rendezvous point for pickup. Renshaw and Lawson would be waiting for her in the Village Inn car park, three kilometres from the mansion.

As she moved deeper into the party, the last thing she did was blend in. The guests, predominantly made up of Mathis' go-getter office people, were dressed to impress. Blight was in bike leathers, as tight and revealing as a second skin. A blight didn't blend—it attracted. She spent the next few minutes picking up full drinks and leaving them on window sills and behind plant pots. She chatted, mingled, and played the game. When the crowd she was talking to went to the cocaine mountain, she went with them, as natural as you like.

She was about to help herself to her first line of coke when a member of house security stopped her. She'd reached for a fifty-pound note on the coke-laden table when the firm hand had grasped her wrist. She looked up, ready to deliver a biting remark, but paused when she saw the guard. She licked the note that had been used before and tucked it into her top pocket. Although it wasn't good manners to take them, they were there to be stolen. She was goading him, but the guard didn't react.

'Mr Mathis would like a word in his private chambers,' he said.

'Can't keep the boss waiting, can we?' She cast a longing glance at the cocaine, knowing the expectations of her undercover role.

She was going into this assignment with her eyes wide open. Getting hooked on drugs as part of her cover was a foregone conclusion and the grim reality she had to face. She would endure a detox facility when the operation concluded. But she had a part to play and it had to be flawless.

'You can have as much candy as you like later,' the guard said. She caught the way his eyes roamed her body before returning to zombie-neutral. He was prime beef and if the opportunity presented itself, it would be no hardship to play with him later.

Blight sighed, pulling her hand away from his. 'Lead the way, McDuff.'

They walked through the house, and she took in her surroundings checking it against the blueprint in her head. The Mathis mansion was an ultra-modern marvel, unlike the traditional historic estates dotting the shores of Lake Windermere.

Jerod Mathis was a powerful figure whose reputation preceded him. Meeting him alone would test her nerve and her ability to maintain her cover. This was the moment she had been preparing for. Game on with her not-very-charming charm offensive.

The guard led her past the grand staircase to the lift. As they ascended, she caught him looking at her in the mirrored wall and met his gaze with an open invitation. He was on duty and looked away, but he'd be back. Their cards had been laid face up where they could both see them.

They reached the top floor and walked down a corridor lined with artwork and expensive furnishings. At the end of the hall, double doors opened into Mathis' private suite. The guard knocked and opened the door, pushing Blight in ahead of him.

She stepped inside and felt the shift in the atmosphere. The suite was luxurious, with floor-to-ceiling windows showing off the lake in all her majestic beauty. A moorhen late to its roost, swam below, leaving a straight trail in the water behind her.

The suite was furnished with sleek pieces—a leather sofa, a glass coffee table, and no doubt a massive king-sized bed. A fireplace crackled, casting strange light over the room. Shelves lined one wall filled with books and artefacts hinting at Mathis' diverse interests. He'd done well for himself and that didn't happen by stupidity. Blight made a note not to underestimate him. He wasn't a boy strutting around the streets of Barrow any more. She noted Chris Stapleton playing in the background, a pleasant contrast to the R&B blasting downstairs.

Mathis stood near the window with his back to her. He was over six feet, exuding an air of authority and menace. He spoke without turning. 'I thought it was you.'

Blight felt a flicker of unease but buried it beneath her practised bravado.

'I didn't think you'd recognise me. It's been a long time.'

'Little Tammy Logan. I often wondered what happened to you.'

'My name is Blight. That's the only name you need.'

'Is Keeley Norton not good enough for you?' He looked thoughtful, and she was floored. He knew her names—all of them. And Blight thought back to her time living with Scorch in his filthy bedsit. She'd killed a man when sex wasn't enough for him. He'd beaten her, and she'd had to run, but not before she'd put a kitchen knife through him. Jerod Mathis was the only one who knew about her past. She'd left him that night fourteen years ago. He was strung out on a bed drenched with sweat. Tammy was worth more and bought her way to a new identity. She'd got clean once, she could do it again when the time came.

Mathis was framed in the blackness outside the picture window, one hand raised and she heard ice singing in a glass. Whisky—without the e—on the rocks. A good Scottish blend, she smelt it. He kept her waiting and took his time to turn, and when he did, he had a sardonic look on his face that was hard to read. 'Where do you go to my lovely? When you're alone in your bed.'

'What?'

'I can look inside your head.' Mathis' piercing gaze met hers, and he nodded. She remembered her grandma. The smell of her kitchen. The smell of her death, and the scent of Tammy's shift in circumstance back then. 'I'm not the only one who's changed. We've come a long way from Highway Close.' She knew him. He was bigger and ripped, but she knew his body. She'd pleased him in the night. They had a code, and that transcended time or status. Her secret past was safe—for now. The man she'd knifed would stay buried. She challenged Mathis with her return stare. He was the first to back down.

Blight crossed her arms. She didn't like that he knew her legal name. But it was out there on the street. While she preferred Blight, she hadn't tried to hide it. That would have been folly. A person with no identity to trace is a target. He knew her name but, she was still standing. That said, he clearly didn't know she was a cop. Nothing could track back to her career. She gave herself a pep talk. Relax, don't show any signs of stress. 'I aim to please,' she said.

Mathis' laugh was a dangerous sound. 'I hope you do. Because if you're as good as they say, you'll be a valuable asset. But if not, this won't end well.' He let the threat hang in the air, unexplained but clear.

'I can deliver. I never disappoint.'

Mathis studied her, then nodded. 'Good. Let's talk business.'

Renshaw had told her to pump him for information about the next consignment drop.

Renshaw was a fool.

In that conversation where he'd played the big man, Renshaw had shown himself up for the rookie sergeant he was. The difference between Norton and Renshaw was that she knew the drug world. You don't go into the first meeting with a higher-ranking gangster and ask questions. Not unless you wanted a hole in your forehead.

Blight walked a tightrope. One misstep meant disaster.

But once, a long time ago, she had been Tammy Logan.

And Tammy Logan had killed a man.

Chapter Thirty

Blight strode back into the party room as though the mansion, and everything in it, belonged to her. People had seen her being taken away by the guard and she was gone a good hour. In that time, most of them would have lost the knowledge of their own names, never mind what she'd been up to, but every detail had to be played on the off-chance that somebody did notice. She came back to the party which meant two things. She wasn't dead, and she'd had sex in Mathis' private rooms. The latter wasn't true.

She smiled. It was the expression of somebody who had just scored points off every person in the room. She went straight to the depleted cocaine mountain and did a bump. A quarter of it was gone. Personal supplies will have been topped up, but how could a hundred people get through so much cocaine in an hour?

Lascivious minds would conclude that she'd been chosen for a sexual liaison with Mathis. It suited her to let them think that. Her heart pounded with adrenaline and relief. She'd walked out of Mathis' lair without a hitch, but the encounter had left her on edge and needing a hit. After holding herself steady for an hour, she released the bruxism buildup and knew she was gurning. She needed that bump.

Scorch Mathis was a dangerous man. Being in his suite felt like standing on the edge of a razor blade in bare feet.

The party was bouncing. People danced to EDM's high-energy beats, perfect for keeping the party lively. They swayed with their hands above their heads in a hypnotic altered state. Every track sounded the same to Blight but was a staple in upscale parties for its ability to create an electrifying atmosphere.

The high was getting to her and she laughed as a thought hit her. Unbidden, she imagined DCI Nash in this situation. She didn't know him well enough to judge, but she imagined him in the groove of the dancers. She grinned, though to be fair, he was in pretty good shape and might be able to bust some decent moves. Before leaving the station, he'd given her a list of dos and don'ts as if this was her first rodeo. She had no idea what made her think of that pompous fool, but he was attractive. She laughed out loud and the person next to her started laughing too. The last thing she needed was a daddy crush.

Blight's eyes swept the crowd, noting the extravagant display of designer clothing and the careless indulgence of the guests. A man caught her eye because he stood out. What the hell? This dude was like a hippy throw-back from the 70's. He was at the edge of the dancefloor free-dancing. He brought to life the phrase, dance like nobody's watching, and she thought somebody would need an ambulance if he kept bouncing around like that. Nobody looked bothered by him and she wondered if they were too high to notice.

The guy stopped dancing. He stared at her and brought his finger to his lips. He smiled and the thought came into her head that this stranger had her back. It was ridiculous. As if a buffoon like that could help her. He lowered his hand and went back to his crazy dancing.

In a roomful of suits, this guy was unkempt and barefoot. He wore a flowery shirt and tight jeans, his hair was wavy and past his collar and his body had a life of its own. She blinked, and he was gone. Looking around for him she thought the crowd must have swallowed him.

This was a far cry from the other end of Mathis' operation, where underprivileged kids from refugee families were forced to deal on the streets. She amended that thought. If the latest kids coming forward were anything to go by, Mathis was getting bold and any kid was fair game for distribution. She'd even heard a murmur in the canteen that Nash's family were being threatened. His wife must be beside herself with worry for her grandkids. She forced herself to relax, blending into the atmosphere, and standing out at the same time. Nash didn't wear a ring. For Christ's sake stop it, she told herself.

She felt the strong effect of the drugs and alcohol and went in search of water to clear her head and flush the toxins through her body. Water bottles were readily available to the guests, so as long as she was seen drinking alcohol as well it didn't look out of place. Vodka over ice fed the plants and water topped up her empty glass.

Her mind raced with details of her conversation with Mathis. He'd tested her, probing for weakness, but she held her ground. Every gesture was calculated, convincing him that she was an ambitious player in the game.

She went to the floor and danced, another way to rush the crap through her system. The weight of the last double bump pressed down on her and sharpened her wits, making adrenaline bounce in time to the music. The casual way they treated drugs was her world again. She could cry for getting dragged back into the scene she'd left behind a long time ago—but if she did, it would be the drugs talking. The cocaine on the table, and the bullseye notes used as sniffers—this was her reality. She knew the price she'd pay. She was hooked again and it was a grim spectre but a necessary evil. She would die to get these bastards off the street and make it a safe place for children.

She hadn't been saved when she was prostituted by Mathis at fifteen. But she didn't blame him—he was just a rung on a ladder. She had a single line of vision, just like back then. This time around she'd take out the cook, help cut the supply chain and end the misery. It was worth a stint in recovery. Turner had said Nash would be livid when he found out the length of her sacrifice, but that was a bridge to cross. This was the assignment she'd chosen.

She stopped at a gilded mirror and her lip curled at the absurdity of what had paid for it. Her braids were only slightly messed up after her visit to Mathis, and her revitalised make-up was flawless. She looked like a woman who had just repaired her look after sex.

She wouldn't let anything, or anybody, stand in her way. Not Mathis, not his goons, and certainly not the drugs playing pinball in her circuitry and making her heart pound. She could handle it.

She did a lap of the room, dancing, chatting, flirting and looking for the hippy she'd seen earlier. Before it was obvious that she hadn't been back to the cocaine table, she went. Her eyes locked with the good-looking security guard. He gave her a nod, an acknowledgement of her newfound status. She reached for a rolled-up bullseye and took another hit.

Mathis' arm slid around her waist from behind. She knew it was him. She'd noted his cologne and estimated his weight, within a kilo. Looking down, she recognised the decal on his suede shoe from earlier. Her only reaction to his arm snaking around her was to stagger. Not enough to lack class, but a little nod to his excellent hospitality. 'I thought we might continue our chat over breakfast tomorrow,' he said, his voice a smooth purr.

Before she straightened from the table, she pushed her bottom into his stomach. It would do her position no harm to be seen with him. 'Really? Are we going to go there again? It's been a long time, Jerod.'

He laughed. 'As tempting as that sounds given the new curves, it's strictly business, babe. My associates will be joining us.'

Blight's stomach churned. She knew what breakfast meant. She'd be expected to do more coke, and he'd push more substances to test her loyalty. She knew his MO, and his army all ended up on crystal meth and Chaos eventually. She couldn't refuse. She smiled, and nodded, masking her unease. Turning, she leaned into him for the room to see, and whispered, 'It will be my pleasure.'

Mathis' smile widened as he handed her a glass of champagne. 'Enjoy the party. But remember, you'll be brought to the dining room at eight sharp.'

Blight accepted the drink, the flute was cool against her palm. She took a measured sip. It was a high-quality fizz. Jerod Mathis was the real deal, he didn't cut corners. No Prosecco was masquerading as its French cousin here. 'I'll be ready,' she replied. Her plan to escape was scuppered and with no way to contact

Renshaw at the Village Inn, she was alone for the night. They'd factored this eventuality into their plans. The rookies wouldn't come in all guns blazing—at least she hoped not.

Blight felt some twisted relief. On the upside, she had a good chance of leaving with the bike they'd hired, the next day. This was better for keeping her cover intact and she wouldn't need the story of why she'd left before the party finished. Hell, it would probably be going three days from now.

The opulence of the mansion was like a dame with no knickers. The crystal chandeliers cast shadows over the room while the bathrooms were full of partygoers puking up indulgence. The air was redolent with the scent of expensive perfume mingling with the tang of illicit substances. She hated that already it was a smell that she was growing accustomed to again.

Laughter and loud conversation grated on her nerves and screamed over the music from the DJ in the corner. Every detail oozed excess and luxury. It gave her a headache. She needed another bump to get through this. Dependence was clawing at her nerve endings and she wondered when the first time was that she needed it rather than just doing it for show. It was weeks ago.

Grabbing another champagne from a passing waiter, she lifted it to her lips but didn't drink. She let the bubbles tickle her nose before lowering the glass. It was okay to ease up. Others were hitting their ceiling, so it was acceptable to be seen with a water bottle, and without a drink in her other hand. She lost the glass behind the alabaster buttocks of a naked statue.

She was sociable, laughing at jokes and engaging in banter. Half an hour later, she accepted another champagne, pretending to sip before putting it on a windowsill when nobody was looking. She projected an image of casual enjoyment, blending in with other partygoers.

The fifty notes were scattered around the table like discarded playthings—but fewer than there had been. Blight picked one up, twirling it between her fingers as she watched others indulge. She cut a line and lowered her head to join the kids at the trough.

Her eyes rolled, no pretence in her enjoyment. Damn, it felt good. Welcome back, old friend. Her ears were attuned to pick up information—her senses heightened. Drugs were everywhere—lines of cocaine left on the back of Mathis' chairs and pills of many colours, like Joseph's coat, scattered on almost every surface.

She passed a group of men discussing shipments and territory. It was important and she filed the details away for later. A woman in a red sequined dress boasted about her connections, and Blight noted the names she spouted. Tongues were loose. 'Were all friends here.' There was much to learn, and information dropped like ice cubes splashing into bourbon.

She laughed at jokes that weren't funny, pretended to be interested in vapid conversations, and her thoughts focused on the mission. She had what she came for—but wanted more coke, the high hadn't dropped but she knew it was coming.

At the table, she thought about walking away. This wasn't work. This was needed. She wanted to fight it, but couldn't resist the pull of the light hitting the grey.

The notes on this side of the table had all been taken, so she pulled her key fob from her pocket rather than doing it directly off the mirrored surface. She cut her line and as she bent her head, a breeze came from nowhere. It was as though somebody had blown her coke away. She loaded it again, and the same thing happened. She stood up, confused and looked around.

There was no breeze. It was a hot sticky mess under the overhead lights and with the heat of all the bodies in the room and from other people crowded around the table. She looked at the bloke next to her but he was oblivious. Maybe she didn't need a hit so badly after all.

As she walked away, she saw the hippy again. He was leaning against a doorjamb. He shook his head at her in reproach and then smiled. She walked over to him, but when she got to that side of the room he was gone. Tosser.

She stood near the window overlooking the private jetty and took a moment to appreciate the view. Her mind drifted to the escape route it offered. She couldn't be complacent. The night had gone well, but she wasn't safe. Things could still go south and taking Mathis' small outboard motor boat to the jetty on the other side of the lake would be her quickest way out. She filed that away, another detail to keep in mind.

Blight continued her careful dance of observation and subterfuge. She was aware of Mathis watching her from across the room, his gaze a reminder of the precariousness of her situation. But she didn't falter.

Chapter Thirty-One

She was in the belly of the beast, and she would do what it took to bring it down. Her eyes scanned the room for her next target.

She noticed a low-life office operative eyeing her from across the room. He was full of himself, with greasy hair slicked back in a poor attempt at style. He wore a cheap suit that couldn't disguise his seedy nature. She imagined him hitting the phones and chatting bullshit at the unsuspecting. Fast-talking, not letting the target get a word in. Potential client refusal was a failure when he needed another sale on the target board.

'With these domain names, I can guarantee you'll hit the front page of Google, my friend. My next call will be to your leading competitor, and if you don't take them in the next five minutes, I can guarantee, he will. He's already shown an interest but I don't like his attitude. Look, let me level with you. Somebody has just released three premium domains onto the market and I've been lucky enough to snag them. I'm selling them to you for a song, my friend. Three hundred pounds apiece and they're yours. No. You know what, I'm going to do you a big favour. Two fifty. I'm taking your credit card details now.' Like anybody cared about Google these days, Blight thought. She'd read their script in the briefing room and it was awful. Their sales tactic was brutal and aggressive. There were only two ways to end a call. Either the target bought, or the target hung up. Mr Smooth here, would bully them on the phone until they did one of the two. And this was supposed to be the legitimate side of Mathis' business.

She walked towards the bathroom knowing she wouldn't get halfway there. Her hips swayed more than usual, not that she needed to catch his attention. His eyes lit up as she passed, a sleazy grin spreading across his face.

'Hey there, gorgeous,' he said. 'Enjoying the party?'

'Absolutely. But it's only as good as the company.'

'Name's Brandon. What's a beautiful woman like you doing in a place like this?'

Oh God, save me from this moron. 'I'm just looking for a little excitement.'

Brandon reached into his pocket and pulled out a baggie of tablets. 'Here, this will make things a lot more interesting.'

He held the tab up to the light as if examining it, and then poked out his slimy tongue. He put the tab on the end and raised his eyebrow at her in invitation. She met Brandon's gaze and just about managing not to gag, she took it from his tongue. Sliding it past her lips, she made a show of rolling it around her mouth, moaning as she pretended to savour the taste.

'Mm, that's good,' she purred, leaning closer to Brandon.

It was a wonder he didn't trip over his hard-on. 'Wait until it kicks in. You'll fly.'

Blight gave him a conspiratorial wink and turned her head in a delicate cough. Her hand came up to her mouth. In a practised motion, she spat the pill into her palm and slipped it into her pocket. Wiping her lips, she turned back to Brandon, maintaining her seductive smile but wanting to punch him. The job should pay sleaze money. 'My God, that's good gear. I was just on my way to the bathroom. So, see you later, big boy. You be good now.' That jerk had nothing to tell her.

'Hey, hang on. You can't leave me now.'

She was already over him.

Blight worked the room, using her charm to extract information. She drifted around the groups but mostly drew people to her. She listened to conversations, guiding them towards topics of interest.

People splintered off towards dawn. Blight couldn't be among the first to leave—it would look suspicious. And she couldn't be the last, drawing unnecessary attention from security. She timed her departure, slipping away in the middle of the exodus.

The makeshift sleeping area had commandeered the ballroom. It was filled with cots and sleeping bags and felt like a teenager's summer camp, though the dim lighting and murmurs of conversation gave it an underworld atmosphere. Somebody was being sick in a bucket, and several double-humped camels moved in the dance of sex.

Blight chose a cot in a far corner, away from the main cluster of people. Her boots were the only items she removed. She slipped the knife out, unrolled her sleeping bag and slipped it inside the liner, her eyes scanning the room for potential trouble. The tight leather suit was hell, but she had to be ready to move at a second's notice. She hadn't been comfortable taking her boots off, but if she didn't it would have looked suspicious if they weren't at the foot of her cot. Most people appeared to be sleeping naked or in their underwear, but some opted for the modesty of keeping their day clothes on.

Blight had no intention of sleeping. She felt sick from the drugs and alcohol but was a master of self-control. Supine meditation would keep it down.

As she lay in her sleeping bag and settled, she felt a stab of unease. She saw somebody watching in the dim light from across the room. She couldn't make out their features but her instincts flared, warning her to be alert.

Blight pretended to adjust her sleeping bag, using the movement to check her surroundings. The other partygoers were either already asleep or too intoxicated to care. The watcher, however, was focused on her.

She turned onto her side, facing away from the observer, and closed her eyes. But sleep wasn't on her mind. She was vigilant and ready to react. She couldn't afford to let her guard down—not for a second.

As she feigned sleep, her mind kept her awake—albeit fuzzy—with the night's events. She'd gathered valuable intel, but the watcher kept her on edge. She was in enemy territory, surrounded by potential threats and although she couldn't see him, she felt his eyes on her back. She was better at her job than anyone else in that room.

Her thoughts drifted to Nash and his warning to keep herself safe at all costs. He was a strange clashing meld of character, with shades of endearing warmth and frigid aloofness. He came across as a stern father figure to the team, and yet she'd seen him in action in the interview room where he was like granite. Nash fascinated her and more conflict awaited from his direction when she went back to base. He wouldn't understand the sacrifices she had to make or the lengths she'd go to maintain her cover. She pushed the thoughts aside.

Blight didn't need a father. She'd managed this long without one.

She lay still, listening for noise in the room. The muffled sounds of the party were still bass-pounding in the distance, but her focus was attuned to the shuffling footsteps approaching her cot. From a ten-foot distance, she could smell the alcohol on his breath and she was aware of a list to his stance due to the effects of the drink. He was quiet enough but was doing a poor job of creeping. She almost laughed. This idiot would never make it as a police officer.

Despite avoiding as much alcohol and as many drugs as possible, Blight hadn't escaped unscathed. Her head swam, the room doing helicopters across her vision in a disorienting slur of movement. She made her eyes follow the room to steady it. Now wasn't the time to lose a grip of her senses. She gritted her teeth. She had to maintain control. She was in a fight-or-flight situation, and the option was chosen.

The sleazy office guy from earlier reached her cot. His breathing was heavy and uneven. He was a silhouette and loomed over her as he reached for the zipper of her sleeping bag. Blight's hand tightened around the thin blade. She had the element of surprise.

As he unzipped her bag and reached inside for her breast, Blight's eyes snapped open. She moved fast, despite the haze clouding her mind. In a fluid motion, she sat up, rolled him over, straddled him, and pressed the blade to his throat. The manoeuvre would have been easier in anything but the skin-tight leather suit.

'Touch me again and I'll slit your throat,' she hissed, her voice dangerous.

The sleazebag's eyes opened in shock. His body was rigid beneath her and it had nothing to do with sexual desire. His bravado had vanished along with his wood and was replaced by fear.

'What the hell?' He stammered and Blight thought he might be about to lose control of either his bowels or his bladder.

Her grip tightened on the knife, the cold steel pressing against his skin. 'I should have warned you not to underestimate me. Now get out of here before I carve my name into your face.' Blight put her finger to her lips to silence him. She didn't need more unwanted attention.

He nodded, his eyes never leaving hers and she eased the pressure on the knife, giving him enough room to scramble from underneath her. He stumbled to his feet, his hands raised in a placating gesture.

'I thought you were up for it,' he said.

'Of course you did.' Blight glared at him, her eyes burning with fury. 'You come near me again, and I won't be so forgiving.'

She wasn't sure what happened next. No matter how many times she replayed it, she couldn't make sense of the way the pervert's body lifted from the floor and was thrust backwards so he flew several feet across the room. Was she hallucinating?

He turned, looked at her in the gloom, and practically ran for the exit. Blight watched him go, and she steadied herself. The adrenaline helped clear her head. She felt almost sober and the room had righted itself, but she must have been more stoned than she thought. The adrenaline had done in a minute what would take the normal recovery process a couple of hours. But she still had some time before the alcohol was out of her system, so she needed to stay vigilant.

Nobody else seemed to have noticed the tussle or the way the guy had been blown across the room. Most of the partygoers were either passed out or too intoxicated to care. She settled with the knife in her hand under the sleeping bag and practised meditation to stay awake. She visualised the effects of the drugs and alcohol as waves washed over her body. They lessened in intensity over time. She would deal with the consequences of her actions later. For now, she had to survive the night.

Chapter Thirty-Two

Nash hadn't taken any time off since the Diamond Light Operation began. The guys were over for dinner, and he'd felt obliged to invite Turner and his wife, Lucinda. The guilt he felt at his relief when they'd declined due to Lucinda being unwell soon passed. Now he could enjoy himself.

Nash's house was the best on the island and others around it bowed to its sophistication. With the two imposing towers and veranda looking out to the ocean, it was as iconic a landmark as the Round House building.

The living room was spacious and lit by the ambient glow of strategically placed lamps, casting warm hues on the beautifully papered feature wall. A leather sectional couch dominated one side of the room, flanked by armchairs facing a coffee table crammed with snacks. An impressive array of liquor bottles winked at them from the corner bar. Shelves lined with books and mementos from their travels filled the remaining space, adding personal history to the room. Kelvin's deceased wife smiled at them from a photograph on the mantelpiece.

The scent of delicious offerings wafted in from the kitchen, where Kelvin was in charge of the hors d'oeuvres. Kelvin and

Nash were fierce rivals in the kitchen and everybody agreed that, between them, they put on one hell of a spread. Tonight, Kel was in his element, whipping up an array of finger foods ranging from stuffed mushrooms to spicy chicken wings while Nash chatted with their guests.

He was mixing drinks at the bar. 'Who's ready for another round?' His voice carried over the soft jazz playing in the background. He wore a casual button-down shirt with his sleeves rolled up, revealing the muscular forearms that were his pride during his rugby days.

Conrad Snow and his wife, Natasha, lounged on the couch, looking at home. While Nash showed no favouritism at work, the six had formed a social group that met at each other's houses a couple of times a month. Sometimes Nash invited the team but the core reprobates were here tonight. Conrad, a handsome man with long blond hair and a pleasant laugh, recounted one of his infamous stories, his hands illustrating the finer points. Nash appreciated how unassuming he was. He never mentioned his gift unless he was asked. Natasha was elegant and laughed at the right moments, her eyes sparkling with amusement. As well as working a few shifts at the village pub, she was an art curator at a prestigious gallery in Ambleside. Her refined tastes were evident in her subtle dress sense. Tonight she wore a blue maxi dress in soft cotton that was simple but flowed with yards of material.

Molly's mind was sharper than her tongue, but only just. She sat in one of the armchairs with her boyfriend, Danny, perched on the armrest beside her. Molly's laugh was infectious, her brown curly hair bouncing with every chuckle. Danny, a roofer seemed out of place until he laughed and his easy-going nature made him blend in seamlessly. The group spanned a couple of generations, but they clicked and were just right. 'How have you coped with this one all week, Si? She's had a right cob on with this new girl starting,' Danny said.

Nash shook a cocktail shaker and laughed. 'Blight has been a blight on all of us. She's aptly named.'

Kelvin came out of the kitchen with a tray in each hand. 'All right, everyone, dig in. We have more chicken wings, and some mini quiches with my extra special touch.' He put the trays on the coffee table after Danny had made space. 'A little dribble of Tabasco,' Kelvin winked and Molly dived in.

Conrad grabbed a third stuffed mushroom. 'If I could cook like you, I'd never leave the house.'

'Go easy with them, they have a dribble of my extra special touch.'

Nash started singing the Tequila tune, and at the appropriate place they all sang 'Tabasco!'

Natasha nudged Conrad. 'You barely leave the house as it is. Too many invisible playmates.'

The room laughed, and Nash handed Molly a gin and tonic. 'Thanks, boss. Just what I needed.'

Nash grinned. 'Anything for my best detective.'

Danny raised his beer in a toast. 'To good friends and fast food with a special touch.'

'Hear, hear,' the group chorused, clinking glasses.

'Don't you dare lump my cuisine in with takeaway junk. You won't get my extra special touch anywhere else you know.'

'You keep your special touch away from him.' Molly laughed, gnawing a chicken wing to the bone.

They discussed everything from office gossip to Max still being around. He often came through to show Nash he was still there. Nash threw in sarcastic comments and anecdotes that had everyone in stitches. Silas at home with Kelvin and under the influence, was a very different man to the hardened detective in a stiff suit holding rank in the briefing room.

Molly leaned over to Nash, lowering her voice. 'Did you hear about the latest screw-up in Records? They lost an entire case file.'

Nash shook his head. 'Of course they did. If it wasn't for us cleaning up their mess, the department would fall apart.'

Natasha looked up. 'You two always have the best goss. It makes my art exhibitions seem dull. But you'll never guess who bought a Corcoran today?' They went on to discuss the celebrity tourist who had bought from Natasha.

'I love the police, timeless band,' Danny said.

Conrad grinned and shook his floppy hair from his face. 'See, and she calls her job boring. I'd take an exhibition with Sting over some of the stuff we deal with any day.'

'Don't let him fool you,' Nash said, handing out another round of drinks. 'Conrad loves the thrill. It's why he joined us as a consultant.'

'And we all know what you felt about that arrangement, Si,' Natasha said with a smile. 'Arty-farty bollocks was one of the phrases Con brought home with him. Oh and Con by name, con artist by nature, is another direct quote. Though sometimes I wish he'd bring a little less excitement home.'

Conrad had his say on the matter. 'You unbelievers are the bane of my life. And you're no better now, Nash, it doesn't matter how much my helpers save the day—you still have to find your logical explanation for everything.'

They all laughed. Nash hadn't taken well to Conrad's tenure in the department and still struggled with that element of the work.

'How have you been getting on, Danny? Your normal usually sounds like a movie plot. I never knew being a roofer could be so interesting. I'm sure you make half of it up.' Nash ensured that Danny was brought into the conversation so he didn't feel left out.

'You would not believe what we see above everybody's eyeline,' Danny replied. 'And it makes for good pillow talk.'

Molly elbowed him. 'Watch it, slate boy. I've got a pair of handcuffs with your name on them.'

'Misappropriation of police issue, will not be condoned Detective Brown,' Nash said with a wink.

Kelvin groaned, feigning disgust. 'All right, Molly. No need to ruin our appetites.'

'I've never heard you complain when ours come out,' Nash said.

This time they all joined Kelvin in a communal groan.

The easy banter made the hours fly by. These were his people—his family in the special sense of the word. Despite the danger and stress of the job, moments like these made it all worthwhile.

The jazz moved over to make way for classic rock, and Kelvin did a mean air guitar. The solicitor was always the first to let loose after being in a formal suit all day. Nash got there, but it took longer. Conrad and Natasha snuggled closer on the couch, while Molly and Danny bickered about who was the smartest.

Kelvin kept the food and drinks flowing, ensuring everybody was taken care of. Nash was three martinis in and beyond caring.

'Let the peasants help themselves,' he said, waving an olive on a cocktail stick. 'Who invented these green things? They are foul.'

'You keep putting them in your drink,'

'Well, a Martini is only a mart or a teeny without them, isn't it?'

Conrad waved his hand to impart a message from Max. 'He says it's time for bed old man.'

'And what would he know, he's dead' Nash said. 'Tell him to get back in his coffin.'

'He says no offence taken,' Conrad laughed.

When he stopped, he listened for a second and then said. 'I don't understand this message but he says, "Do your job detective. I can't keep protecting the new firecracker for you." He's gone now.'

'When he comes back you can tell him I do my job just fine without his interference, thanks,' Nash laughed.

He went to the bar where the martini was switched to a bourbon when nobody was looking. It wasn't often he let his guard down and, in the company of these friends, he felt enough trust to be silly. The pressures of the job meant that he had a position to maintain in the community. He'd struggled with being himself and the thought that a member of the public might see him do the macarena filled him with horror. God forbid that he should be seen as human human. The role he forced on himself of acting like a stern, straight, pillar of the community could wait until tomorrow. Tonight was about laughter, friendship, and a respite from the stress of their everyday lives.

He caught Kelvin's eye and raised his glass. 'To love, friends and alcohol.'

Kelvin grinned. 'And to the macarena, Alka-Seltzer and paracetamol. Another couple of hours and I won't envy your team coping with your mood tomorrow.' He gave Molly a sympathetic look, but she'd have her own hangover to deal with.

Chapter Thirty-Three

As they clinked glasses, Nash smiled. It was a good night. Conrad turned to him. 'So, what's the deal with this new officer, Keeley Norton?'

Nash's smile tightened. He took a sip of his bourbon, choosing his words carefully. 'She's an interesting addition to the team. She has a lot of experience, and isn't afraid to get her hands dirty.'

Molly let out a noise similar to a snort. 'Interesting? Is that how we're playing it?' She rolled her eyes, putting her drink down with a thud. 'The woman's a nightmare, Nash. Admit it.'

'She's unconventional. But she's been effective in the past, or so I'm told.'

'She's a sodding bulldozer. The only thing she's effective at is leaving trouble in her wake. Did you see the way she strutted into the briefing room? It was like she owned the place. And the attitude. God, don't get me started on that.'

Danny loved stirring the pot and riling his girlfriend up. 'It sounds like she's peeing on your pitch. I can only imagine how that's going to work.'

He knew she'd rise to it. Molly shot him a withering look. 'I love it when someone waltzes in and acts like the rest of us are expendable. She's got a superiority complex bigger than Hoad Monument.'

Kelvin tried his hand at peace-making. 'Maybe she's asserting herself to show she's got what it takes?'

'There's a difference between asserting yourself and being a complete arse. I know she's my SO, but I can't stand the bitch. She doesn't respect anyone. Not me, not Nash, and certainly not the protocols we have in place.'

Conrad chuckled, enjoying the show. 'She's made an impression, then?'

Nash rubbed the back of his neck. 'I know she's a lot to handle. But Turner vouched for her, and we should give her a chance.'

Molly wasn't having it. 'He's another one with tickets on himself. And Norton doesn't deserve a chance. She thinks the badge puts her above the law. She held a girl at knifepoint, for Christ's sake, Nash. She put a broken bottle against a young girl's throat. And we have to play nice because Turner says so? Bollocks to that.'

Natasha sympathised with Molly. 'She sounds dangerous.'

'She is,' Molly said. 'But not in the way you think. She doesn't care about collateral damage. She's the kind of cop who'll bulldoze through a case, put us all in danger, then piss off, leaving the rest of us to pick up the pieces.'

Nash steered the conversation back to steadier ground. 'We're on the same team. We'll find a way to work together.'

Molly was unconvinced. 'Good luck with that. Unless she gets a serious attitude adjustment and a muzzle, we're in for a rough ride.'

Danny was still grinning. 'At least it won't be boring. Can't wait to meet her.'

Molly shot him a withering glare, but there was a hint of a smile at the corners of her mouth. 'You can keep well away from her. She's mental.'

Conrad, the king of toasts raised his glass. 'Here's to surviving Keeley Norton. May she not get us all killed.'

The group laughed, but Nash knew they had a point. Norton was a wildcard, and wildcards were unpredictable. But he was stuck with her. Being so deep undercover was dangerous and he hoped her methods would pay off.

He decided to share some crucial information with Brown before the morning briefing. If nothing else, he wanted to ease her frustration and show her that Norton's presence wasn't in vain.

He glanced around the room, ensuring the others were engaged in conversation then called Molly. 'Can I have a word in private?' he asked.

She disentangled herself from Danny. 'Sounds ominous.'

They moved to a quieter corner of the living room, away from the chatter and Nash leaned in, his voice serious. 'I'm about to tell you something confidential that doesn't leave this room. It might help you see why Norton's involvement is so important.'

'What is it?'

'She uncovered vital information at the Windermere party. There's going to be a major drop this Friday night. The Barrow squad will be shadowing GMNT. It's big, Molly. We're planning to intercept the consignment on the A590. And we would've missed it if it wasn't for Norton.'

'All hail Queen Blight.'

'Stop it. It's getting old now.'

Molly's scepticism gave way to intrigue. 'Is it a major drop? How much are we talking?'

'A significant shipment. This could be the break we've been waiting for to dismantle their operation. If we can intercept the product, we'll have the evidence to swoop on the heads of the organisation. It's a two-fold swipe. We want the cooks. Take them out and it stops production stone dead. But we need to dismantle the organisation from the top tier. As soon as we've radioed to Manchester that we've stopped the truck, they'll pass it up the chain and go in hard to round up all the major players.'

'So we do the work and GMNT's home squad take all the glory?'

Nash laughed. 'Something like that, but who cares who gets the medals if it cleans our town?'

Molly processed the information. 'And Norton's involvement is key to this?'

'Yes. She's got an in with Mathis and his crew. Her ongoing intel is crucial to the operation. And you have no idea what she's giving to achieve it.'

Molly saw Nash stiffen and pounced. 'What?'

Nash held up his glass. 'I've said too much. Look. I know she's rough around the edges, but she gets results. I want you in on this, Molly. She's going to need support and I'm counting on you.'

'Why? She doesn't strike me as the type of woman who needs a sisterhood.'

'She's going through some stuff. Like I said, I've already told you too much. We have to live with her for the time being. It won't be forever. We need to leverage her connections and her ability to blend in with the criminals.'

Molly pouted, showed awareness of her childish stance, and altered her expression. 'What about Mathis?'

'We get him at the same time as the Manchester sting.'

'I still don't trust Blight.'

'After what I've just discovered, I don't either, but we work with what we've got. This operation is too important to fail. I need everyone on board. Especially you.'

Molly put her head on Nash's shoulder. 'I wish you'd tell me what you've got on her, maybe I can help.'

'Nice try, gossip monger.'

She laughed, 'Okay. I'll keep my feelings in check. But if she steps out of line, I'll call her out.'

'I wouldn't expect anything less.' A smile played around his lips. 'Let's hope it doesn't come to that.' Nash heard something and looked around. 'What was that?'

'What?'

He scanned the room and looked confused. 'Nothing. I thought I heard something, that's all. Come on, let's get back to the others.'

Conrad was at the bar mixing a drink but stopped. He held a scoop in the ice bucket and froze. He had his back facing the room. Nash couldn't see his expression, but the stillness of his body was unnatural, like one of those glitches in the matrix videos you see of people, frozen in time.

The voice that came out of him belonged to Max Jones. *Row, row, row your boat, gently down the stream.*

Nash knew not to touch him. 'Snow, are you all right?'

Conrad turned around. His face was in partial shadow, but it looked as though his features had darkened. The voice had changed again and Max was gone. This time an image accompanied the song. The face was there and then gone, but Nash saw a child of colour in that nano-second. Snow's blond hair was shorter. The waves he loved, had turned into tight curls. His voice changed into a pre-pubescent soprano with a thick African accent. 'Merrily, merrily, merrily, merrily. Life is but a dream.'

Conrad snapped out of it and looked at the glass he held, the ice scoop in his other hand. 'Top-up, Nash?'

Chapter Thirty-Four

When he burst into Bronwyn's office, Nash made it clear that he was there for trouble—and Brown's face was no kinder. They didn't bother knocking and he pushed the door open, the wood slamming against the wall with a force that made Lewis jolt up from her desk in alarm. This was a sanctuary of calm and greenery and Barrow Division knew better than to burst in with anything but good energy.

'What's going on?' Lewis asked.

Nash didn't wait for an invitation to sit and pulled out a chair. 'We need to talk about Norton.' His voice was tight with barely controlled rage.

Lewis sighed, leaned back in her chair and picked up a pen to twiddle. 'Before you start, DCI Nash, I suggest you lose the attitude so we can get somewhere.'

Nash let go of some tension, 'I'm sorry but this is unacceptable. And frankly, DCS Lewis, I'm surprised you're supporting the tenure.'

Molly sat down, her eyes blazing. 'She's lost it. She's in a bad way.'

'Elaborate?' Lewis said.

'Do you know she's using?'

'I assume you're talking about Officer Norton. Go on,' The DCS neither confirmed nor denied Brown's accusation.

'This morning, I went to the bathroom and heard Blight being violently ill. She was puking her bloody guts up, and I don't mind telling you, I nearly lost my breakfast. I was going to knock to ask if she was okay when I saw she hadn't had time to lock the door. When the toilet flushed, I looked around it to see if she was okay and I saw her doing a line of coke on the cistern. Ma'am, I couldn't believe it. We've got a cop doing drugs in our station.'

Lewis didn't sound surprised or give any indication that it was news to her.

'I pulled out my cuffs to arrest her and she said you knew about it.'

'This is an internal issue and will go no further than this office. Is that understood?'

'But she can't continue to work here.'

'Is that understood?'

Brown opened her mouth and said, 'But,' then closed it again when she saw Lewis' glare. Nash interrupted with, 'Yes, ma'am.'

Brown looked at Nash as if he'd gone mad. She tried to get her point across again. 'When she came out she looked awful. She's not well.'

'We'll see that Agent Norton gets the support she needs.'

Nash had been biting his tongue. 'Come on, Bronwyn. What are you playing at? Everything about your tone and demeanour says you're giving us the brush-off. You can't ignore this.'

Brown looked Bronwyn in the eye and wouldn't back down. 'I confronted her about it, but she ignored me, splashed her face with water, and took a tablet. I'm pretty sure that was illegal, too. Does Superintendent Turner know he's brought a junkie to work on our team?'

Lewis rubbed her temples, her red nails scratched against her skin. 'Watch your mouth and remember where you are, Brown.'

Nash interjected, his voice furious. 'How can you turn a blind eye to this? It's too much. It goes way beyond deep cover. She's compromising herself, my team, and the case.'

'Nash, I'll level with you, this operation is vital. We need to gather intel, and we're aware that Blight has to go to certain lengths to secure that.'

'Certain lengths? She's snorting drugs from dirty toilets.' Nash felt a surge of anger and he was so enraged that it took him a second to get his words out. 'Are you saying you're aware of her taking illegal substances—that you condone it? At what cost? Her health? Her sanity? She's supposed to be one of us, not a liability.'

'This is a unique case. It has been handled and given clearance by our legal team working in conjunction with the IPCC. Certain protocols have been put in place by the Police and Crime Commissioner to safeguard Norton.' Lewis' tone softened. 'I know it's hard for you to understand, but Superintendent Norton went into this fully aware of her role and with her eyes open. She's been forced into regular drug use to maintain her cover, and this has caused her to become addicted over the months she's been infiltrating this gang. We have an exit arrangement in place that will take immediate effect after the case closes. Nobody is happy with the extreme boundaries of this operation, least of all her. But please. I need your absolute discretion. Norton is being as discrete as possible and you two are in the perfect position to help her and protect her well-being.'

Molly looked exasperated. 'She's spiralling. If we don't pull her out, she's going to be lost in this mess. It's not right.'

'She's working under the influence and riding that big motorbike. She could kill somebody. I don't see how the force can turn a blind eye to this,' Nash said.

Lewis shifted her gaze between them. 'We've spoken to her about that and she's assured us that she never rides her bike when she's just used.'

'And you'll take the word of a woman who's strung out on God knows what?' Nash said.

'We're so close to the end. I need you with me. Soon, we'll get Norton the help she needs. Rest assured that she's under constant medical attention and is on medication, as you saw Molly, to keep her on an even keel. You don't need to know any more than that. But you do need to be effective colleagues and support her.'

'Not easy, ma'am, she's bloody obnoxious. It'd be like trying to get close to a rattlesnake.' Molly said, crossing her arms in defiance. Nash had to agree with her.

He couldn't get his head around the fact that Bronwyn was going along with this madness. 'We need to stop this. Get her some help, now, Bronwyn. Not next week or next year. Anything but letting her destroy herself. You'll have her blood on your hands if you aren't careful.'

'I'll talk to her. I can give her a key to the disabled toilets so that she has some privacy. I had no idea she was that poorly. I have a meeting with her and Turner later, but every time she comes in it has to be in handcuffs. We'll see if there's anything else that can be done. We can't bring her in too often because it'll red flag her to the gang.'

Nash's expression was hard. 'Do it soon. Before it's too late.'
'I will. I promise.'

Lewis shifted from the frustration of having divulged more than was intended, to a sombre tone. 'What Blight is doing isn't easy. As part of her undercover work, she's taken certain substances for some time. This isn't something she wanted, but it's necessary to maintain her cover.'

Nash felt a cold chill run down his spine. 'What, weeks? Months? It sounds pretty advanced if she's sniffing up from a toilet to get through the day. How long does it take to get hooked on this rubbish?'

'Yes, Nash. It's been months, mainly while she was living in a squat with members of the criminal world in Bolton. She's been remarkable. She's sacrificing her personal health and well-being because she believes in this mission. She wants to take down Mathis and the entire operation. Despite her difficult exterior, Blight is a hero. She's putting herself on the line to stop more children dying.'

Molly's face softened, but her eyes were sceptical. 'When you put it like that. I suppose it's pretty brave.'

Lewis leaned forward. 'She's incredible. She knew what she was signing up for. She's aware of the risks, and she's committed to seeing it through. Norton's one of the best we have, and she's doing this because she knows the impact Chaos has on the streets. These drugs are destroying people and it takes a strong unit to stop them.'

Nash struggled to reconcile the image of tough, mouthy, Blight with the reality of her dedication and sacrifice. 'It's hard to see her going through this.'

'I understand, Nash,' Lewis said gently. 'But we have to trust her. She'll get the best care when this is over. We'll make sure of that. But right now, she's deep in the guts of the crisis, and she needs our support more than ever.'

Molly said she was conflicted and vented her feelings before she found a quieter space in her head. 'I get it, boss. But it's hard to be near. Can't she be moved back to Manchester and work the case from there?'

'It's hard for everybody. But remember, every time she does what she has to do, she risks her life. She's buying us time and leverage, and every bit of intel she gathers is getting us closer to shutting them down.'

Nash looked at Lewis. 'This is immoral and you're forcing me to go along with it. But, we'll support her and try to cushion her addiction from the rest of the team. We'll see this through. But the moment it's over, she gets help. No delays and no excuses or I'll take this to the IPCC myself.'

Lewis gave a grateful smile. 'She'll get the best private care.'

Nash felt an odd balance of disgust and admiration for Blight. He was disgusted at the thought of anybody taking drugs, but knowing what she was doing it for was selfless and incredible. Blight's sacrifice was immense, and it was hard watching her struggle.

Chapter Thirty-Five

Lewis looked at Brown. 'Would you mind giving us a moment alone? I need to discuss some operational details with DCI Nash.'

'No problem. I'll get back to work,' she snapped. Nash saw that Brown had wound herself up and was put out. She'd be hard work until she settled down.

Lewis waited for the door to close behind her before speaking. 'We need to talk about Friday's operation. Is everything in place for the interception?'

'All set. The Barrow squad are coordinating with GMNT, and we've put our best officers on it. But there's something you need to know about Mathis. He's been clever and has timed the drop to coincide with rush hour traffic. It's the perfect smokescreen, but there'll be mayhem on the roads. The congestion will make it harder for us to track the vehicles, and it'll give them more opportunity to slip away. We'll have to be on the ball.'

Lewis fiddled with her hair and dislodged a strand from her tight updo. 'He's a slimy piece of work, but there's no way he's scheduled this. There's somebody else at the local helm and he's always one step ahead of us.'

'Don't underestimate Mathis. He's thorough. Considering it's his livelihood, he despises anybody who takes drugs. To him, users are a lower species, a lifeform not worth considering. That's why he's happy to supply them. He has no qualms about profiting off the weaknesses of others because they deserve what they get for not being as strong as he is. He was a young addict but put himself through withdrawal. The fact that he did it without intervention makes him superior and he thinks everybody should be able to do it. However, as rotten as he is, even he has his morals. Did you know he donates a lot of money to the refugee centre he recruits from?' Nash asked.

'Another business strategy?'

'Apparently not, Blight says that it's guilt. He wants to save the ones strong enough to resist the pull of the drugs.'

'Bless him, he's a regular Robin Hood. Let's go easy on him. He can serve his stretch at Center Parcs.'

Nash pulled a face. 'Of course, I'm not suggesting that. All I'm saying is he has hidden depths and not to dismiss him too lightly.'

Lewis's expression hardened. 'It just makes him more dangerous. He has no qualms about destroying lives because he feels superior to his clients. It's a twisted justification for his actions.'

'Exactly. Twisted morals aside, he's smart and ruthless. We need to be on our game. Everything has to go well on Friday.'

Lewis stood up, pacing the room to think before wheeling around on Nash. 'Has everybody been given their positions?'

Nash refused to look away under her intense stare. 'Yes. We'll tail the traffic back between the M6 and the roundabout for Devil's Bridge. Every car will be checked in case they've changed their plans, but we know they're coming in a white Transit. Every van will be stopped and searched regardless of colour.'

'At that time of day, won't it tailback further than the motorway exit?'

'If it does it does. We'll close a lane, drop the speed to fifty, and put in traffic controls.'

'All right. I'll double-check everything on my end. You do the same. Let's be ready for whatever they throw at us.'

Nash stood. 'We'll be ready. This ends on Friday.'

With the operation looming, every decision carried pressure. Nash felt it as he stood at Lewis's desk, arguing his case. The scent of jasmine wafted through the air from an essential oil diffuser and contrasted with the smell of coffee and sweat permeating the rest of the building.

Lewis sat behind her desk moving things for symmetry as her brow furrowed listening to Nash. When satisfied with the layout, she leaned back in her chair, steepling her fingers in thought. 'Just one more thing. Is Bowes ready for this? I have reservations about him being part of the takedown. His inexperience could jeopardise the operation.'

Nash's frustration simmered just below the surface. 'I get your concerns, but Bowes has proven himself. He handled the family attack case. And he got some crucial information out of one of the kids during the interview process—if it wasn't for Bowes, we wouldn't know that the local Mr Big is a security guard. And don't forget the Ulverston Sting. He did an excellent job that night. I know he plays the fool and acts out, but he's up to the job. Bowes is shaping up to be a good cop.'

'Even so.'

'I must say, Bronwyn, your hypocrisy is off the scale. If we can overlook an officer taking illegal substances in the bathroom, I think we can let Bowes loose to do his worst.'

'I take your point, so let's not dwell on it. But be aware that one good sting and a bit of luck in an interview doesn't prepare him for something this high-stakes.'

Nash realised that Lewis wanted the last word, but he wouldn't have a member of his team put down. 'He's got the instinct we need. He might be inexperienced, but he's sharp and dedicated. He's not just lucky; he's good. And, he's got the team's trust. That's enough for me.'

Lewis was silent for a moment. 'All right, Nash. If you're confident, we'll go with your recommendation. But understand this: if Bowes' inexperience leads to any mishap, heads will roll. And yours will be the first.'

Nash nodded, feeling the tonnage of her words settle on his shoulders. 'Understood, Bronwyn. Bowes won't let us down and hopefully, your Norton won't either.'

He received the look.

Nash left Lewis' office to the fading scent of jasmine and went back to the busy operations room. As he opened the door, the noise hit him like a truck. He called Bowes over for a pep talk. The lad was capable, but the stakes had never been this important. Nash forced a smile. 'You're in, Bowes. But it's high pressure. Just know that the success of this mission is on all of us. We've got your back.'

Bowes grinned. 'Do I get to swing a gun around?'

'Good God, no. And it's those wisecracks that make us worry.'

'I'm just messing. I won't let you down, boss.'

'Don't be a dick and make me regret bringing you in on this. I've spoken up for you and put my reputation on the line. Less messing and more thinking.'

Nash saw the flash of pride on Bowes' face as they rejoined the team. Running the plan through his mind, Nash's blood pressure rose another couple of notches and he couldn't wait to get out of the office to run the stress away along the beach.

Bowes was reviewing details with Renshaw and Brown. 'How'd it go with the boss?' Brown asked Nash as he looked up from the documents spread across the table.

'Fine. Let's go over the plan again. We need to be ready for anything.'

They gathered around but Nash couldn't shake his unease. They had a solid team. Relax, he told himself.

The next few hours were spent anticipating every possible scenario and by the time they wrapped up, Nash was confident. The operation was risky, but with the right preparation, they stood a chance of bringing down one of the most dangerous drug operations in the country.

Jerod Mathis, the second in command of the supply chain for everything north of Manchester, was only a secondary target, but Nash wanted to take the slimy git down. However, the shadowy figure above Mathis was the real kingpin orchestrating this end of the operation. He was a mystery. They found out that he'd come into town recently to oversee the distribution. It irked Nash that they had no solid leads on his identity. He didn't like loose ends, and this one added a new level of complexity to the sting. Stray ends brought the possibility of danger.

Nash had pulled the files on members of Jerod's gang and sat at his desk. They'd interviewed the low-level operatives, but all they knew was that the mysterious boss masqueraded as a security guard. It was too vague. The team was cross-referencing every business that used them, from pubs to the job centre. 'As if he's going to take a job there,' Molly had laughed. 'That would be brazen.'

'Exactly,' Bowes argued. 'If he's ballsy enough, that's exactly the type of place he'd put himself. Where better to find kids needing a bit of coin?'

Nash spread mugshots and notes across his desk, trying to join some dots.

Patel was cross-referencing the SIA licence database. Every security guard in the country was supposed to do this training. It wasn't foolproof, and people slipped through the net with fake certificates, but there was every likelihood that their man was listed.

Renshaw put his head around the door and sensed Nash's agitation. 'Any luck, boss?' he asked, as Nash motioned him into the office.

'Not much. We know Mathis is second in command, but this guy above him is a loose cannon. We've got to identify him before Friday. Every time we interview one of these low-level thugs, it's the same story. He looms large over them as the ultimate threat, but none of the street crews claim to have ever seen him.

Phil Renshaw leaned over the desk to look. 'He could blend in anywhere. He might be a bouncer at one of the clubs or a warehouse guard, even working at one of those posh estates in the Lakes.'

Nash drummed his fingers on the desk. 'No, we know he's based in Barrow. That much we do have, but that's what makes it difficult. We don't have a name. He's faceless and we've nothing concrete to go on. Timing the drop to coincide with rush hour traffic gives them perfect cover and tracking them will be chaos, every pun intended. Thank you very much.' He winked.

'But what we do have is methodology. He's probably insinuated himself into a place with kids. We should concentrate on venues that bring him into contact with young people,' Bowes said. Give a lad a bit of praise and he'll shine, Nash thought.

'We need to change our approach. If we can't identify him, we should tighten the net on the people around him. Someone has to know more than they're letting on. Let's bring them all in again and turn up the heat.'

Nash considered the suggestion. 'We've only got two days. Is it throwing good resources after bad?' he asked.

Molly disagreed with the suggestion. 'The local scallies have given us what they've got. If they had more, one of them would have broken. Boss, we've got to find this guy. We should focus on staking places where security guards come into contact with young people, like job agencies, local bars and cinemas.'

'That's a better idea, Brown. At least it's a start. We're cross-checking the lists of known associates with employees at these places. It's a long shot, but it might give us something.'

Molly nodded. 'I'll work with the guys on it. We need every angle covered. Barrow isn't that big, and this man's hiding in plain sight.'

'Has there been any word on the cook now that we have a name for him?'

Renshaw answered. 'We only have the nickname, Acetone, but GMNT thinks they've tracked him down. They've got eyes on and he'll be taken in with the big fish, as soon as we have the shipment. Manchester will be on standby.'

Nash felt good as he left to take up the new lines of investigation. They had to find the local head of distribution. The two dealers on the next tier down from him had been squeezed until they squeaked but didn't give anything up. Nash had surveillance on them, but they were probably onto it as they hadn't put a foot wrong in over a week. The station's overtime hours were racking up to terrifying proportions and every hour had to be justified.

Mathis was slippery, but the real mastermind around town was even more dangerous. The clock was ticking, and they had forty-eight hours to uncover his identity before the drop that Friday.

As they delved into the files, scouring for any missed detail that could lead them to Mr Big, Nash had a niggle in his gut. He remembered a security guard acting out of character and accessed his memory training for the penny to drop. He called Renshaw and Brown and told them to bring Russ Lee in. He was the security guard involved in the disturbance outside the supermarket two weeks earlier. The lad was a little scroat barely out of nappies, but the more Nash thought about it, the more he felt that Lee had been on something that day. But, their Mr Big? Surely not. He pulled the records to check the details of the incident.

Chapter Thirty-Six

Nash was being swallowed by a stack of paperwork when Lawson knocked and burst into his office.

'Sir, someone's asking for you at the front desk. They're causing a disturbance,' Lawson blurted out.

Nash put his pen down and locked the confidential files he'd been working on in the top drawer of his filing cabinet beside the bottle of good malt that only came out at the end of every successful case. 'Who is it?'

'I don't know, but she's upset.'

'Thanks, Paul. Tell her I'll be right out.'

Lawson walked away, leaving the door open for his boss to follow. Nash heard him humming a song, but couldn't remember where he'd heard it recently. It took him a second to put words to the childish tune. Row, row, row your boat. For goodness sake, it was like working in a preschool. He put it out of his mind.

As he rushed to the front desk, he was aware of a woman's voice raised in distress. He opened the door separating calm from the rabble of noise and saw Zola with tears streaming down her face. Honey was by her side, equally upset. The poor kid looked terrified and buried her face in her mother's leg. But that didn't prevent Nash from seeing the cut on her cheek and a bruise forming. If somebody had hurt her he'd have them locked up for a long time. The sight of them looking so traumatised infuriated him.

'Nash. Get my dad,' Zola screamed when she saw him. 'You have to do something to get Serena out of here. They've locked her up.'

Nash didn't understand. He motioned for Lawson to clear the area of onlookers and drew Zola and Honey away, his tone calm but firm. 'Zola, let's take this somewhere private and we'll sort it out.'

He led them to a visitor's room, a small space designed to be comforting, with soft lighting and cosy chairs. He picked up the remote control to put the cartoon channel on and to give Zola a minute to compose herself. After pressing buttons and getting nowhere, he gave up in disgust. 'Too many damned choices,' he said.

Zola collapsed into one of the chairs, her sobs wracking her body, while Honey sat beside her with silent tears streaking down her face. He handed Zola the box of tissues from the table and pressed the remote control into her other hand. She needed to pull herself together for Honey's sake and distracting her with a task was a good place to start. 'Here, find the Disney channel, for Honey, please. It's beyond me.'

'I'll do it, Mum,' Honey said, giving Nash a look reminiscent of Bronwyn Lewis's worst despairing glance. He got it—old people.

Nash pulled up a chair and sat facing them. He waited until Honey shuffled to the end of the sofa, put her thumb in her mouth and was absorbed in *The New Adventures of Winnie the Pooh*.

'Zola, I need you to tell me what happened.'

Zola tried to steady herself and wipe her tears. 'It's Serena. They say it's drugs, Nash. She got into trouble at school. My little girl was involved in a fight, and they called the police. It's not like her. You know that.' He patted her hand but let her talk it out. 'When I got there, they'd already taken her away. I had no idea that the person she'd hit was Honey. I can't believe it.'

Neither could Nash. That shocked him and he didn't hide his reaction in time. He sucked in air through his teeth and Honey looked up from the sofa. As her thumb left her mouth, it made a popping sound. She rubbed her cheek. 'Serena hit me,' she lisped.

Bowes tapped and came in with a bowl of ice cream. 'I heard that there was a brave little girl in here who likes Raspberry Ripple.' Nash shot him a grateful look as he left.

Zola looked traumatised but Honey was comfortable. With the arrival of ice cream and her TV programme, she was resilient and had bounced back the way youngsters do, but adults have forgotten how to.

'Serena's only eleven, Nash. She doesn't belong in a cell,' Zola said.

He leaned forward, his voice gentle. 'I know you're scared. But at least I can take that away for you. Serena isn't in a cell. She'll be with a female officer in a room like this one. They're designed to be safe and comforting. I know she's a good kid, so don't worry. We just need to figure out what happened.'

Zola shook her head, tears still flowing. 'She shouldn't be here at all. What's happening to us?' She dropped her voice to a whisper. 'Drugs, Silas. Drugs.'

Honey spoke, her voice small and shaky. 'They hurt Serena. One of the boys threw a rock at her. She was trying to protect me. They said bad words. Racist words, like the ones you told me about, Mum. And then Serena got mad.'

Nash felt protective at the thought of anyone hurting the girls. He patted Honey's knee, and took Zola's hand, squeezing it. 'We'll get to the bottom of this. Kelvin's on his way and we'll sort it out together.'

When Kelvin rushed in, his face was heavy with worry as he looked at his daughter. 'I'm here, sweetheart. It's okay. We'll get Serena out, I promise.' He glared at Nash as though it was his fault and then seemed to see the error of his ways and reached for his hand.

Nash glanced at the camera on the wall and pulled his hand away from Kelvin's. It didn't go unnoticed by his partner.

Zola clung to her dad, her sobs subsiding and Nash stood up, giving Kelvin a nod rather than his touch. 'We need to stay calm and figure this out. Serena's in the family room with an officer. We'll iron out the details and find out what happened.'

Nash's expression was serious but kind. 'I need you to trust me, Zola. We're going to fix this. Serena will be allowed to go home soon, okay? We just need to take her statement.'

The woman was terrified. Nash saw the toll it was taking on her. She'd lost weight. His trained eye took in more details. Her hair hadn't been oiled and was more frizzy than usual. She was particular about her nails, but one was broken, the gold varnish chipped. In trying her damndest to keep her children safe she'd forgotten to look after herself. He wondered how Greg was coping.

Zola nodded, her eyes red and puffy. 'Okay.'

Chapter Thirty-Seven

Nash went to the family room where they interviewed children. Who were the boys that hurt Serena and Honey?

When he reached the juvenile holding area, he was met by Officer Patel, a seasoned officer with a calm demeanour. 'Sir, good to see you. I heard about Serena. She's with Officer Woods. But with respect, given your conflict of interest, you know you can't be directly involved, right?'

'Yes, but I can be her responsible adult, there's no law against that and I won't interfere with the case.'

Patel looked dubious, while not breaking any rules, it was a grey area. But Nash was his superior, and he smiled and patted his shoulder. 'You know how this goes, sir. Other than stating your name for the tape, you won't be allowed to intervene.'

Nash nodded. 'Thanks, Mo. Can you fill me in on what happened?'

'From what we gather, there was an altercation outside the school. Some boys were bullying Honey as she waited for her sister. Serena had been held up in the cloakroom, we can imagine what for, and she was late getting to the junior school to pick Honey up. It's just around the corner and they were allowed to walk home together. It's only five minutes away.'

Nash thought he detected disapproval in Patel's tone, but when he looked up, Mo smiled at him. He understood how hard this was.

'When Serena didn't turn up, rather than telling a teacher, Honey wandered off to find her. Things escalated and turned nasty outside the gates. The staff called us when it got physical. But by the time we arrived, Serena had a bloody nose and was pretty shaken up.'

Nash clenched his fists, anger bubbling inside him. 'And the boys?'

'They're being dealt with,' Patel assured him. 'I've got kids, Nash, and I could kill the bullies that did this. But Serena threw the first punch, so they soon backed off.'

'How did Honey get hurt?'

'Clammed up like a crustacean. But the older kid's got some anger issues, Boss.'

Nash tried to control his frustration. 'Brown's going to interview her. But can I have a word to tell her it's okay and that her Mum and Grandad are outside?'

'Course you can, boss. But please don't put me in an awkward position.'

Nash patted him on the arm. 'You got it.'

Serena looked small and scared in the big chair, and Nash's heart ached at the sight of her.

'Serena,' he said, stepping into the room. 'It's okay, I'm here.'

Serena looked up, her eyes wide with fear and ran into his arms. 'Grandad Si.'

He sat her down and knelt beside her, taking her small hands in his. She'd never called him that before and he could only imagine what Imani would make of it. But the warmth in his chest was an unfamiliar feeling he'd never experienced. 'Your mum's here to take you home, okay? But first, we need to know what happened. You don't have to tell me, though. My good friend, Molly, is coming to talk to you, and you've been getting to know Jackie, haven't you? She can stay too if you like.' He smiled at Woods.

Serena sniffled, her voice trembling. 'They were picking on Honey. I told them to stop, but they wouldn't. One of them threw a rock at her, and I hit him. I didn't mean to hurt anyone, I just wanted them to stop.'

Nash nodded, his heart breaking for her. 'But that wasn't all that happened was it, sweetheart? Something happened to Honey didn't it?'

'No,' Serena dropped her head and played with her fingers in her lap.

'Molly's going to come to talk to you about that. But you don't have to worry, she's nice, and it's all going to be okay.' Woods stepped over her rank to flash him a warning look. Nash could jeopardise the case if he got involved with this witness.

He left them to it, but not until she was playing Roblox with Jackie Woods, and was laughing. He went back to his office with a heavy heart. Serena's involvement in a fight was troubling, but there was more to the story. Patel was waiting for him in the corridor.

'Any updates?' Nash asked.

Mo nodded, looking grim. 'We got some new information out of the mother. It turns out that Serena wasn't defending Honey. She hit her sister herself.'

'Yeah, I know. They told me.'

'That's not all, Nash. Not by a long chalk. The eldest one forced that little tot to hide drugs in her schoolbag.'

Nash felt a cold knot tighten in his stomach. 'Chaos? Zola had said as much but they couldn't talk in front of Serena. Where did it come from?'

Mo sighed. 'From a dealer higher up the chain.'

Nash balled his fists before he had time to think about it, but he kept them at his sides. 'Steady, Patel. You're very close to crossing the line there. Serena is not a dealer.'

'Not by choice, of course not. But, like all the kids out there, she was following orders, Nash. They forced her to deliver the drugs and she panicked.'

'That's as maybe, but watch your choice of words, Patel.'

He put his hand on Nash's arm in an expression of understanding. 'We know she didn't want to. When her sister said she'd tell her mother about them delivering drugs, Serena was scared and hit out. Then she hid the gear in Honey's bag. The poor kid's as much a victim in this as her sister.'

'Thank you, Mo.' He ran a hand through his hair, frustration boiling under his skin. He had a hunch that the kids had been caught up in something bigger than schoolyard bullying. Especially after Nikki Moor, the girl who had to hide in a workman's van had almost got herself killed by these thugs.

After Patel left, Nash went to his office, drew his blinds, and sat quietly with his fingers steepled on the desk. He wasn't aware of thinking about Max, but he felt his presence. Sometimes he could hear him without Snow acting as a conduit. It was probably his mind telling him what Max would do in this situation, but he heard it as clearly as when Mo Patel had spoken to him.

Now what, Si?

'I've no idea.'

Noah's here. He says you've got to stop them.

'God dammit. Can't you see I'm trying?'

Okay. Keep your hair on.

'Is it going to work on Friday, Max?'

What am I, a tea-reading gypsy?

'A pain in the arse is what you are.'

Here, give the kid this. It'll help.

A blue teddy with a Pride-coloured heart that the team had given him, tottered, wobbled, teetered, and fell face-first from the top of his bookcase. Nash had no idea what the hell it was doing on display. He kept it hidden in his cupboard, the world didn't need to know his business. He scooped it up and opened the cupboard door, but the soft fur soothed him. It would do the same for Honey.

'Thanks, Max,' he said. And felt stupid talking to himself.

Tell them it's to share or Serena will feel excluded.

'You should have provided another one, then.'

One day, my friend, we will sit down and I'll tell you how this ghosting gig works.

'You can sit down? You'll tell me you stand up to pee, next.'

Max was gone—or Nash had cleared his mind.

Back in the visitor's room, Kelvin was holding Zola, while Honey was engrossed in the TV, but she had red-rimmed eyes and still looked scared. An empty crisp packet had joined the empty ice cream bowl. When Nash went in, he held the teddy out to her. Honey grinned, the shine of the bruise standing out on her cheek. Her sister had some right hook. Honey grasped the teddy tight and hugged it to her chest. Her thumb found its way back to her mouth. Nash thought she was too old for thumb-sucking and wondered if it was a recent habit. Children often regressed to an easier time when they were traumatised.

He was shocked when she mumbled the row boat song, she must have heard Renshaw humming it, or he heard her—but Nash didn't think Honey had come into contact with him.

He reassured Zola that all was well and within minutes, while they talked, Honey was asleep with her sore cheek resting on the blue bear.

'Serena's okay,' Nash said, giving Zola a reassuring smile. 'But she's a confused and angry little girl and she's going to need some help to get her over this.'

Kelvin's face darkened. 'What do you mean, Si?'

'She may need counselling when this is over. We can make a referral if you need it.'

Kelvin nodded his thanks.

'They hurt my girls,' Zola whispered, her voice trembling. 'They made them do terrible things. How could they do that?'

'We've got those boys but we're going to find out who's behind this,' Nash said. 'For now, we need to keep Serena and Honey safe. It's half term in a week, so I suggest you keep them off school until then. I'll square it officially, so don't worry about that. When's Greg due home?'

'He's on his way.'

'Good.'

Kelvin nodded, his jaw set. 'Thank you, Si. I know you'll keep them safe.'

As they left the station, Nash was determined to protect Kelvin's family. When they went outside for some fresh air, Nash put his arm around Kelvin's shoulder. But only for a minute until he shuffled his hand back into his pocket. Kelvin said he understood how conflicted Nash was with being a gay man in that environment. Kelvin tried to get it.

Nash smiled, 'Serena called me grandad,' he said.

Chapter Thirty-Eight

Nash spoke to Brown as he collared her eating a cream cake in the staff room. He marvelled at how much rubbish that woman could eat without putting on an ounce. He only had to look at her cake to need an extra hour in the gym. He didn't eat junk and worked out most mornings before his shift. He was in good shape and intended to stay that way. He'd even spoken to Kelvin about doing the 40-mile K2B run the following May. He pulled himself out of his thoughts. He was smiling at the memory of Kelvin's look of horror at the thought of the Keswick to Barrow race.

'Brown, I need you to conduct the taped interview with Serena. She trusts you, so she'll be more likely to open up.'

Brown stuffed the last piece of choux bun in her mouth. 'Of course. I'll wash my hands and be with you.'

As she was going, Blight strode to her locker with a rucksack over her shoulder. She barged into their conversation without any polite niceties.

'Renshaw just told me about the new witness. Nash, I need to interview the girl. Let me handle it.'

The girl. Nash bristled. She didn't even know Serena's name without looking at the file in her hand. Blight looked awful. She was shaking and had a sheen of sweat over her face that looked greasy.

Molly's nose turned red with fury. 'Are you serious? After what I saw in the bathroom, you want to talk to a vulnerable child? You still think you can swoop in and take over.'

Blight cast a shifty look at Nash, who held up his hand to referee. He wanted to appease Brown but turned to Blight. 'Why do you think you should take the interview, Keeley?'

'Jesus. How many times? It's Blight. You need to use my street name. It's not difficult. Look, I know what the kid's going through. I can relate to her. And I think she'll respond to me better than anyone else right now.'

'I don't know, she's fragile,' Nash said.

'Who do you think tipped you off about Shelly Myers and the Gibsons, and you didn't even act on that in time?'

Nash remembered the note left on his desk and was shocked.

Molly scoffed, crossing her arms over her chest. 'This is ridiculous. She's a child, not one of your informants. And after what you did to that girl in the pub, you're not fit to be around children.'

Nash thought Molly was about to combust. She was right to be furious, but something in Blight's expression made him pause.

Give her a chance. She needs to prove herself.

'All right, you can do the interview. But don't mess this up. Serena's been through enough.'

Blight nodded and turned her back on Brown. If she knew about Nash's connection to Serena, she didn't let on. 'Let me just remind you who is SO here. I don't need your permission Nash but you chose the right girl for the job.'

Molly's mouth fell open. 'You can't be serious. Blight's been compromised. She's in no state to handle this.'

Blight ignored Molly's outburst. 'I'll get changed and be back in a minute.'

Molly was apoplectic. 'She's not stable, and she's going to make things worse. What was all that creeping up your arse about?'

Nash rubbed the back of his neck. 'I know you're angry, Molly, and you have every right. But Blight has a point. She might connect with Serena in a way we can't. Give her this chance.'

Molly shook her head. 'How many chances do you expect me to give her? You saw the state she's in. The woman's a mess. She's strung out. You know damned well that, "Be back in a minute" means she's going to do a couple of lines in her private toilet. I hope you know what you're doing, Nash, for Serena's sake.'

When Blight left the disabled toilet and locked the door behind her, she was like a different woman. Nobody had seen her in anything but the skintight leather suit, more suited to an adult video than a serious biker. But her face was scrubbed clean until it shone across her cheekbones. The sheen of greasy sweat was gone and she smelled of handwash. She wore capri jeans, a simple hoodie, and trainers. The rose tattoo Snow had told them to look for wrapped around her ankle and disappeared up the hem of her jeans.

Brown went for the jugular. 'My god, I thought the gimp suit was glued on. It was about time you washed. I don't reckon much to your hygiene regime.' She made a point of turning her back as Blight had done to her and she leaned against the booking desk.

Nash sighed but didn't have time to react before Blight made her move.

She charged across the room at Brown.

Caught by surprise and expecting an assault, Brown straightened and turned raising her arms. Blight stopped with the precision of a thrown knife an inch from Brown's face. She brought up her hands, wagged them in front of the lower-ranking officer's eyes, and shouted, 'Boo.'

Brown squealed, stepped backwards, overbalanced and fell into the swivel seat beside the desk. Blight grabbed both arms of the chair and Brown had to plant her feet on the floor to stop Blight from spinning her around.

'Stay in your lane, bitch.'

'What?' Brown asked. Her voice was feeble.

'Get out of my face,' Blight hissed, 'and I'll stay out of yours. Last time of telling before you get put on a charge. I am your superior officer.'

'That's enough,' Nash said. 'Blight. Your witness is waiting, ma'am.'

Nash watched as she disappeared down the hallway, her backside swaying and her long legs moving to their own beat. Blight was trouble, but damn, she was a fine woman. Even he could see that. There were going to be fireworks between those two. They'd been one-all before she went into the bathroom, but Blight had to make it a two-one advantage in her favour. She reminded Nash of a young Cher. But brass neck aside, he hoped he hadn't made a mistake by trusting her with the delicate interview.

Minutes later, while Nash was still facing the brunt of Brown's fury, Blight reappeared with a Jigsaw tucked under her arm. She put the index and middle fingers of both hands into her mouth and whistled at Brown as if she was calling a dog. Nash winced.

'Well, are you coming or what? This bastard's got two hundred pieces, and I've got the patience for about two of them. You seem like a jigsaw type of girl, to me. Dowdy.'

'Me?' Brown said. She looked at her clothing as though that explained the jigsaw remark.

'Duh. You wanted in, didn't you? And the kid knows you. Ready?' Blight asked. Her voice was steadier than her appearance suggested. She wiped her arm across her forehead.

'Yeah, sure,' Brown replied. 'Just try not to scare her, all right?'

Blight didn't bite back when they got to the children's room. But her expression softened as she pushed the door open and smiled at Serena.

Nash watched them go, feeling the tension between his staff like a physical weight. Brown was furious but he understood Blight's ability to connect with Serena. Kids would either love her or be scared stiff. Time would tell if he'd made the right call.

Chapter Thirty-Nine

Nash watched through the two-way mirror from the room next door and turned the microphone on. Serena sat on the couch, her knees pulled up to her chest and he heard Blight telling Brown to take a chair by the door. The room was designed to be comforting, with pastel walls, plush toys, and soft lighting. Despite the welcoming environment, Serena's face was pale, and her eyes were red-rimmed from crying.

'Hey, Serena,' Blight said. So she did know her name without looking at the file. 'I'm Keeley. Can I sit with you?'

Serena nodded, her eyes darting to the door as if expecting someone else to come in. Blight moved slowly. She sat on the edge of the couch, giving Serena plenty of space.

She didn't look at her or speak again until she had emptied the jigsaw onto the coffee table and started looking for straight edges. When it was clear what she was doing without needing to give instructions, she passed a pile across the teak tabletop and left them in front of Serena.

She still didn't speak and Serena didn't move, but Nash was aware of her watching Blight with curiosity. She found the first corner and held it to Serena.

'Thanks,' Serena's voice was tiny—a whisper, but at least she'd spoken. The technique rested on the witness speaking first. The piece was blue, a flash of sky that fit in one of two places. Serena laid the first piece in position on the table. Blight had allowed her to make a decision and take charge and then she spoke as Serena sifted through her pile for more edges.

'See her over there? That Molly? I bet you like her, don't you?'

She didn't look up but Nash saw Serena nodding.

'Well kid, there's no accounting for taste. I suppose somebody's got to like her and it might as well be you. But, damn, she's a lazy one. She'll sit there all day if you let her. Shifty eyes if you ask me, but I reckon you should tell her to pull up her chair and give us a hand.'

Nash smiled. Her approach was good. Every time she put Serena in a position where she had to take action, the little girl would grow in confidence. The aim was to draw her out until she had the courage to talk.

Serena's face brightened and she waved Brown over. Nash saw the eleven-year-old relax, she was at ease with Brown there, too. He was impressed. Blight carried on talking. It was a gentle tone floating across the movement of Molly coming over and joining in. The vibe was simple. No big deal here. Just three girls, shooting the breeze.

'I know you're scared.' Blight's voice was soft. 'But I promise, we're here to help you.' She pointed at Molly. 'Even her and they reckon she's not as useless as she looks. She can take a man down as big as your daddy.'

'Do you know my dad?' Serena found her voice.

'Well, no. Okay, so not your dad, but I bet Molly the Moo Cow could take down all the bad guys in Barrow with one punch.'

Serena giggled. 'Not all of them.'

'Hell yeah, man. Don't let that floppy wrist and dopey expression fool you. She's a ninja.'

Molly glared at her, and Blight kept up her chat. 'Whatever happened today, it's not the end of the world. It's not like running out of Cheesy Wotsits. Come on, now that would be a big deal. Right?' She put up her hand to high-five, and Serena didn't leave her hanging. 'Atta girl. We can figure it out together, okay?' she said.

'Am I going to prison?'

Serena's lip wobbled and Molly jumped in. 'No love. We just want to find out what happened. Your mum's outside waiting for you.'

Molly reached across and touched Serena's hand, but it was Blight that she looked to for confirmation. 'Yeah,' Blight said, attaching a row of three pieces to Serena's sky. 'What she said, but not as wet.'

Serena nodded, but she didn't speak. Blight kept her tone reassuring. 'We get that things have been tough. And we know they made you do things you didn't want to. They made you very angry. I get it. I'd want to high-five them...' Serena looked up startled, but Blight kept talking in the same flat tone. '...in the face with a chair.' She winked and Serena laughed. 'You feel like you're stuck and there's no way out. But there is, Serena. We just need to talk about what's been going on, so we can help you.'

Brown had cottoned on to the jigsaw distraction. She gave Serena a puzzle piece and pointed to a vertical run of clouds.

Serena looked at Blight, her eyes filled with fear. 'You're not like the others,' she whispered. 'You don't talk like a police lady.'

Blight smiled gently. 'That's because I'm not just a cop today. I'm your friend. And Honey—no, that's your sister—and Serena, when you've got Keeley Norton as your friend, you can do any damn thing you want to. I want to understand what you're going through. Can you tell me what happened today?' While Nash didn't condone her poking Brown or some of her colourful language, it warmed his heart to see Serena laughing and opening to her. A softer approach would have made the girl break down until she felt too small to speak.

Serena's eyes welled up with tears, and she shook her head.

'No? You can't tell me? Oh sister, we need to find that voice of yours. Put that jigsaw down and stand up. And you, slacker. Come on. Up you get. Molly, your ass will turn to lard sitting on it all day.'

They all stood up.

'We are lionesses.' Blight said in a loud voice. She looked at them and

raised her hands and her voice.

'We are lionesses.'

They didn't respond.

She waved her arms in the air.

'Come on. We are lionesses.'

Molly joined in and Serena giggled. Blight made claws of her hands and Molly copied her. This time Serena joined in. They said, 'We are lionesses,' three more times.

'Let's shake this station up. Are we ready to roar?' Molly looked doubtful, but Serena was all over it. Buoyed with excitement she shook her hands and was the first to roar. Blight and Molly had to play catchup and soon faces appeared at the square window in the door to see what was going on. The team had piled into the surveillance room to watch. Blight led them in a lion dance around the room. Nash saw the blush on Molly's face and guessed that she knew her colleagues were watching her from behind the mirror. She'd get some ribbing for this. When they had worn themselves out, they sat down and Blight motioned to the jigsaw. 'Never leave a job half done. Now then, Miss Serena, who has been messing with my lioness?'

Her voice was shaky and Blight clawed the air. Serena raised her voice. 'They made me do it. They said if I didn't, they'd hurt me and Honey. I didn't want to, but they forced me. They wanted me to put the stuff in her bag because it would be safer than mine as she's younger.'

Blight nodded her expression serious but understanding. 'Did they make you hit her, too?'

Serena started crying and Brown gave Blight a warning look.

Serena shook her head. 'No. Honey's only little, but she knew it was bad stuff. She wouldn't take it, and we had to go to people's houses and give it to big men. It was scary and Honey didn't like it. Dave and Joey were across the street watching, and Honey was shouting at me and making people look. I was scared Sir would hear and come out of my school because Dave and Joey would be mad, and then they'd hit her more than I could. My little sister's got a real big voice. I was scared and I panicked. So I hit her to make her do it.'

'You poor thing.' Blight touched Serena's knee. 'Who made you do it, Serena? Can you tell me their full names?'

Serena glanced at the door again and Blight moved her comforting hand to her arm. 'It's okay. You're safe here. Nobody can hurt you now.'

'Dave Roberts and I don't know Joey's other name,' Serena whispered. 'They told me to hide the drugs in Honey's bag. They said if I didn't, they'd hurt her. But, it was me. I hurt her.'

Nash's heart ached for her.

'Thank you for telling me, Serena. You've been very brave. We're going to make sure Dave and Joey can't hurt you or Honey ever again. But I need you to be honest with us about everything, okay?' Blight said.

Serena nodded, tears streaming down her face. 'Okay.'

Blight continued the interview, gently guiding Serena through her story. They drew a map together and Blight made it fun adding the houses that the sisters visited. 'Like Dora the Explorer on an adventure,' she said.

When she was sure Blight had Serena's confidence, Brown excused herself and slipped out to join Nash who was still watching through the mirror. Blight was getting excellent intel.

'She's doing well,' Nash murmured, more to himself than Brown.

'She's brilliant,' Brown said, surprising both of them. As the interview progressed, Nash noticed that Blight's tremor lessened as she concentrated on the job.

When Blight let Jackie Woods in to take Serena to her mum, she looked drained but relieved that she'd got what they needed. As she came out, she glanced at Nash, who gave her a nod of approval. Molly was still sulking but muttered a grudging, 'Good job. You did great.'

'We did great. We're a team,' Blight said.

She managed a faint smile before heading towards the disabled toilet. Brown said she probably needed a moment to collect herself after the emotional ordeal. And this time when she smiled, it was without malice. 'She was amazing with Serena. But my stance on this hasn't changed, Boss. She doesn't fit in here,' she said.

'I know.'

Chapter Forty

Nash felt ridiculous. The stupid Pudsey Bear hat perched on his head was itching, and he fought the urge to scratch. Outside the briefing room, a poster read Children in Need with instructions on making Nash look like an imbecile. A yellow bucket sat on a table next to the poster, with some donations from his team covering the bottom. As they trooped in, they deposited their contribution and pointed to the activity they wanted Nash to perform with them.

Patel was kind and chose a fist bump with a glitter-fingers cascade. That was painless. Bowes, being Bowes, demanded a squeezy cuddle that nearly cracked Nash's ribs. But the worst offender so far had been Brown, who insisted on doing the Cheeky Girls dance with him. The memory of his awkward, flailing movements alongside her smooth gyrations made him cringe.

Blight, was a different story. She strode past the bucket without a glance, muttering, 'What is this, Kindergarten?' Her disdain was palpable.

'The fun sponge has arrived,' Molly said and Nash sighed, knowing he'd hear about her opinion later, and in a more direct manner.

Lewis and Turner had similar posters outside their offices. They embraced the spirit of the day with good humour, but varying degrees of reluctance. Blight, had been given a storage area to use as a makeshift office—her rank dictated one. Her poster was covered in red marker with the scrawled addition, Don't even think about it. Losers.

Nash had reason to go to her office once—that was enough. It was an OCD sufferer's worst nightmare. Official files bore coffee rings, which offended him enough, but the mess, the disorder, the rubbish and the half-eaten sandwich made him want to run. She'd aimed paper and tissues at the waste bin, missed, and left them in a semi-circle around it. His face must have shown his disdain because she was quick to bite at him. 'I don't like organised. I want it to look like craziness dropped in and threw up in my filing cabinet,' she said.

This morning, the incident room filled for his briefing and Nash appreciated the camaraderie. Despite the embarrassment, the team had come together for a good cause. It reminded him what he'd put together and built, and why he loved this job. Even when the stakes were high and the stress was nearly unbearable, it was better than anything else he could imagine.

Nash addressed the room. 'Listen up, team. Thank you for your contributions. I think we might have beaten last year's effort, and if we haven't I'll make up the difference myself.'

'And starve all those moths in your wallet, boss. That's cruel,'

'And that merciless jibe has just cost you another quid, Bowes. Go on. Walk of shame. In the bucket.' Bowes checked his pockets, walked to the bin and dropped all his loose change in 'Now I can take the mick out of you all day, sir.'

'My cross to bear, Bowes, and all in a good cause. Now, let's get down to business.'

The shift in the atmosphere was immediate. The team straightened in their chairs, the playful grins replaced with focused expressions. Nash removed his hat and set it aside. The briefing was critical as a precursor to the sting scheduled for the next day and there was no leeway for jovial distractions. They had little time and a lot of ground to cover.

He outlined the plan, detailing roles and responsibilities and ensuring every member knew their part. The information gathered from dozens of interviews was invaluable—it was time to act, and it had been a long time coming. The team were pumped. Nash felt the familiar surge of adrenaline.

After the briefing, the team dispersed to finalise preparations. Nash saw Blight coming and tried to escape, but she cornered him. The woman was terrifying. She crossed her arms and raised an eyebrow. 'You know this isn't a circus, right?'

Nash chuckled. 'Sometimes a bit of fun helps keep the stress at bay.'

'Make sure you're focused tomorrow. You won't be needing the stupid hat—or a dick stuck to the middle of your forehead.'

Nash was only used to being outranked by Lewis, and she was enough to cope with, but he couldn't suppress a grin. Blight was his personal nightmare, sent to make his life a misery, but there was a tiny flame, somewhere inside him that said he should like her. He fought the urge and took in her appearance. Gaunt. She looked more like an addict with every passing day.

'And I thought I was the party pooper. Are you, okay? Can I do anything?'

She straightened her posture and pushed back her shoulders. 'I'm fine. Hanging in there.' She smiled and Nash saw appreciation for his concern. Despite her noble reasons, Nash had seen the stigma around the station—the looks.

Everybody knew about her addiction now, the cat was well out of the bag. They could see the decline in her physical health, and Nash could only imagine what it was doing to her mentally. They all knew the good place it came from, but still, there was that desire to distance yourself from it as though it could be catching.

He put his hand on her shoulder and she inclined her cheek onto it. A moment of vulnerability but it was less than a second before she walked away.

He had faith in his team. They rose to any challenge and Blight was a short-term asset. He'd never admit it, not even if somebody pulled his nails out with pliers, but he'd miss her when she was gone. He returned to his desk to tackle the mountain of work that had greeted him at seven that morning. Laughter somewhere in the station warmed his spirit.

He was late home. Not knowing when he'd get away, he'd rung Kelvin from behind a mile of folders and asked him to hold dinner and they'd make it together when he got in. But he opened his door to the comforting aroma of spaghetti sauce and was overcome with gratitude. Kelvin met him with a garlic kiss and packed him off to the shower. Nash was too tired to suggest Kelvin join him and luxuriated under the too-hot water.

Kelvin was busy in the kitchen when he came down in loungewear. Their playful banter filled the room and Nash knew what total happiness felt like. He appreciated the normalcy of home life after a job that was anything but. He'd spent years alone, and then two more in a toxic relationship. He never expected this life, and, even now, he expected to wake up to days where work was all he had.

Kelvin laughed and said interfering was in Nash's bones when he went to the stove and stirred the sauce before tasting it.

'Needs more pepper,' Nash said. He reached for the mill. Then froze.

Row, row, row your boat.

He turned to the sound and saw Noah Ross in the corner of the room. He was smiling at Silas, and his legs were intact. The prosthetic blade was gone. Nash blinked, and during that heartbeat, Noah disappeared.

Confused and unsettled, Nash heard the second line of the children's song and turned to see Max in the other corner. His eyes bore into him, *You need some shopping, Nash.*

Nash frowned, trying to decipher the cryptic message. Before he could answer Max had vanished.

Kel caught on to Nash's tension. 'Was that Max?' he asked.

Nash nodded. 'Yes. But I'm too tired to talk ghost rubbish tonight. Come on, let's get dinner on trays. It smells amazing.'

Nash ground some pepper and picked up his spoon, dipping it into the sauce for a taste. He almost spat it out and grimaced. What had been delicious a minute before was inedible. He saw the salt cellar beside him. It was empty. Somehow the entire contents had been dumped into the pot, ruining the meal.

You need to go shopping.

'Damn it, Max,' Nash muttered. 'God, it's like having a child around. You're even more of a dickhead now than when you were alive. What did you do that for?'

He waited for Max to respond but there was nothing. It was November and a draught blew under the kitchen door. But it was just a draught. 'He's ruined dinner,' he said to Kelvin holding up the empty salt pot.

'Why would he do that?' Kelvin looked suspicious and Nash knew he was concerned for his state of mind. More than once, Kelvin had put Max coming through to Nash down to the stress of the job.

'Why does he do anything? Because he's a dick? Because he's bored? You tell me. I'll nip to Star Select and get a chicken from their hot food counter. And some coleslaw and crusty bread will go nicely with it.' Nash paused. It looks like I'm going out after all.

'I'll go,' Kelvin said.

Nash was already putting his coat on. 'No. I won't be long. You stay here and get a bottle of wine breathing, I could do with it after the day I've had.' He kissed Kelvin and grabbed his keys, stopping by the door to put his outside shoes on.

At the mention of chicken, Lola, wound around Nash's legs, meowing as if she hadn't eaten in days. Nash bent down to pet her. 'All right, Lola. You'll get some, too. Even the cat was too clever for her own good.'

As he drove, Nash thought about Noah having two legs, and Max's cryptic message. The visions were more frequent and intense. He wondered if it was stress or something more. Up to now, he'd only been able to speak to Max through Conrad Snow—and when he was tired and this cranky, his rational mind still told him that it was hogwash. However, for the last month, he'd been hearing Max in his head and now he was seeing him, too. He needed to speak to Conrad about it. The lines between reality and his subconscious were blurring.

Chapter Forty-One

The cool air in the supermarket was a chilly contrast to the car's heater and Nash wanted to get done and back home. He grabbed the coleslaw and a tiger bread loaf. And as an afterthought, he picked up some extra treats for Lola to please her. His last stop was at the hot food counter for the chicken and as he walked, his mind worked on the case.

He wasn't looking where he was going and almost bumped into the young security guard they had brought in for questioning. Nash felt a pang of guilt. They had been barking up the wrong tree regarding the lad. And when he proved his innocence they'd let him go without charge. He glared at Nash as he walked past.

As Nash watched, the guard's boss caught up with him and clipped him around the head. He told him to get back to work. The boy's shoulders slumped, and he returned to the car park. The stance of the older guard was aggressive, certainly not the impression of the happy-go-lucky character he'd put across to the police on previous occasions. Everybody loved him, but did he have a different side to him when he thought nobody was looking? It didn't sit well with Nash.

He waited for his chicken to be bagged at the deli counter and saw Liz and Andy Gibson. Andy was still walking with a limp, but he was happy to see them holding hands and laughing together.

'Hi?' he said.

Liz smiled back. 'Inspector, Nash. How are you?'

'I'm good, thanks. Picking up dinner. How are you doing?'

Andy nodded. 'Better. We're taking one day at a time. Have you caught them yet?'

'We're working on it, Mr Gibson. And when they're under lock and key, nothing will give me greater pleasure than ringing to tell you in person.' He put his hand on Andy's shoulder to offer sincerity. 'I hope we'll have more for you, very soon.' He made a mental note to tell Bowes that he'd seen Liz and Andy and they looked well. It would please him.

At the checkout—Nash hated queueing, but loathed the self-service tills even more—he looked out of the window. It took a second to see further than the bright shop reflected in the darkness, but he saw a black car pulling up. The older security guard looked around before approaching the tinted window to speak to the driver. Nash focused on his groceries and thanked the cashier as he collected his bags.

As he walked to his car, he saw the guard again. He was going to his hut with a canvas bag. It could have been his lunch, and the people in the car might be looking for a parking place, but the guard's furtive behaviour set Nash's instinct on edge. He wouldn't have given it a second thought but for the guard looking around before approaching the car. Nash knew shifty when he saw it, and this was as shifty as a burglar up a squeaky drainpipe.

He loaded his groceries. His policeman's nose was rarely wrong. He took out his phone and dialled.

'Renshaw, it's Nash. Bring the security guard at Star Select in for questioning. And you'll need a search warrant for his hut.'

There was a pause on the other end before Renshaw replied. 'We've already had him in. He's clean. Never so much as a parking ticket and alibi's for the relevant dates.'

'Not that one. The older guy.'

'What? Barbosa?' Renshaw laughed. 'Boss, it's not him. I don't know what intel you've received, but he's the nicest guy you'll ever meet. My kids love him.'

Nash rubbed his temples, he'd had enough. 'Bring him in.'

Nash didn't need any more than the tone. 'Understood, boss. I'm on it.'

He ended the call and started his car. The urge to go back to the station was strong, but the smell of hot chicken was stronger. He'd ring to follow up later. He knew he was onto something and sometimes, small hunches led to big breakthroughs.

The next day, the incident room was buzzing with news. They'd caught Mr Big. The loveable security guard in his fifties had been apprehended and arrested on the spot after drugs and money were found stashed in his hut. He'd tried shifting the blame onto the younger guard, but after Nash's tip-off, Renshaw and Patel weren't buying it.

Jake Barbosa had been stripped of his phone at the scene so he couldn't alert anybody. He was cooling his heels in the cells waiting for his initial court appearance the next morning. They had enough to hold him.

Despite Nash explicitly forbidding it, Blight went to the cells. She told Nash she wanted to see if she could get anything more out of Barbosa, even if it wouldn't be admissible in court, but Nash knew she wanted to gloat. He saw where she was going and followed her. This could end badly.

Barbosa looked confused when he saw Blight. His face lit up. It was clear he thought that one of his three next-tier agents was there to help him. Blight was ballsy, so it wasn't a stretch for either him or Nash to assume she could walk in and demand his release. Nash watched from a distance, ready to intervene.

Blight flashed her warrant card at Barbosa. 'After months of working for you, we finally meet in person, Mr Barbosa. Do you know what we call you around here?' She didn't wait for a reply. 'No? We call you, Mr Big.' She laughed. 'Big belly, that's about it.'

Barbosa's eyes widened in shock. 'You've got to be kidding me. You're filth?'

'No, you're the filth, I'm the one that's going to clean you up. Yeah, I'm a cop. And you're a bitter disappointment. You don't look so impressive to me. Just a tired old has-been. You're done, Barbosa. We've got enough on you to put you away for a long time.'

Barbosa looked flabbergasted. 'One of my distributors is a cop? I'll have you taken out. You hear me. You're dead meat.'

Blight smirked. 'Yeah, yeah. Tell it to all the dead children, fatty. You're a coward and a joke.'

Nash stepped in, sensing the situation escalating. 'That's enough. Let's go.'

Blight's eyes flashed. 'I'm not going anywhere. I'm going to smash his fat face in.'

Nash put a firm hand on her shoulder. 'This isn't the way. We've got what we need. Anything you get under duress would be inadmissible and you'll damage the case. Let's go.'

Barbosa watched with a grin on his face. 'You think you've won? This isn't over.'

Nash ignored him and guided Blight out of the cell block. He felt the tension radiating off her.

'Why did you stop me?' Blight demanded when they were out of earshot. 'I could have got more out of him.'

'We have protocol and code of practice for a reason.' Nash was calm. 'We've got enough to hold him. Anything you get now wouldn't hold up in court and you know it.'

Blight clenched her fists. 'I want to make sure we have everything. I might not have met him, but I know how he operates. He'll slip through our fingers.'

'He won't,' Nash reassured her. 'We've got him. Focus on doing this by the book, ma'am.'

Blight was visibly trying to calm herself. 'I hate feeling like we could be missing something.'

'I know. But we've got this. Trust the process.'

The news of Barbosa's capture spread fast. Officers were talking in hushed voices all over the station, exchanging facts, pockets of gossip, and speculation. It was their first significant win and a breakthrough in dismantling the criminal network.

'Can you credit it?' Jackie Woods whispered. 'We got Mr Big. I can't believe it, he plays darts with my son every Thursday.'

'I heard he tried to pin it on the other guy. Pathetic,' Lawson said.

Brown and Renshaw reviewed the evidence, preparing for the next steps. Patel was talking to Mason, and they looked up as Nash came in.

'Everything okay?' Brown asked, noting the tension between him and Blight.

'All good,' Nash replied

Renshaw brought over a sheaf of papers for Nash to review. But as he held them out, Blight pulled rank and took them out of his hand. She gave him a withering look that could melt flesh.

'My mistake, ma'am.' Renshaw said and Nash felt sorry for him. He struggled to adapt to the new chain of command too and found it hard to accept Blight as his superior. Was it her clothing, her age, or the fact that she was off her face?

It didn't matter who held the reins. Despite the bumps in the road, their work was paying off. Nash swallowed his irritation.

Chapter Forty-Two

By Friday, nerves were shredded. Tension and anticipation coated the team's expectations like a black treacle too thick to sink into. Nash was hopeful. They had to believe that today they were winners.

The dual carriageway from the M6 was a hive of activity, with roadblocks strategically placed every 500 yards to intercept vehicles and search them for smuggled contraband. Drivers on their way home from work, or going to the Lake District, were stressed by the delay. It was the start of their weekend and crawling along a tailback wasn't how they wanted it to flow. Every car was stopped and the drivers were PNC-checked. Their vehicle details were run against the Police National Computer. Officers did an inside sweep through passenger windows and car boots were searched before the vehicle could be waved on. This was a covering-all-bases process because the consignment was expected to come in by van.

Checking every vehicle had been the subject of debate. They had intel that the Chaos was arriving by Transit, so checking cars and wagons was arguably a waste of resources. But the cartel was smart and things could change. Nash argued that this was their one chance and every precaution had to be taken. Lewis worried about cost, budget, and getting the public's backs up. Turner wanted results and sided with Nash. It wasn't worth risking. They had one shot at this. Lewis had concurred and signed the relevant papers.

Every van coming off the motorway was meticulously searched. The sounds of engines idling, doors slamming, and raised voices put everyone on edge.

Turner and Nash moved with authority, shouting orders and ensuring the operation ran well. Turner was a veteran of countless manoeuvres like this and had a commanding presence that made the team more efficient. Nash was proud of them. While Turner moved fast, Nash was methodical. He had a keen eye for detail and missed nothing.

'Check the back of that van again, Lawson.' Turner barked, pointing at a black Transit that had pulled into the checkpoint. 'You didn't lift the carpet. Don't leave anything unsearched.'

'Copy that,' Lawson replied, opening the van's rear doors and beginning a second inspection.

Nash moved down the line of the roadblocks double-checking the search protocols. 'Make sure you inspect the wheel wells and undercarriages,' he instructed another team, his voice carrying over the din. 'We can't afford to miss anything.'

The sun was a memory in the sky. The light was dull and the officers shone strong torches into murky vehicles, making passengers shield their eyes. Officers in high-visibility vests moved efficiently, their faces set and determined.

Woods had been talking to a driver through his cab window for too long.

'Look. What's all this about? I have to be in Scotland in four hours,'

'I'm sorry, sir. We are giving service vehicles priority for clearance.'

'Well, that's not good enough. Who's going to tell my boss when I miss the ferry? You lot don't give a damn. What are you looking for?'

Nash told Woods to continue the search. He took her place and spoke to the man who was still shouting. 'Sir. Please let my officers continue the search. Holding them up is only delaying you further.'

The disgruntled lorry driver had another moan, and when Woods gave him the thumbs up, Nash waved him on without addressing his stream of complaints. 'Have a good evening, sir. Drive safely.'

The dual carriageway was usually a bustling artery of traffic, but the vein was clogged and progress was slow. Nash walked along one of the checkpoints and saw Bowes. He masked his inexperience with his determined expression as he inspected a green sedan. His gloved hands methodically searched the boot's interior.

'How's it going, Bowes?' Nash called out. He stopped to watch.

'All clear so far, sir. No sign of anything suspicious.'

'Good. Pick up the pace. Let's keep them moving.' Nash clapped him on the shoulder. Despite reservations, Bowes was proving his worth.

Turner walked over to Nash. 'We've had a few hauls of personal supply, but nothing substantial.'

Nash nodded. 'We can't let our guard down. Mathis is a slippery bastard, but he'll have done his homework and expects a clear run.'

Turner looked at his watch. 'The window's closing. We need to stay sharp.'

Nash scanned the sting, taking in the roadblocks, his officers, and the vehicles waiting to be searched. 'Everyone, stay focused!' he shouted, his voice cutting through the noise. 'This is it. We catch them today, or they get away.'

The officers redoubled their efforts, moving with a renewed sense of urgency. Each vehicle was subjected to a rigorous inspection, with officers using mirrors to check undercarriages and sniffer dogs to find hidden drugs.

Nash and Turner coordinated the operation well, their eyes scanning for unexpected trouble. The tension was palpable, but so was the determination. They were close, and they knew it.

One of the GMNT officers put his hand up. He called out, 'Here.'

Nash and Turner rushed to the checkpoint, where a nondescript van had been pulled over. The dogs indicated a find. The officer pointed to a hidden compartment in the floor, where packages wrapped in plastic were being pulled out and photographed.

'Get it all open,' Turner shouted, signalling for more officers to help.

As a second compartment was pried open revealing the contents inside, Nash's excitement turned to disappointment. There were drugs. The officer held up two packages of a brown substance, but they only amounted to a couple of pounds in weight. A few thousand quid's worth at most. The rest of the haul consisted of counterfeit tobacco and booze. They'd been to Belgium for a weekend pick-up. The driver and his mate were taken to the side of the road, searched and arrested. They were just a pair of chancers.

'Damn it,' Turner cursed. 'False alarm.'

Nash's jaw tightened, and he quelled his anger. 'Secure the evidence and take them into custody,' he ordered, trying to salvage a semblance of success from the situation. 'I doubt they're of any use, but there's a chance they might have some valuable intel on our lot.'

The officers processed the scene, but the mood had shifted. Rush hour had passed and the initial excitement was gone. A feeling of letdown and irritation seeped in but nobody used the word failure. Nash exchanged a look with Turner. They were running out of time.

'It's not over yet. Stay sharp, everyone,' Turner called out, trying to rally the team. 'We're not beaten, yet.'

Nash looked down the line of vehicles. They had to keep pushing, even as the odds slipped away from their grasp. They couldn't afford to let their guard down now.

A council wagon came down the line putting out lighting poles that created long shadows across the dual carriageway. Despite the tailback, the traffic on the motorway end was thinning, and Nash's unease mounted. Something wasn't right. He pushed the thought away. The team had meticulously planned the operation to coincide with the heaviest traffic. It was based on information that the cartel drivers were using the confusion to provide cover for their smuggling operation. Yet, it was six o'clock, and the optimum window was closed.

Nash watched as another van was flagged down and searched. Officers moved along the vehicles with mechanical precision, their expressions still held hope that this was the one, but it was tempered with a colourwash of resignation.

'It doesn't make sense,' Nash said, mostly to himself. 'The gang was coming during heavy congestion for a reason. They wanted the least chance of being noticed. We're missing something.'

Turner caught his words. 'What are you saying, Nash?'

'We've messed up. The traffic's thinning, and we're out of time. If they were going to make a move, they'd have done it by now.'

Turner's face hardened. 'Keep stopping traffic. We're not giving up. Not yet.'

'We've got to face facts. The optimal time has passed. We're wasting our resources.'

Turner shook his head in denial and reminded Nash of a gambler chasing that big win. Just one more bet. 'We keep going. We stop every damn vehicle until we're sure.'

Nash was frustrated. 'With respect, it's time to reassess. Maybe they had a tip-off, or we've missed something.'

'Got a drug dealing worm in your department, have you, Nash, because I know my guys are committed?'

Nash bit back the response that Turner had brought Blight with him, and she was already hooked on drugs. He had to force it back, it would have been an unfair and childish jibe to score points. 'I trust our combined team, implicitly,' he said.

Turner's eyes were like steel. 'We stay the course. This operation is too important to pull the plug now. If they have been tipped, they could be banking on us losing hope and leaving.'

Nash looked at the faces of his officers. The frustration was etched into their expressions, but they kept working. He felt the collective exhaustion and mounting doubt the drop in adrenaline brought. But he understood Turner's resolve. The stakes were high, and the pressure immense.

A car was waved through after being cleared. Its driver flicked the bone against his closed window as he drove past. Renshaw moved forward, but Nash put his arm on Renshaw's wrist to stop him. 'Let him go.'

Nash saw impatience growing in the queue. But they had less than fifty vehicles left to herd through. New ones were joining the back as they came off the motorway but fewer of them. He glanced at Turner. 'We've been out here too long. If they slipped past us, we need to regroup and come up with another plan.'

'And what if we're one car away from catching them? One more vehicle could be the break we need.'

Nash looked at the stream of cars, a sense of futility washing over him. 'Or it could be nothing. We've had one false alarm. We need to be smart about this.'

Turner glared at him. 'Fine. Give it another fifteen minutes. If we don't find anything by then, we'll call it.'

Nash nodded, though his gut told him it was already too late. 'Fifteen minutes, team,' He shouted and heard it being passed down the line. He watched as another car was pulled over, the officers going through the same routine, their movements slower now. The weight of failure pressed down on them all with the creeping sense of the bad guys winning again.

As the minutes ticked by traffic dwindled. The sky was dark with the approach of evening. Nash checked his watch. 'All right. Good work, everybody. Let's wrap it up.'

The operation brought disappointment, but they had to pick up the pieces and figure out their next move.

They dismantled the roadblocks and the remaining cars were allowed through. Nash walked over to Turner and clapped him on the shoulder. 'We'll get them.'

Turner nodded, his expression grim. 'Yeah, next time.'

Nash watched the dual carriageway returning to normal. Every detail had been accounted for, yet they'd come up empty-handed. He saw the shift in Turner's posture. His frustration boiled over. He was livid and turned on Nash, his voice echoing across the empty road.

'This is down to you. We should have had them. All the other cogs in the wheel will be stood down, as well. Don't you realise how far up this sting went? He kicked a cone and they watched it turn over and roll down the road. Turner bellowed at Nash, his face red with fury. 'You couldn't organise a piss-up in a brewery.'

Nash's anger rose in retaliation. Earlier, Turner had accepted the failure, but now he pointed the finger of blame anywhere so long as it couldn't land on him.

'We did everything we could. Sometimes we have to accept that things don't go according to plan,' Nash said.

'That's not good enough,' Turner shouted. 'We had one job, Nash. And now they're laughing at us.'

Nash was annoyed that he was being yelled at in front of both teams and tried to keep his voice steady. 'With all due respect, sir, screaming at me isn't going to change what happened. We need to figure out where we went wrong and how to fix it.'

Turner stepped closer, his voice dropping to a dangerous whisper. 'Don't talk back to me, you impudent shit. Your team are nothing more than an unprofessional rabble of country bumkins. We should never have trusted you with a serious operation. You're responsible for this mess.'

Nash squared his shoulders. 'I am aware of my responsibilities. I also know how to get the best out of people, and this isn't it.'

Turner glared at him before wheeling away and Nash wanted to kick him up the backside when he turned his back. He felt the team watching him after being publicly dressed down. Their disappointment and confusion added to Nash's despondency. He looked up, visibility was bad in the gloom, but he saw a boy standing in the middle of the road. It was Noah. He looked sad. Nash blinked and Noah was gone.

Something was niggling at the back of his mind, a sense that he was missing something crucial.

He focussed. The noise of the dismantling operation faded into the background as he strained to listen to his thoughts. Like a whisper in his ear, he heard Max's voice as clearly as Turner's had been seconds earlier.

'Row, row, row your boat.'

Nash froze. He thought Max had been taking the piss about the cruise Kelvin wanted him to go on, but he realised that the stupid song had significance to the case. Think. He'd heard it everywhere for days but had been too distracted to attach importance to it. Why was it coming to him now? Instead of pushing the distraction aside, he welcomed it in. This had happened to him before during The Florist case. A song had played in his mind but he hadn't listened to his subconscious. This was Max's way of reminding him of it and coming at him with a song that meant something. Or maybe it was his crazy mind again—either way, he was listening. The feeling persisted.

He closed his eyes. The words repeated like a mantra. It didn't make sense, but there was a connection that was just out of his reach.

Nash opened his eyes, scanning the scene. Turner was still fuming and barking orders at the remaining officers.

It hit him.

Nash turned back to Turner. 'Sir, I know what we missed.'

Chapter Forty-Three

Nash was stunned by the realisation. 'I didn't listen,' he said, his voice urgent and sharp. 'They're coming across Morecambe Bay by boat.'

Turner stopped mid-shout and stared at Nash. 'Don't be ridiculous. Those are treacherous waters. Remember the Chinese Cocklers? It's twenty years ago this year, you know? They'd never risk it when coming by road is so much easier.'

'Think about it,' Nash's mind was racing. 'The setup was a red herring to distract us. They aren't stupid. They know you've been snooping around up here. They timed it to coincide with rush hour to keep us occupied. The real drop is coming in by water. I'm certain of it.' He refrained from mentioning that two persistent ghosts had been telling him about it for a week.

Turner wheeled around reaching for his phone. 'Damn it, Nash, if you're right we need to act fast.'

Nash nodded, punching numbers into his mobile. It depends on the tide. We might be too late.' He searched the number and dialled the Coast Guard, his fingers flying over the keypad.

'Coast Guard. This is an emergency. I am Detective Chief Inspector Nash from Barrow Station. We believe a major drug shipment is coming across the bay tonight. I need all available units on standby. When's high tide?'

The voice on the other end crackled with urgency. 'Understood, DCI Nash. The tide hasn't turned yet. It won't be high enough for a crossing until 20:13. We'll scramble and be ready to intercept any alien vessels.'

Nash's heart pounded in his chest. 'Thank you. Keep us updated on any sightings, please. We'll coordinate from here. We're on our way. I'll be with you within the hour.' He hung up. 'The Coast Guard is on standby. We need to get units to the coast and watch the waterways. If they try to land prematurely or get into bother, we'll be ready for them.'

Turner nodded, the earlier tension between them dissipating in the face of the new opportunity to hang the bastards out to dry. 'Let's move. We can't let them beat us again.'

Nash barked orders to the team, mobilising officers to the coast. 'Team, we've got intel that the shipment is coming in by boat. Get back to Barrow, reconvene at Rampside, and cover every possible landing point. I want eyes on the water and everyone ready to move.'

The team sprang into action, the urgency reviving weary spirits. Nash felt the thrill of the chase mingling with the fear of repeated failure. If he was wrong and cost the department more money, he'd look a fool. But they still had a chance to intercept the shipment and bring down the network behind it.

When they got to Rampside, Nash deployed the officers along the coast, positioning them to cover the most likely landing points. He checked in with the Coast Guard, who reported no sightings, but the tide was still rising.

Nash scanned the dark horizon, his eyes straining to catch any sign of lights. The minutes ticked by and every officer was sitting on a knife edge waiting for something—or nothing—to happen. The dealers would make their move soon.

'Stay sharp,' Nash fixed his gaze on the water.

The sea looked deceptively calm, but Morecambe Bay was an angry lady of wild temperament. She could go from millpond to destruction in a minute. They had to be ready for anything. This could be a rescue mission as much as an interception.

We're ready for you, Nash thought, his resolve hardening. Bring it on.

The coastguard brought them welcome mugs of strong coffee. Nash and Turner were locked in a heated debate, their voices echoing from the walls of the utilitarian space. Their return from the motorway should have taken an hour with the additional run along the coast road to Rampside. They did it in under forty minutes, speeding on blues and twos as they left the failed motorway operation. The concentration needed for safe driving at considerable speed had left them frustrated and snappy. Maps of Morecambe Bay were spread out on the table, their edges curled in the salty air.

'It's obvious, sir,' Nash said, jabbing a finger at the map. 'You're right that the shortest route would be from Arnside to Greenodd. But that's not what they'll do. It doesn't make sense because it wouldn't get them through the roadblocks we set up. They'd be walking right into our net.'

'Not if we'd already shut up shop and gone home—as we have. They'd think we wouldn't expect them to take the direct route because it's too obvious.'

'We can't afford to think that way. These guys are too smart for that. If we want to catch them, we have to think like them. They're not going to risk a direct route when they know we've been active on the roads.'

The Coast Guard, a middle-aged man with a weathered face and sharp eyes, nodded. 'He's right. If I was coming across and didn't want to be seen, I'd take a longer but more discrete route. Humphrey Head to Rampside would be ideal. It's less obvious and avoids the traffic detailing. Safer too, there's some terrible undercurrents out there and treacherous rips on the outgoing tide that would make docking difficult.'

Turner's expression was sour. 'Fine. But we need to be ready for any eventuality. This is our last chance to get this right.'

They bent over maps and Nash traced the route with his finger, his mind racing, flying ahead and visualising the crossing. 'Look here,' he said, pointing to a narrow channel past Rampside and around the headland, running adjacent to Roa Island road. 'I think they'll head for here. They aren't going to come to the main pier. They'll know it isn't manned 24/7, but they'll have done their homework and get that boats can be called out any time. This is the perfect spot for them.'

'It makes sense,' Turner said.

'I'm right. I can feel it in my gut.'

The Coast Guard marked the map with a pen. 'We'll position our boats here, here, and here,' he said, indicating points along the channel. 'We'll have them surrounded before they can react.'

Turner crossed his arms, his face set. 'How much longer?'

Nash ignored him and keyed his microphone. 'All units, listen up. All focus on the water. We're anticipating a route from Humphrey Head to Rampside. Boats are moving into position without lights. Get ready to move out and coordinate with the Coast Guard. If he tells you to move, you move.'

Nash looked out to the water where five white foamy wakes gave the guard boats away. They would be seen better from this side of the bay, but anybody looking closely enough on the other bank would see them, too. He hoped the marks were too occupied loading the shipment to be looking out. With the bluster of the wind, there was no sound reaching them from the motors, and at least that was something to be grateful for. He watched as they cut their engines, and as the foam lines sank into the tossing waves, the coastguard boats became invisible.

On land, officers waited, ready to spring—nothing to go for yet. They were tightly wound.

The team had the advantage of surprise and the element of strategic positioning. They just needed to be right. Turner came over to Nash, his voice serious. 'You'd better be right about this, Nash. We can't afford another failure.'

Nash met his gaze. 'If I'm right, you'll take the credit, but don't worry, you've got your scapegoat if I'm wrong.'

'Insubordination again, Inspector Nash.'

'Yes, sir.' It was many years since Nash had to take orders and he didn't much like it. He'd been too comfortable at the top of operations.

It's good for your pompous ass, Nasher.

Every detail was covered. Boats were ready at the key interception points, and officers were briefed on their roles. The operation was set.

Nash stood by the water's edge, with the biting wind violating his hair and biting into his lower spine. He looked at his watch.

The apparent calmness of the scene was deceptive, masking the storm of activity.

'Time,' Turner shouted over the mic. 'All units in position.' His voice crackled over the radio.

All units in position, Max echoed as though he was in charge as well. Nash shook his head to rid himself of the voice.

He went back into the guard house and stared out of the observation window, his focus sharpening. 'Let's bring them in,' he said in a steady voice. 'It's all or nothing.' He felt icy sweat trickle from his neck to his waistband. All this was on the say-so of a couple of ghosts. He wished he was at home with Kelvin. Suddenly salty spaghetti didn't seem so bad.

He couldn't see anything on the water.

Chapter Forty-Four

The tension in the coastguard's office was unbearable. This sting was Nash's call, and he'd made a difficult decision based on subtle nudges from a ghost. He was basing his future career on subconscious fancy and the cruel tricks his grieving mind played. If he was wrong his position would be in jeopardy. Despite the stress, and still always trying to deny him, Nash felt Max's presence. It was a comforting reassurance. He was certain about this.

Turner, who had belittled Nash in front of the team seemed contrite. 'Sorry Nash. Tensions ran a bit high there. No pissing contests here, eh? Look, we'll have to get together for a drink sometime.'

Nash would rather poke his eyes out with a blunt stick, he ignored the drink idea. 'Think nothing of it. Let's concentrate on the task at hand.'

'Of course, but I've had a better idea. Let's have dinner. I'm sure your wife will get on famously with my Lucinda, she's a real people person. Not like me,' he said and laughed awkwardly.

Nash was amazed that the office gossip hadn't reached Turner's ears. He was silent, hoping Turner would drop the subject, but his superior was oblivious to the hint.

'What do you say, Nash? Dinner at Salvanna's tomorrow night. My treat to say thank you for a job well done. What's your wife's name?'

'Kelvin.'

It took a second. Turner blinked. 'Oh, I'm sorry. I didn't realise.'

Nash kept his tone neutral. 'Why would you? I don't wear a slogan, and I'm not especially fond of Madonna.'

Turner cleared his throat, shifting around on his feet. He clapped Nash hard on the back—a proper manly slap. 'You're a funny guy, Nash. My offer stands, and I'd like to show my appreciation. I just won't order flowers for Kelvin.'

The room fell silent again, the monotony only broken for the length of the brief conversation. George, the Coast Guard, was still trying to hide a grin. 'Kelvin,' he muttered, 'flowers,' and he laughed, turning it into a cough.

Five minutes later, George spoke up, his voice tense. 'Ladies, we've got blinking lights coming towards us, 0.00723 degrees East from Humphrey Head.'

He was a character and Nash saw Turner bristle. Nash had heard it all before and grinned at his Super's awkwardness.

George raised his binoculars, focusing hard. 'I see a vessel with an outboard motor leaving the shore, about half a mile from the dock.'

Nash's heart rate quickened. This was it. He turned to his team, his voice steady but urgent. 'All right, everyone. Showtime.'

The coastguard's voice crackled over the radio. 'High tide. Outboard incoming. Everyone, be ready.'

Nash felt a surge of adrenaline. He exchanged a look with Turner, who gave a tight nod, clearly embarrassed by the earlier faux pas but focused on the operation.

The team moved into position, everybody taking up their assigned roles. Nash felt the responsibility for the operation's success on his shoulders. Max was here. A silent friend who bolstered his resolve.

Arrr, shiver me timbers. That be a mighty storm comin' our way.

'Shut up, fool,' Nash muttered.

'What?' Turned asked.

'I said, we should be up soon.' Nash had his binoculars trained on the vessel leaving Humphrey Head and they covered his blush. They watched from the observation room as the boat's motor churned the water, sending up a spray as it sped away from the shore.

The coastguard's voice came through the open channel again, though he was speaking to his officers in the boats. 'Hitting the mark in five… four… three… two… one. Go, go, go!'

The coastal team powered their boats and roared into action out of the pitch darkness. Nash watched as the operation unfolded, every move calculated. Boats moved, cutting off escape routes and it put him in mind of sharks homing in on tuna while officers on land closed in to receive their suspects.

Nash's heart pounded as he scanned the scene, looking for any sign of trouble. The drug runner's boat was coming towards them fast. As he watched, a flash of movement caught his eye. Two figures fought on the deck, and somebody on the suspect boat threw something overboard. Nash couldn't make out much, but his body lurched forward as he watched something come up. thrashing in the water, he realised it was the second person.

'Man overboard,' George shouted into his radio, directing his team to intercept. 'Target on the move.'

Nash had just witnessed attempted murder.

'Boarding team prepare to engage,' George commanded.

The patrol boat crews moved fast. Grappling hooks secured two vessels together, and three officers leapt onto the smaller boat. The sole suspect, a man in his late thirties with a weathered face and a look of desperation, tried to resist but he was overpowered and subdued.

'Suspect One secured,' an officer reported.

Nash's eyes were aching with trying to focus through the binoculars as he watched a guard boat fishing the drowning man out of the water. He looked heavy and they had trouble hauling him over the side of the boat.

'Suspect Two on board.'

Nash watched them roll him and cuff him behind his back.

'Second suspect secured.'

Nash adjusted the focus wheel on the binoculars. The boat was closer. His eyes shifted to the packages the other man had been trying to dump. They were lying on the deck. He counted eleven waterproof duffel bags that looked heavy. The officers secured the bags and signalled the all-clear.

'Packages secured. Proceeding with retrieval.'

Nash directed his attention to the shore as the scene unfolded on the water. His team swept the area, ensuring nobody was waiting for the suspect boat on land. The drivers would be here any minute. They'd be watching for the motorboat to leave Humphrey Head and would time their arrival to coincide with the docking. Sitting around would make them conspicuous. Renshaw keyed his mic and Nash heard a tinge of excitement when he said that a white van had just driven along Roa Island Road and, as predicted, was heading toward the inlets they'd marked off on the map. He said he'd keep Nash informed regarding the suspect van's movements. 'Oh shit. Too late, boss. They've seen the intercept.'

'Wait,' Nash instructed. 'Don't move yet. Let them come right in.'

The drivers, assumed to be Jimmy and Rob in the accepting van, saw the coastguards bringing in the boat. The driver screeched to a halt and tried to turn the van in the narrow road.

'Go. Go. Go.'

Nash's team were on them in seconds, surrounding the vehicle and securing the suspects.

Renshaw sounded breathless. 'Two males secured and cuffed,' he said over the mic. 'Permission to take them into custody, boss?'

Nash looked at Turner but the GMNT operative knew who Renshaw was referring to and motioned for Nash to respond.

'Good work, Renshaw. Take them in.'

Still alert for trouble, the coastal boats guided the suspect vessel inland to the disembarkation ramp that gave the hamlet its name.

Nash's heart pounded as he watched the scene unfold from his vantage point in the coastguard's office. Every movement was precise, every step calculated. Boats docked and the remaining officers on land closed in on their target.

The coastguard's office was frenetic with each person playing their part in the operation. Nash watched the monitors, tracking the officers and ensuring that the perimeter bank was secure. The calm efficiency of his team, in conjunction with the excellent work of the coastguards, made his heart sing.

'Perimeter secure. No additional suspects found,' Patel reported.

Nash allowed a moment of relief and stretched his body. He hadn't moved for several minutes and was stiff. The operation was going well, but it wasn't over. Every detail mattered. They needed all the suspects in custody and the evidence collected. Turner patted him on the back and he smiled at him. George was unscrewing the cap from a bottle of whiskey. 'I think this calls for a celebration, don't you, gentlemen?' Nash was driving and declined, but Turner accepted his glass and swished the contents around before drinking. Nash swallowed in his dry throat and reached for his cold coffee.

He went outside to the ramp. He needed to see this through personally. The suspects were being led off the boat in handcuffs, flanked by officers.

'Good work, everyone,' Nash said. He looked at the captives, one of them soaking wet, and both wrapped in silver insulation blankets against the freezing temperatures. 'You're in a lot of trouble.' He turned to Patel, 'Read them their rights and get them in,' he said.

The suspects remained silent, their jaws clenched. It would take time to break them down, but they had what they needed. This was one pincer of Operation Diamond Light. The heads of manoeuvres still had to be apprehended at their various locations. Nash hoped it was going as well as his branch had.

'Let's get this wrapped up,' He said to the team. 'Make sure everything is logged and secured. We don't want anybody getting off on a technicality through sloppy policing. By the book, folks.'

The officers secured the evidence and Nash took a moment to reflect. This was a significant win, but they had to keep digging until they dismantled the operation. He went to say goodbye to George, shook his hand warmly, and offered his thanks.

Nash's thoughts were interrupted by Turner, who'd been overseeing the clean-up from a distance. 'Good call, Nash. You were right.'

Nash nodded, the tension easing from his body. 'Thanks, Turner. We all did our part.'

Turner extended his hand, and Nash shook it firmly. Despite the awkwardness, they'd worked together effectively.

'About that dinner,' Turner began, but Nash cut him off with a smile.

'For now, let's enjoy the victory. We can talk about tomorrow, tomorrow.'

Turner laughed, a genuine sound that broke the remaining tension. 'Fair enough, Nash.'

Nash was contrite. Things had been heated but there was no need to be churlish. 'However, when we're finished at the station, I happen to know that Kel has the stew pot on. You have not lived until you've tasted my other halves' Irish stew.'

'Is that an invitation, Nash?'

Nash clapped Turner awkwardly around the shoulder and they walked to his car together. 'If you can eat at a country bumpkin table, I reckon it is, Mark.'

'I am bloody starving, man. Let's crack on.'

Chapter Forty-Five

Turner gave the order to move in on Mathis. They had Barbosa in custody and it was the final takedown of the key players.

Under the cover of darkness, a team of officers surrounded the sprawling property on Lake Windermere. They were in riot gear and their movements were silent and coordinated. They'd received a tip-off at the station. Their informant had struck a deal for leniency in exchange for information that Mathis had smelled a rat after the grass had been attacked at the party. He would only be sentenced to a few months for dealing. Nash said he'd put in a good word in his written report for him to be placed as close to Cumbria as possible so that his family could visit. Nash wasn't forthcoming with the fact that he'd have done that for him anyway, but he was grateful for any information he could get. And if that meant playing a little You Scratch My Back, then sobeit.

The informant told Nash that Blight attacking one of Mathis' workers was enough to make him check his CCTV footage of that night. Mathis had said Blight looked pretty wasted by the end and wanted to know where she'd got her burst of sobriety from. The informant said Mathis didn't believe the kid until he saw Norton palming the pill he'd given her. Norton was good, but Mathis watched her leaving too many drinks on too many windowsills. She was standing on the periphery of every conversation—and the grass said, Mathis knew a cop when he saw one. The informant told them he was preparing to flee.

Another race ensued that night as special ops teams rushed to apprehend Mathis before he could escape. Nash and Turner exchanged a look, the Irish stew was simmering and Nash felt the day would never end.

He'd get one of the lads to run them home later, but as hungry as they were, they couldn't leave until they had word that Mathis was in custody. He took the celebration bottle out of his desk drawer and poured them a couple of fingers each.

To a lesser degree, they needed to know that Gloria Burnette and Barry Barlow on the next tier down had been caught as well. The cells were going to be buzzing and the custody staff kept busy that night. The prisoners would be rattling bars and screaming the place down.

Nash was surprised to hear that Alesha Cordon—otherwise known as Blue—had turned on her gang after being ousted by Blight and she'd been a useful source of information. That girl could talk when it was in her interest and she was in an interview, rattling off names and addresses like a trained parrot. At this point, they wouldn't have been able to shut her up if they'd wanted to. Blue's verbal diarrhoea was proving useful.

Mark Turner, Bronwyn Lewis and Nash sat in Lewis' office watching a wall-mounted screen. They were live-viewing DCI Bold's bodycam as the action in Windermere unfolded. Mathis was like an eel, but they had him cornered.

'Move in,' Nash whispered as if Bold could hear him. His voice was barely audible over the sound of Turner's breathing. They were both frustrated. By the time they got back to the station, the special ops team were already on their way to Windermere to head Mathis off. They'd missed out on his takedown, and Turner was furious.

Regular Action man isn't he, Nasher?

It was late and Nash wanted to get home for dinner, but he'd have given that up in a heartbeat to be the one to kick in Mathis' door. He'd been a thorn in the detective's side for years.

They watched the officers advance, their weapons drawn and ready. They moved in formation keeping low to the ground, and securing the estate perimeter. There were no land escape routes for Mathis, and Norton had warned them about the Jetty and said that's how he'd try to leave.

'Norton should be here to see this,' Nash said. 'We wouldn't have anywhere near as much intel on Mathis if it wasn't for her.'

'She's with Lawson and Brown on the last of the Barrow arrests,' Bronwyn said. She didn't take her eyes off the screen and sipped her whiskey as though she didn't know it was in her hand.

'Are you going soft on my Valkyrie,' Turner teased.

'Hardly. I'd just rather have her where I can keep an eye on her,' Nash laughed. But he was. There was something about her resilience that made him like her.

As they watched, Mathis crept out of the ground-floor French doors at the back of the mansion. He had a leather suitcase in each hand.

'Maxwell-Scott luggage,' Bronwyn, murmured. 'Tasteful and expensive.'

Mathis straightened up as he crossed the lawn and made it to his jetty on the edge of the estate. He was confident until he was met by a wall of officers pointing guns at him. The look on his face was a picture as he realised there was no escape. Nash thought it was ironic that when it came to it, this man normally surrounded by his horde of sycophants out for what they could get, was alone.

'Police! Jerod Mathis, get on the ground. You are under arrest. Get down with your hands on your head. Now,' Bold said. His voice was hard and unwavering.

Mathis looked scared, and Nash knew that frightened men were at their most dangerous. The suspect put on a defiant front but there was no fight in him. 'You've got nothing on me. You can't touch me.'

Nash knew better. They'd been building their case against him for months, and they had enough evidence to bring him to justice.

He was led away in handcuffs, and Nash felt satisfaction swathe him. They'd taken down all the kingpins and hinges of the operation. Blue was singing sweet songs to them on tape, and tomorrow they would round up all the small-time dealers preying on kids to do their dirty work. The town's children would not be forced into such heinous positions again—and that was all Nash cared about—that and Kelvin's stew. He was amazed that it was still early, not eleven o'clock yet. It felt like the early hours of the morning. He expected Turner to bail on him but he said he only had an empty hotel room waiting for him, as Lucinda wasn't coming until the next morning.

Bronwyn declined the offer of stew and bourbon and said she had to get home to Grant.

'Eight sharp in the morning, you two, so take it easy,' she said, laughing as they almost fell over each other to get out of the station.

Chapter Forty-Six

The next day the atmosphere was electric. Officers still riding the high of the operation were in excellent spirits. Nash had a bad headache and Turner looked green. The incident room buzzed with activity as reports were filed, evidence was catalogued, and the suspects were processed and interviewed.

Renshaw and Patel were at their desks, reviewing the testimony and preparing for the next steps. Patel grinned as Nash came in.

'Everything okay?' he asked, noting that the tension between Nash and Turner had dissipated.

'Never again,' Nash moaned. 'Turner's an animal.'

'It was you that kept saying, "Just one more," before you showed me to your spare room.'

Renshaw laughed. 'We've got everything lined up for Monday. And Barbosa's not going anywhere.'

Nash felt quietly euphoric—very quietly. Noise wasn't good—and he was grateful when Bowes put a mug of strong coffee in front of him. They'd made significant progress, and despite the bumps in the road, their hard work was paying off. They could ease off the gas, take their time with processing, have a moment to breathe, and prepare for court cases with meticulous care and without rushing. 'This has to be airtight, people. No holes. Let's get them through interrogation,' Nash said. 'I want to see what they know.'

The suspect, Jake Barbosa, was brought into the interrogation room. Nash and Brown took their seats opposite him, and an officer stood by the door.

'Mr Barbosa,' Nash began, his tone measured, 'We know you were trying to smuggle dangerous contraband, commonly known as Crystal Chaos, into the county. We have the packages. It's only a matter of time before we find out the chemical compound and then you'll be in a whole world of trouble. You can help yourself by cooperating.'

Barbosa glared at him. His silence spoke volumes. Nash leaned forward, his eyes locked onto the prisoner.

'How hard do you want this to be, Mr Barbosa? Either you start talking or we'll discover what we want to know without your help. And trust me, that won't go well for you.'

There was a long moment of silence. Barbosa's eyes flicked to Brown, then back to Nash. When he spoke, his voice was surprisingly gentle. The man everybody loved, Nash reminded himself and made a point not to be fooled by him. 'You don't know what you're dealing with, inspector.'

'Enlighten us,' Brown said, leaning forward in her chair.

'What's with the ho? Can't you get a man for the job? You insult me, inspector.'

Brown slammed her hand on the desk and Nash smiled. 'I can assure you that DI Brown is one of our finest officers.'

Barbosa hesitated, then shook his head. 'It doesn't matter. You've got nothing on me.' He shifted his feet, then his buttocks and Nash knew he was being deceptive. With three grounding points of contact sitting in a chair; feet, buttocks and back, if a suspect moves any of these excessively, it can be a tell of extreme agitation or even deception.

Nash exchanged a look with Brown. They knew it would take time to break him, but they were patient. They had all night if necessary.

'We want to help you,' Nash said. 'Why don't you start by filling us in on your background? Mexican, right?'

Barbosa looked as though Nash had just slapped him and he spat on the floor. 'Mexican scum. Soy Cuban.'

'Forgive me. I expect life hasn't always been easy for you, Mr Barbosa. Please, tell us about it. We want to understand you and present your case in the best light possible.'

Nash and Brown did some rapport-building, even exchanging minor details of their lives, before moving into the Reid technique. It meant putting forward lesser explanations for his dealing than he was charged with. 'I get that you might not have had any choice in some of the things you did. What with being the new guy in town,' Nash said.

'Ah, the Reid technique. I expected better of you, Inspector Nash. I was warned to watch out for you because you're the big queso around town. I'll tell you what?' he glanced at the tape. 'You want me to give you something. I've got something big, but what do I get in return?'

'Taking into account the good you've done for the town, and the people you've always helped,' Nash struggled to get the words out, and he kicked Brown under the table when she snorted, 'we'll do everything we can to get you a lenient sentence. I'll ensure that our reports show you were cooperative and helpful.'

'Okay. Here's something for you. Roland Purvis is on the payroll.'

Nash was shocked, Purvis was one of the main solicitors in town and had represented many of Nash's prisoners over the years. He was taken aback, but when he thought about it, he wasn't surprised. He'd never liked the man and there had always been something slimy about him. Kelvin was a solicitor too and he couldn't stand him. It was rare that Kel disliked somebody. Trusting Kelvin was like trusting a dog's instincts, they were rarely wrong and if he didn't like somebody, you could bet your arse there was a good reason for it.

Nash leaned back in his chair, scrutinising the suspect across the table. Beside him, Brown flipped through her notes, glancing up to gauge his reaction to their questions. The man was stone-faced and sneered at her.

'Let's go over this again,' Nash said. 'Where were you on the night of—'

Nash sighed as the door burst open making him jump. The sound reverberated through the small room. He reacted and pushed Brown out of the way. A group of officers stormed in, moving with coordinated precision. They tackled Barbosa to the floor, chaos erupting as the table and chairs were shoved aside.

'What the hell?' Nash shouted, standing up, his hand moving towards Molly. Brown stepped back and flattened against the wall to give the men room.

Barbosa struggled, his protest muffled by the noise of the scuffle. An officer pulled out a taser. The sharp, electrical clicking filled the room until Barbosa convulsed and lay still. He was cuffed, his body rigid as they lifted him off the ground.

'Get him out of here,' DCI Bold shouted, and they carried him out of the room, horizontal and unconscious, his face inches from the floor.

Nash watched, his mind racing to catch up with the drama. One of the officers, his face flushed with effort, threw a makeshift shiv down as they carried Barbosa out. It was crudely fashioned from a sharpened plastic fork.

'He was going to use this on you,' the officer said.

Nash stared at the weapon, the reality of the situation sinking in. 'How did you know? I never saw anything,' he asked, his voice tight. He assumed the body language expert, watching through the two-way, had seen some movement that Nash hadn't. He was a better cop than that and should have been more attentive. Brown could have been hurt and that would be on him.

'There was nothing to see. We had Conrad Snow on the phone,' another officer explained. 'He called in, demanding we stop whatever you were doing. He said the man sitting opposite you had a knife down his sock and was about to attack you.'

Renshaw looked at Molly. 'You okay?' he asked. They had history, and the care he felt for her was still apparent. 'You told us to act on anything Snow says without question, boss,' he said to Nash. 'The psychic has come up trumps again.'

Nash felt a shiver run down his spine. He glanced at Brown, who looked just as shaken.

'Snow was adamant. Said you were in immediate danger. Mind, wouldn't we have looked like a load of prize dicks if it turned out to be bollocks?'

'Not as bad as we'd look if he'd have got away with it,' Nash said. He exhaled, running a hand through his hair. 'All right, good work,' he said, trying to regain his composure and control his emotion. 'Make sure Barbosa is secured.'

The officers left the room, closing the door with a thud and Nash sank into his chair. He picked up the shiv, turning it in his hand, the reality of how close he had come to serious harm hitting home.

'We owe Conrad a thank you,' Brown said.

'Yeah,' he agreed. 'Crisis over. Let's get back to work.'

When they concluded the interview and left the room, Nash had created a whole case file of new paperwork for the team to plough through. And the hangover was subsiding. Bonus.

Chapter Forty-Seven

They came out to applause. Word had travelled around the station that they'd caught all the key members of the gang, including the elusive Mr Big. The team wanted to hear the story and gathered around as Brown filled them in on the details.

The overweight security guard in his fifties, Jake Barbosa had been apprehended and arrested on the spot after drugs and money were found stashed in his security hut. He'd tried to shift the blame onto the younger guard, but Renshaw and Patel weren't buying it.

'Barbosa was brought in, stripped of his phone so he couldn't alert anyone, and is currently cooling his heels in the cells, waiting for his initial court appearance on Monday. We've got enough to hold him,' Brown told them. 'We've made significant breakthroughs. But there's still work to be done. We have to make every single charge stick to bring justice for all those lost children.'

They went back to the incident room, where the rest of the team was waiting. The atmosphere was charged with triumph.

'Are you two okay?' Jackie Woods said, pulling out a chair for Molly and then one for Nash. Molly sat, and Nash smiled at Jackie but waved the chair away.

Hey, look on the bright side, boss, almost sticking you means that we've got him on another charge.' Bowes picked up a pencil from the desk and made stabbing motions and the Psycho noise while Brown fixed him with the bog-eye.

'Good work, everyone,' Nash said. 'All right Bowes, settle down. We've made a significant breakthrough, but this is just the beginning. We need to keep the pressure on and see this through.'

Renshaw and Patel were already compiling the evidence and preparing for the next phase. They had a solid case but needed to ensure it was airtight. The drug operation was extensive, and while they'd taken the cream off the top, many gallons of rancid milk floated in dark churns.

'We've got enough to keep them all in custody,' Renshaw said. 'But we need to link them to the larger operation. If we can connect them to the suppliers and distributors, we can take the rest of the network.'

Patel nodded. 'Agreed. We should focus on following the money and tracking the drugs.'

Nash glanced around the room, feeling the responsibility. This was their chance to make an impact. 'All right, let's get to work. Renshaw, Patel, I want you to dig into Mathis' and Barbosa's finances and connections. See if you can trace any transactions or communications that link them to the higher-ups. Look into Purvis as well. He's as bent as a nine-bob note.'

'The Solicitor?'

'Yep. He's been on the cartel payroll for years. He's got the blood of those children on his hands as much as the cooks.'

He turned to Blight who was hovering around and waiting for her opportunity to get the hell out of there. Nash knew the meetings bored her and she wanted to be in the middle of the action. 'Superintendent Norton, May I make a suggestion, ma'am?'

'Sure.' Nash was glad to notice that the chewing gum prop was gone. If we can get together later we could review what we have on the suspects' known associates. See if any of them have connections to the larger operation.'

Blight nodded, 'Got it.' She was the senior officer, but Nash saw that she let him call the shots in his station now that the initial busts were over.

The team dispersed, diving into their assigned tasks with renewed focus, and Nash collected his thoughts. This was a pivotal point in the investigation, and they needed to maintain momentum.

Later that day, Nash and Renshaw prepared to interrogate Mathis. They'd spent the morning reviewing the evidence and formulating their strategy. Mathis was a seasoned criminal, but Nash was confident they could break him.

As they entered the interrogation room, he looked up, his eyes cold and defiant. Nash took a seat across from him, while Patel stood by the door, ready to intervene if necessary.

'Mr Mathis,' Nash began, his tone calm. 'You've been arrested on drug smuggling and possession. You're also charged with trafficking minors and embezzlement. That's enough to put you away for a long time. But we know you're not the mastermind behind the operation.'

Mathis remained silent, his expression unreadable.

Nash pulled his chair closer to Mathis and took a wide position to invade his space. 'We can make this easier for you,' Nash continued. 'Cooperate with us, and we might be able to work out a deal. Help us take down the people you work for, and it could reduce your sentence.'

Mathis scoffed, leaning back in his chair. 'You think I'm going to turn on them? You're dreaming. They are my people.'

Nash leaned forward, a technique to make himself smaller and less intimidating. The idea was to draw the suspect into mirroring the position. Nash knew he wouldn't yet, but he was getting Mathis familiar with the gesture. When Mathis also leaned forward, it would be an indicator that he was ready to confess. 'We already have enough to convict you. It's only a matter of time before we get to the top. The question is, do you want to do life with them, or do you want to make it easier on yourself?'

Mathis' jaw tightened, but he didn't answer.

Renshaw stepped forward, and put a file on the table. 'We've traced your finances, Jerod. We know about the offshore accounts and the payments you've been making to Roland Purvis. It's all here, and it links you to the operation.'

Mathis glanced at the file, and a flicker of uncertainty crossed his face. Nash seized the moment and went for the Prisoner's Dilemma.

'We've had Barbosa in and he's turned rat. Between him and Blue they've given us chapter and verse on you little big shot. You're in so deep that where you are, the fish don't need eyes,' Nash said. 'But you can still make a choice. Help us, and we can help you. Refuse, and you'll take the fall for everything. You call them your people. Do you think they'd incriminate themselves to save you? I can assure you, they won't. Barbosa has already given us you and Purvis.'

'Who?' Mathis tried to get one over on Nash. I don't know a Barbosa.'

'Oh, I think you do. He's one of your so-called people, Jerod. Who are your suppliers?'

'No comment.'

He didn't say anything other than that. Not a word. After resting time in his cells as per his human rights, he was brought back and they went at it again. They played the no-comment game some more. The evidence against him piled up on the table in front of them. Nash and Renshaw were tired but they'd played this game many times before. There was a long silence. Mathis' eyes darted between them, weighing his options. Finally, he leaned forward, his voice tense. Good Lad. Gottcha, Nash thought.

'What do you want to know?'

'Start with your suppliers. Who are they, and where are they based?'

Mathis hesitated, then began to talk. It was slow, but as the details emerged, Nash and Renshaw saw the line of command and the bigger picture forming as Mathis named names they didn't have. His information was invaluable, providing leads and connections they hadn't been able to uncover before. 'Tell Blight that when I get out, I'm coming for her,' He said. 'I know who she is.'

'No you aren't, Mr Mathis,' Renshaw said. 'And that kind of talk is exactly what's going to put you away for life, without the chance of parole so let's play nice shall we?'

As the interrogation continued, Nash knew they were making progress. Mathis was giving them the keys to dismantling the rest of the operation. Slit a snake and it will hiss.

Chapter Forty-Eight

The following days were crazy with people buzzing around the station like worker drones. The team followed up on suspect leads and pieced together the network. Building timeframes and diagrams, they understood the extent and reach of the cartel and worked through to its heart.

Nash coordinated with other law enforcement agencies, expanding their range and resources. The scale of Diamond Light was larger than anything they had worked on before, spanning multiple cities.

Blight's research into Barbosa's associates paid off, revealing connections to several high-ranking members of society that surprised them, including Roland Purvis. They launched more coordinated raids, arresting key figures and seizing substantial amounts of drugs and money from homes and businesses across the region.

The media caught wind of the crackdown, and the story made headlines. The public was aware of the significant blow to the drug trade, and the pressure on the remaining members of the operation increased.

Jonas Scott, the reporter, always managed to be at the final raids with his camera crew.

He'd appear from behind a wall like Wally, bouncing around and waving his microphone in people's faces, peppering everybody with questions.

Bowes ran into him outside a shop that had been raided for fencing Chaos. After being thrown out of the shop, where the owner had been arrested an hour before, the distraught member of staff—only a young girl was visibly shaken. Scott didn't give up and was approaching customers who were prevented from entering while the shop was being searched. He wanted their initial reactions about the owner they all trusted being carted off in handcuffs. But his eyes lit up when he saw Bowes striding towards him.

Scott was a seasoned hack and had many run-ins with the police under his belt. Nash saw Bowes holding up his hand to move the microphone out of his face. He couldn't hear what was being said, so he pushed through the onlookers in case he needed to intervene. It would be interesting to see how Bowes handled the press and if he stuck to protocol or let his enthusiasm get the better of him. When he was closer he heard Bowes inform him that it was a live operation and nobody would be making any statements at this time.

'I understand that, officer but it's in the public interest to know what was found in the shop behind me.'

'A press conference will be arranged as soon as we have something to share.' Bowes wished him a good day and moved on.

As he passed Nash, he gave him a cocky wink. 'I did all right, didn't I boss? Do you know what I wanted to say, though? I wanted to tell him that it would be in the public's interest if I kicked him right in the bollocks.'

The raids continued with private homes and businesses to hit. Operations were meticulously planned, with officers positioned strategically to ensure nobody escaped. The organised raids felt like old hat now and Nash was still blown away by the reach of Chaos. He'd been at charity functions dressed like a penguin with some of these people who'd swapped tuxedos for handcuffs.

Nash was in command, coordinating efforts.

'Positions,' he ordered.

'All teams ready,' confirmation came over the radio.

'Move in.'

The teams converged on the target location. This time it was a warehouse way down Salthouse Road. The Broker's operation was dismantled and as the officers breached the building, the world went mad. The suspects tried to flee, but they were apprehended with minimal bloodshed on both sides.

They'd rehearsed this scenario in training countless times, and it showed. They all moaned about training sessions that took them off the street and stopped them from policing. But the building was secured, and more dealers were in custody. Most importantly, nobody was badly hurt.

Over the next few days, the dust settled. Plea hearings were heard, some prisoners were released onto the street, and others were held on remand.

Nash felt a profound sense of pride in his team. They weren't geared up for an operation of this magnitude, but they'd done it and come out on top. Operation Diamond Light was dismantled, and the key players were behind bars. It had been a long road, but the team were high on success.

The mood at the station was jubilant, and Nash reflected that they'd made a real difference. It was a victory worth savouring.

Nash smiled at each of the photographs of the victims as he unpinned them from the incident board and put them away respectfully in an envelope ready to be filed.

Turner came over with a genuine grin on his face. 'You did good, yokel.'

Nash nodded, feeling the weight lifting. 'Thanks.'

Turner extended his hand, and Nash shook it.

'About that restaurant?' Turner said, and this time Nash smiled.

'As long as you're paying.'

Turner laughed. 'Fair enough, Nash.'

Nash looked around his office. Max's presence had faded, but he expected he'd be back to peck his head. He put his coat on and walked to the main door with Molly. 'Get some sleep, Brown. You deserve it.'

'Are you kidding me? Danny's got tickets for a gig in Lancaster tonight. I'm off tomorrow, remember.' Before they could say anymore, a motorbike roared around the corner and screeched to a stop by the steps. Nash disapproved of the burned rubber tracks on the clean beige cement.

Blight handed Brown a helmet. 'Lift home, bitch?'

'Are you insane? I'm not getting on that thing,' Brown said.

'Are you chicken shit?'

'Are you sober?'

'I'm as sober as the judge who's going to send all that scum down. But I can't vouch for the state I'll be in an hour from now. Small windows, Brown. Small windows until I go to rehab.'

'All right, Amy Winehouse, I'm game. But I hope you know what you're doing with this thing, Blight. I don't like you, remember.'

'Blight who? From now on, you can call me Keeley. Blight died, and Keeley's a nicer person.'

Brown grinned and climbed on the back of the bike, holding onto Blight's waist. And Nash laughed as Norton screeched away from the kerb, almost tipping Brown off the back.

Brown screamed and then shouted, 'Hell yes.'

'Hell yes,' he heard them both screaming into the night as they roared through the police station gates.

Chapter Forty-Nine

The after-case party was a bittersweet affair for Nash. As he mingled among his colleagues and their partners, he couldn't shake the feeling of melancholy that hung in the air. It felt wrong to celebrate when so many lives had been lost, but he understood the importance of closure and camaraderie for the team.

Kelvin stood by Nash's side as they mingled in the crowded room at Abbey House Hotel. Nash loved being able to attend these things with him, and it was hard to believe how lonely he'd found them before he met Kelvin. He wouldn't have made it through the case without his support.

There were several of the victims' families among the guests and Nash wanted to make sure he spent time with all of them. Their presence was a poignant reminder of the lives affected by the cartel.

Noah's mum was there. The outer appearance of her grief was softened by a new hairdo and a fake fur stole around her shoulders. Nash and Kelvin sat with her. The time for offering condolences and showing gratitude for her strength throughout the ordeal was done. Tonight, they laughed about some of Noah's antics. Their shared memories kept him alive. Nash pushed aside the image of his bloated face rising out of the dark water of the park lake and remembered him racking up the balls on the pool table and telling Nash he was going to give him a thrashing. The kid had been picking up the lingo. Tonight they weren't talking about his death, they celebrated his life.

Sebastian White and Aiden Lawson stood together and mumbled through a short speech to thank the team and the town for their donations to the refugee centre. They promised it was going to be better than ever—and clean.

Liz and Andy Gibson were there with their son and Jay Bowes. Their laughter and smiles showed the resilience of the human spirit. Liz was on the gin, and her laugh was contagious. As Nash passed, he heard her say to Bowes, 'I'm not drunk, you know. I'm paranoid that you think I'm awful, after that night.'

Bowes laughed and put his arm around her. 'Well, I bloody hope you are by the end of the night, or I'm leaving you for better company. What do you say, Gibbo?'

The night was filled with laughter and music, but Nash couldn't shake the memory of those who were lost along the way. Their faces haunted him, a reminder of the true cost of justice.

He retreated to a quiet corner, lost in thought and watched Kelvin, fending off lady admirers. Giving himself a break, he basked in a moment of triumph, surrounded by the people he cared about most.

The Abbey House Hotel was a majestic sight. He read a plaque on the wall beside him. The beautiful old building was designed by Sir Edward Lutyens in 1914 but was based around the ruins of a far older gatehouse, part of Furness Abbey, built in the 11th century. He wouldn't remember the details tomorrow, but it was a nice touch.

The hotel fronted fourteen acres of beautiful gardens, and beyond that, lush woodland, rolling hills and the stunning abbey ruins themselves. Nash's first love was the ocean outside his house, but the Abbey and surrounding areas came a close second.

The building carried an old lady aura of opulence and grandeur. Its imposing façade, adorned with intricate architectural details, spoke to Nash about a bygone era.

As guests entered the function room, they were greeted by the rich scent of polished wood and the soft glow of teardrop chandeliers overhead. There would still be many tears left to cry by the grieving family members. For the occasion, one wall had been hung with photographs of the victims. Above the kids' faces was the slogan: *Lest We Forget.*

It was tradition that the victims of any case were the honoured guests in attendance. The events after every major operation were a time for celebration, but the faces of lost citizens were a reminder of what the evening was about.

The function room hailed back to the hotel's storied history, with plush velvet drapes framing tall windows offering sweeping views of the countryside. Tapestries covered aged cracks in the walls, depicting scenes from centuries past, while antique furniture provided uncomfortable seating for guests to enjoy the festivities.

A grand piano stood sentinel, its polished ebony surface gleaming in the soft light as a lady in a long gown caressed the keys. An ensemble of musicians played Bach, and their melodic strings filled the air with elegance.

A banqueting table had been laid out with a feast fit for royalty. Platters piled high with hors d'oeuvres beckoned the guests, and champagne flutes sparkled in the candlelight, waiting to be filled. Nash told Kelvin he would rather have a pint and a mini pork pie but Kel was in his element.

Despite the opulence and the air of solemnity hanging over the room during the speeches, everybody was having fun. Voices were loud and tales grew taller.

Nash felt a swell of emotion in his chest. This was more than a party, it was a carnival of the human spirit and the bonds that united people.

During his speech, Nash celebrated the fact that the major players had been taken down, including Acetone the cook and all the top-tier drug dealers. Production of Crystal Chaos has been halted, and no more would be coming into Barrow. He raised his glass to the faces of the children and everybody stood for the toast. He remembered Lance Taylor, the man plunged into a bath of cold water in an attempt to revive him.

'Lest we forget,' he said.

'Lest we forget.'

He saw Norton hovering and excused himself to speak to her. This was going to be her only party for a while. After the last orders, a car would be waiting outside to take her to The Priory retreat for a residential stay in rehab. Her cover had been blown in Manchester and it would be too dangerous for her to work with GMNT anymore. She told Nash that a new position had been found for her working on the vice team in London.

'I just wanted to thank you for everything, you know.' She rubbed her shoe against the carpet and looked at her feet.

'Always a pleasure and never a chore, Norton. Well, sometimes you were just about bearable. I'm sure you know, you're a bloody nightmare. Seriously though, all that aside, you're a fine officer and a credit to the force. Good luck in all of your future endeavours.'

'Cheers Nash, you weren't so bad yourself once I got used to that stick up your arse.'

She looked choked as she told him that her time in the Lake District had been a happy one overall. But the case had taken its toll. She was a drug addict with a long road of recovery ahead of her. 'I'm tired, Nash. I need an easier life. I'm not even sure that vice is right for me.'

'I get that. But you don't have to decide anything now. Just concentrate on getting well.'

'But that's just it, you see. I am thinking about the future. It's what's going to get me through the next few weeks.' She cleared her throat and looked unsure of herself. That was new.

'I'm picking up that this is more than just party chitchat. Is there something you want to say, ma'am?'

'Yes. Jesus, you're so impatient. I'm getting to it, man.'

Nash covered a smile, he could see this was important to her. 'Well get on with it before the cock crows.'

'What?'

'Spit it out.'

'I was wondering if you might have something for me. Look, I haven't spoken to DCS Lewis yet. I want to—you know—show respect for you, and all that crap.'

Nash made a noise in his nose and Keeley's head shot up to glare at him. 'Are you asking me for a job, Blight?' he asked.

'It's Keeley, remember. Blight was last seen under a pile of the nasty stuff. Yeah. Okay. Stupid idea. Forget I asked. I get it. Scum, that's how you all see me. Well to hell with the lot of you. I don't need anybody. You can piss off. Who'd want a useless junkie on their team?' She spun around and was halfway across the room when Nash shouted after her.

'I would.'

'What?'

'I'd want you on my team, Keeley.'

Nash had to admit that his three-second reaction had been, over my dead body, but he responded that he'd be honoured to have her. She'd have to make an official application, but he would endorse it and recommend her for a role on his team. He explained that he didn't have a place for her and would have to create one if Lewis was willing and could persuade the forces above that the team was overdue for expansion.

Nash hadn't thought about Norton for the placement, but taking on a new detective was something he'd considered approaching Lewis about when the case was over. Norton would be rough, hard work, exasperating—but perfect. Brown would have a fit. And Nash saw many dramas ahead, but he was a glutton for punishment. Who needed a quiet day at work?

'It would mean you being a hundred per cent fit for work, a reduced rank, and a pay cut. How does sergeant grab you?' Nash winked, 'Oh, and I'd be your boss.'

'A year ago, I'd have slit the throat of anybody trying to take my rank, but I can live with that. All I need is a place to lay my head.' Keeley saluted him and laughed behind the light tone, but it had a bitter edge. 'I can go with that, boss. Besides, I'll be saving a fortune on coke.'

'This has come out of left field. No promises but I'm pretty sure the team can take one more member—I warn you though, it won't be the quiet ride you expect.'

She winked at him, 'Good.'

Half an hour later, they all gathered outside to wave her off. Manchester and Barrow alike, she was one of them.

'She's got balls of steel,' Brown said, and Nash had to agree.

They'd done it. And for now, that was enough. He stood in the doorway of the hotel as Brown fastened her scarf around her neck. Their breath made patterns in the air.

He looked up and saw a solitary figure, with two legs, standing by the fountain. Noah raised his hand to wave goodbye. He was already fading as Nash waved back. He didn't think he'd see him again.

'Hang on, I'm not going yet,' Brown said.

'Sorry. I wasn't waving at you.'

'Ghosts, boss?'

'Something like that,' Nash said.

Only two weeks until Christmas.'

'Let's make it a good one, Brown.'

'You've got a cruise to look forward to early next year, haven't you?' She grinned up at him and he realised how small she looked. Small and mighty.

But, Nash had more to look forward to than a cruise.

He smiled and thought about the engagement ring wrapped and ready to slip under the tree.

Nash was ready to bag himself a husband.

Printed in Great Britain
by Amazon